MONA ACTS OUT

MONA ACTS OUT

a novel

MISCHA BERLINSKI

Liveright Publishing Corporation

An Imprint of W. W. Norton & Company
Independent Publishers Since 1923

For information about permission to reproduce selections from this book, write to Permissions, Liveright Publishing Corporation, a division of W. W. Norton & Company, Inc., 500 Fifth Avenue, New York, NY 10110

For information about special discounts for bulk purchases, please contact W. W. Norton Special Sales at specialsales@wwnorton.com or 800-233-4830

Manufacturing by Lakeside Book Company
Book design by Chris Welch
Production manager: Lauren Abbate

ISBN 978-1-324-09520-0

Liveright Publishing Corporation, 500 Fifth Avenue, New York, N.Y. 10110
www.wwnorton.com

W. W. Norton & Company Ltd., 15 Carlisle Street, London W1D 3BS

$PrintCode

Per Cristina, nella sua infinita varietà

Go together,
You precious winners all; your exultation
Partake to everyone.

—*The Winter's Tale*

ACT ONE

PAROLLES

          . . . Captain I'll be no more;
But I will eat and drink, and sleep as soft
As Captain shall: Simply the thing I am
Shall make me live.

1

On the outlines of Milton Katz's accomplishment, the general shape and structure of his achievement, there was a single point of agreement: not even the most fervent of his enemies denied that the Disorder'd Rabble owed to Milton the remarkable good fortune that was possession of 107 Avenue C.

The story now was company legend: how in 1966 Milton found the abandoned glove factory, little more than a burnt-out husk, victim of the decline in women's formal handwear and a suspicious fire. How squatters were occupying the building: an anarchist commune on the first and second floors, a shooting gallery on three, and on the fourth floor, a Maoist revolutionary organization. How Milton and his guerrilla Shakespeare company seized the fifth floor. How the company rehearsed there during the week and put on free shows every Friday and Saturday night for anyone hip enough to know where to go and brave enough to make their way down to Alphabet City after dark, wriggle through 107 Avenue C's boarded-up ground-floor windows, and mount the unlit staircases. How Milton slept in the space to keep it safe from looters, scaring off thieves with prop swords. How the city shut off power to the building, so those legendary early shows were lit by candlelight, hundreds of theatergoers crammed cheek by jowl to watch a samizdat *Hamlet*, *Tempest*, or *Merchant*. How the fire marshal closed the building in 1970, the front entrance sealed in cement and a security guard stationed out front. How Milton lobbied, solicited, fundraised, cajoled, and pleaded, how he and he alone made the company a New York cause célèbre. How an editorial in the *Times* called on the City of New York to find a permanent home for this "intriguing, avant-garde, thoroughly modern theatrical company, who deserve a place in our city commensurate with the place they have earned in our hearts." How Alphabet City was by then more dangerous, more degraded, and less attractive to investors than it had ever been, how the owners were desperate to sell. How Milton assembled a consortium of company supporters who bought the building and sold it to the company for one dollar. How after three years in the wilderness, the company returned to 107 Avenue C, and Milton had a large brass plaque installed in the lobby, and how on it Milton listed the names of the donors who made the acquisition of the building possible. How above the plaque, he engraved the lines from which his company would take its name: "Your disorder'd rabble / Makes servants of their betters."

But half a century after the Disorder'd Rabble's founding, real estate was just about the only terra firma in the nonstop, still-ongoing in-house debate on the subject of Milton Katz. They fought about Milton in the rehearsal rooms, the admin offices, in the dressing rooms, at fundraisers and at after-parties. That Milton wasn't dead made the whole debate that much more intense. The idea of Milton just sitting at home in exile . . . his hair unkempt . . . maybe even drooling—the thought of Milton neglected in his old age would rile up those who still loved him. "We should do something for Milton," they would say, as if discussing the renovation of the crumbling statue of some long-forgotten Civil War hero. "It isn't right about Milton. After everything he's done." The very same thought—of

Milton lingering, judging, lounging around in his bathrobe—would produce a wave of equal but opposing outrage among the Milto-phobes, who favored tearing down the damn statue in its entirety. Between the extremities of love and hate there was no common ground, no place for nuance. Just mention his name and all the old wounds would reopen, and the two camps, like baboons startled by thunder, would squawk and abandon peaceful grooming to bare their fangs and fist each other vigorously upside the head.

If only Milton would just have the common, human decency to die! Then everyone could settle down. The people who, despite everything, still loved Milton could go back to remembering him fondly; the people who, despite everything, resented him could let it all go; and everybody, wherever they stood on the subject of Milton, could trade their best Milton Katz stories over post-show saketinis at the Get Bento Box.

Sometimes the debate over Milton took place in the space of a single soul. Mona Zahid, for example, had a toe in both of the rival camps: when the company squabbled over his reputation, she was an out-and-out, unabashed Miltophile. Asked to quantify her debt to the man, she would have spread her arms wide and said, "Milton made me." But she was happier, she had discovered, with Milton out of her life. This made her feel treacherous, unsure of herself. She was not sure that she was a better actress without Milton (it wasn't a judgment for her to make) but she was certainly a freer, more spontaneous one. Milton had been for decades of her life a boarder in a psychic spare bedroom. Now that he was moved out, she enjoyed the extra space. Milton had opinions on every-thing. Not visiting him avoided the question, sneering, knowing, and judging all at once, "And how's it going with your doctor?"

The doctor in question was Phil, and Milton had not approved of the marriage—*and why should Milton even have had a vote?* Still, for a long time, she had been planning to visit Milton, she sincerely had. Then she had felt guilty about not visiting him. Then she had justified her guilt—she wasn't Milton's daughter, after all—and then she had forgotten her guilt, and then more months had passed. It had been who-knows-how-long since she had visited Milton. Maybe even a year.

2

A stripe of spotlight-sunlight draped across her eyes. She blinked. Her first waking emotion of the day was irritation. She had pulled down the blinds at night, intending to sleep in, and Phil, who had left the house early, had pulled them back up. Then she remembered her dream. It had been very funny. "That's not meat, that's Milton!" She should write that down. She had been so outraged—that was funny too. And there had been the joke about Milton's penis, something about a side dish.

Now Mona was a little more awake, and none of it made as much sense as it did just a minute ago. Barney, sensing that she was conscious, climbed on the bed and burrowed his snout into the small of her back. She wanted to drift back to sleep and laugh again but she was hopelessly awake. She heard Sheila snap, "Well, I don't know where your glasses are." A moment later, there was a loud and improbably long bellowing noise. That was Bruce blowing his nose. Then he turned the television on and she could hear the angry voices.

Mona flopped back onto her pillow, the day already feeling like defeat. She leaned over, rummaged through her bedside drawer, and found the small yellow bottle containing the last of her sister's hospice kit. She opened the bottle, shook out two pills, and swallowed them.

Mona had exactly six pills left of the stash Zahra had left her. She had started out almost a year ago with one hundred and fifty, plus the lollipop thing. Only a dope fiend, Mona thought, could understand the self-discipline implicit in that last sentence: a lesser woman than herself (not that Mona was being judgmental, mind you) would have surfeited on happiness in weeks. She would have been addicted herself but for the fact that she simply could not act under their influence: she couldn't stop grinning, at low dosages, or, if the dosages were high, she slurred. Milton had stepped in immediately when, years ago, she tried to act while high. "You're flat and out of tune," he said, mid-rehearsal. "Go home and come back better." Implicit in this was a threat. So Mona kept the yellow bottle in her bedside drawer, breaking out a pill or five now and again when she didn't have to work and didn't think she could get through the day otherwise. She could indulge today because she didn't have a show until Friday night.

Bruce's voice boomed through the closed door. "I can't find them *anywhere*. Are you sure you packed them?"

"Is she *still* asleep?" Sheila said.

Mona shook out another pill and swallowed it too.

How small the apartment seemed to Mona with her in-laws on the prowl! Bruce and Sheila occupied the apartment as if it were their own—which, in a sense, it was: Phil and Mona had bought the apartment from them when they migrated south after Bruce's retirement. It was Phil's childhood home, a pleasant, roomy, somewhat dilapidated prewar six in Morningside Heights. Phil and Mona were able to swing the deal only because Bruce and Sheila had deeply discounted the sales price, with the expectation that they could use Phil's office with its comfy foldout couch as an occasional New York pied-à-terre. "You'll never see us," Bruce lied. "We've had enough of the city," Sheila fibbed. They had flown in the night before, letting themselves in after midnight with the extra key.

How long, Mona wondered, could she hide in the bedroom, pretending to be asleep? After a certain point, feigning sleep was like feigning a coma, then you were just feigning death.

Mona lay in bed waiting for the narcotics to work, thinking wistfully about her phone. It was locked in the mailbox in the lobby. The idea was that she'd only be able to get at her phone by dressing herself sufficiently to ride the elevator, so she wouldn't look at it before bed or first thing in the morning. She had banished it from her bedroom because of the advertisements for real estate, mainly. Every time she saw one of those stupid advertisements for real estate, she felt like Barney when he saw a squirrel: she had to tug at the end of the leash and bark. Mona figured that over the last year she had taken the virtual tour of half the available housing stock in Manhattan. One house inevitably led to another, each more empty and more beautiful than the last; none of the apartments featured Bruce and Sheila. Mona was aware that her desire to explore empty apartments was a compulsion, and *still* she couldn't stop, no matter how many times she swore that she would put the phone away in five minutes exactly, until finally, bleary-eyed, she drifted off to uneasy sleep. Locking up the phone had been an emergency intervention.

Barney whimpered and rolled on his back. There was a fine brisk breeze blowing, slipping in through the crack of the window, full of sea smells and roasting meats. A fat pigeon, sassy and proud, strutted around on the fire escape. Barney studied it attentively. He began to nudge at her collarbone with his wet nose. Mona thought, "Daffodils / That come before the swallow dares, and take / The winds of March with beauty." She didn't know why she thought that. The words just made her glad.

3

On the one hand, Sheila was *happy* to see Mona in the morning; on the other hand, Sheila was happy to see Mona in the *morning*.

"Good morning, lazybones!" she cried.

Sheila was already, despite the early hour, dressed for her day in a pink sweat suit, her hair carefully lacquered with hairspray, a slash of lipstick in place. Nobody had ever embraced spry old lady life with quite the enthusiasm of Sheila. She preceded Mona into the kitchen. Across her butt, in bright large letters, was the word JUICY.

"Welcome back, Sheila," Mona said.

Mona found the remote control on the counter and turned the television off. Rachel, her niece, home from college for the holiday and asleep on the couch, had remarkably slept through the noise.

Then Mona poured herself a cup of coffee. As always when Bruce and Sheila made the coffee, they used the wrong kind. The pair of them must have gotten down right onto their creaking knees and delved like cunning ferrets to the back of the cupboard, slipping past the aged ramen, traversing the great wall of antique cereal, to the place where expired coffee lived in an old Maxwell House tin, when just inside the refrigerator door there was not one but two bags of fresh beans from Whole Foods. Mona imagined the two of them chuckling at their daring complot. Mona would have thrown out the pot and started all over again, but then she would have had to have a twenty-minute talk with Sheila about why she was throwing out the pot of coffee, and she would need to drink a pot of coffee before she could have that conversation.

Mona wondered if she had really medicated herself properly before leaving the bedroom. She wanted to be positively soused with happiness. The coffee wasn't just bitter and tasteless—it had no kick to it. Mona felt as if she had hitched the wagon of her consciousness to a skinny gray mule. She and Ol' Bad Coffee had acres and acres of stony conversational ground to plow this morning. Mona knew how the morning would go; it always went the same way. In a moment—Mona would so rather not talk about it—there would be a question—here it came!—about whether Mona was enjoying her new show. "Why, yes, yes I am," Mona answered, and wondered why she found it so difficult simply to tell the truth. She reckoned that a good half of what she said was a lie, in one form or another. Sheila asked if Mona's back was still doing that thing Mona had once complained about a decade ago; and whether Aaron ate beets. Mona didn't know, but she thought she might look like a bad mother if she said so. Before she could answer, Sheila said, "I found a recipe online for roast beets with burrata and thought about you. Aren't you the one who likes burrata?" Mona tried to remember what burrata even was, while Sheila recalled a long-ago holiday that she and Bruce had taken in Puglia, where burrata was apparently produced in vast, fluffy clouds, and how fun that vacation was until Bruce's wallet was stolen on the train.

Then Sheila said, "People are so funny."

Mona knew from experience that this was Sheila's way of changing the subject. Now Sheila would begin an anecdote that would not be funny, featuring herself as protagonist in the latest installment of the multi-episode podcast entitled *How Sheila Was Insulted by Her Book Group Again*. Every episode featured a ferocious middle-school-style feud rifting "the Gang" into warring factions of peeved old ladies, which argument Sheila would recount to Mona in meticulous detail.

Mona flicked the reins at her mule. He thought sadly of the carrots and mash back in the stall.

"Are they?" she said. "I love funny people. But I rarely meet them. Who's the funniest person you ever met?"

But Sheila was not fooled. "Can I ask you a question? Where do you buy your smoked salmon?"

"Nora Weiner wasn't happy?"

Nora Weiner was Sheila's nemesis, her counterparty on the side of darkness.

"Well, people are just so funny. We had my book group last week at my house, and before the Gang came over, Nora Weiner sent me two whole pounds of smoked salmon. From Russ and Daughters."

Mona was always confused by Sheila's stories, which involved slights and insults so subtle as to be inexplicable outside the context of the prison yard or the court at Versailles.

"That was nice of her, wasn't it?" Mona said.

Sheila's flashing eyes revealed that it wasn't nice, it wasn't nice at all. Apparently Nora Weiner's salmon was a shot across the bow of the battleship that was Sheila's hospitality.

Despite the acrimony of the group, Sheila was forever badgering Mona to join them, as if the cycle of argument and reconciliation was as fun as salsa dancing. Mona was supposed to sit in on the sessions via Zoom, which Nora Weiner's daughter-in-law just loved to do. "We read classics too, you know," Sheila said, implying that Mona's reluctance to join was the result of being some kind of highbrow snob. In recent months Sheila had begun sending Mona copies of whatever the group was reading from Amazon, the books piling up on Mona's bedside as a testament to her inadequacies as a daughter-in-law and wife.

Mona thought about those unread books while Sheila talked. She was just getting into the meat of her story—"Now isn't that the funniest thing you've ever heard?" she said all over again, the word "funny" used to describe an emotion probably more like hurt or sorrow than good humor—when Bruce toddled into the kitchen. There was something in his manner that suggested a strong-willed three-year-old, a defiant thrust of his chin.

"Oh good morning, lovely ladies!" he cried.

Barney rushed to Bruce's side. Barney's passion for Bruce was inexplicable, the stuff of family lore. Barney ran around in small circles, then threw himself on his side and cried. Bruce rubbed Barney's head and said, "Oh you son-of-a-gun you, you son-of-a-gun." Those words thrilled Barney, who rolled on his back and squirmed, shaking his head from side to side, his tail waving wildly.

It was thanks to Bruce that Mona had met Phil. Since long before Mona had joined the Rabble, Bruce had been on the board of directors, one of those gray-haired eminences that legally ran the theater but in practice did little but fundraise their brains out and approve Milton's contract and sort out the theater's complicated real estate deals. When Mona joined the Rabble, all eighteen members of the board had set to work at finding Mona the husband they believed she needed. She had been flooded with offers to meet nephews, sons, and junior colleagues. Bruce had invited Mona to a dinner in this very apartment. Phil had arrived with a bottle of very good wine and a pleasing air of emotional stability. By the end of the evening, they were having sex in Phil's childhood bedroom, Phil ostensibly showing her his high school memorabilia. "So you want to see my yearbook?" was still, even after all these years, Phil's preferred way of initiating a romantic encounter.

Bruce pulled a high-backed stool up to the kitchen counter, while

Sheila continued to talk about her book group. Bruce glowered at her. He didn't like it when his wife monopolized the conversation, or if she conversed at all.

"Would you like half a bagel?" Mona asked him.

"A bagel?" he said suspiciously, as if breakfast were some sneaky ploy on the part of his enemies.

"I've got plain and sesame."

"Plain, I guess."

Mona reached for the bag of bagels and a serrated knife.

"So how was the flight?" she asked.

"Well, it was so funny . . ." Sheila said, hoping to get back to her story. She was growing desperate. Like Mona, Sheila could hear the timer of Bruce's patience ticking. When it sounded, she would be abandoned by the conversational herd like a sick and boring wildebeest and no one would listen to her again all day.

Mona sliced the bagels and inserted them into the toaster. She took a swig of the second-rate coffee and felt a shiver of sympathy for Nora Weiner, always eating Sheila's cheap-ass smoked salmon at what was supposed to be a gourmet book club. Mona wondered if she could make it out the door and down the hallway and into the elevator before Bruce and Sheila could get off the stools on which they were so precariously perched. Mona had chosen the stools precisely because in the Crate & Barrel showroom they had looked like they would be inaccessible to the elderly. Mona could make it to the elevator, she figured, but what then? She was in a bathrobe and slippers.

It was too late. The toaster announced that the bagel was ready, and Bruce's timer sounded also, not with some dire knell, but with the words, "Mona, I read something that would interest you."

4

There was a yellow Post-it note on the counter. It read, "Ulti-mate." Had it read, "Ultimate!" or "Ultimate…" Mona would have known that things were fine with Phil. Nine days out of ten he would have added a little heart, or sometimes, if he was feeling goofy, a sketch of himself, smiling. But the underscore—heavy, solid, and unrelenting—told her that she and Phil were still fighting.

Both Mona and her husband held grudges that to the outsider would have seemed trivial, or even incomprehensible, but were in fact deep icebergs of discontent.

For his part, Phil was upset that Mona had not gone out to the Hamptons to play Ultimate Frisbee with his high school chums and their kids, as she had agreed. Phil and the Chums had been close as teenagers, drifted apart, and then in the age of Facebook and the group text, become close once again. When Mona and Phil were first dating, Phil and his friends would meet up on Thanks-giving morning in Sheep Meadow, the way they used to as kids. Then Mona would show up for an hour or two with a cup of cof-fee, and wander home when she started to feel like biting some-one. But a few years back, as more and more of the friends had moved out to various suburbs, the event, in the interests of traffic and parking, was relocated to the lawn of Ralph Perrimeno's house in Bridgehampton.

It was only the kids who could sustain interest in running around a muddy field tossing a Frisbee for more than a half hour, so in recent years the adults treated the game as an opportunity to stand around, drink coffee, and vape pot. They would talk about how weird it was that they were turning into their parents; their parents, in turn, had turned into their grandparents, and their children were beautiful aliens. There was always a lot of talk about investing, the subject naturally encouraging everyone to look hope-eyed at the host. Ralph had been this fat, not-too-popular kid back in high school, who had made a boodle in finance. (Mona was sure that she wasn't the only member of her social circle to drop into incognito mode to submit the shameful phrase "Ralph Perrimeno net worth" to the judgment of her search bar, or looked up the Zestimate® on his numerous tacky houses.) Now all of Phil's friends hung on his every word, hoping that Ralph would drop some hot stock tip, thus baptizing them in cascading showers of cash. Ralph, for his part, displayed an almost admirable simplicity of spirit, wanting nothing more out of his long weekends than to relive the worst years of his adolescence and gloat over his success. Uniquely among the Chums, Mona suspected, Phil actually *liked* Ralph, enthusing with genuine geeky enthusiasm about how impressive his car collection was, as if Ralph, in acquiring a half dozen vintage Jaguars, had been clever rather than rich.

Mona's refusal to attend Ultimate (or any of the other Chum-related events that pimpled up over the course of a year) had been for a while now a source of tension: Phil wanted Mona not only to present herself at these events, but exuberantly to enjoy herself. She just couldn't do it, no matter how she tried. It wasn't that the Chums, even Ralph Perrimeno, weren't nice or something. They were nice enough. They just made her feel so lonely. They talked for hours about building out wine cellars and filling them with Sangiovese and Hungarian varietals from Ralph's snooty-ass wine dealer, who asked you to fill out a ten-page questionnaire and whose minimum order was a half dozen cases.

Mona was always getting in trouble when the Chums got together, offending them somehow, like when she taught all the kids at the Memorial Day Brisket Roast to walk around limping, drooling, and palsied. Mona had in mind Richard III, but Melanie McDowell, who apparently had kissed Phil in high school, asked Mona to stop, saying that she found imitating the physically challenged problematic and offensive. "It's also very difficult, if you want to do it right," Mona said, which Melanie McDowell pretended not to hear. Then there was the Camping Trip Incident, where Mona stayed in the tent the whole time binge-watching *Shoah* on her iPad.

Mona had a newspaper article on the fridge, held in place by a magnet shaped like a panda bear. She had found the article attached to Zahra's fridge cleaning out her apartment. It felt like it had been left there for her, both a commentary on her sister's life and a warning on her own. Mona could pass hours puzzling over its significance. In its entirety the article read:

'MISSING' WOMAN MYSTERY SOLVED

A mix-up at the Glen Marnoch distillery led a group of Brazilian tourists spending a rainy Saturday night searching for a missing woman who was actually with them the entire time.

The group was visiting distilleries and had stopped to enjoy drinks at sunset. A head count revealed someone was missing. The woman, who had changed her jacket and scarf, didn't match the missing person's description and pitched in to help look.

Confusion ended just before dawn when they figured out that the "missing" woman had been with them all along.

Whenever Mona found herself around Ralph and the Chums, she found herself transported to a distant Scottish loch, where an unnatural mist rose up from the black water, blotting out the hills, the sun, herself. Frisbees were flying and Chums were asking Ralph what he thought about the pharmaceutical sector, and she heard herself shouting her own name, only to hear it echoing back in the fog.

MONA AND PHIL had been arguing over the Chum question for several years now, Mona wavering like a leaf on the tide between tentative agreement and absolute refusal to attend these events, but the issue had seemed to come to a decisive resolution just last week in "marriage counseling." Mona put quotation marks around the phrase because the "counseling" was something Phil's mother had bought them off Groupon for Christmas last year. Sheila had got them ten sessions, not on account of any particular crisis, but because the sessions were 72 percent off. Sheila had never seen couple's counseling at such a good price before. Mona had been dubious about the whole enterprise until the "counselor," this older guy with a ponytail who called himself Dr. Billy, asked them five minutes in if they minded if he blew a little bud while they talked. Mona had to admit that Dr. Billy was actually a pretty good counselor, chiefly because he looked so upset at any sign of tension that Mona and Phil would just back off out of basic human decency whenever they approached any maritally sensitive subject. He worked out of his apartment in the Sixties on the far East Side, the walls of which were covered with hand-painted portraits of naked women with jungle bush and big butts, some of them posing on the very couch where Mona was now sitting. Mona was trying to figure out if the couch was actually hygienic when she heard Phil denounce her unwillingness to spend time with his friends.

"I just don't get it, how a woman who has three roles in repertory can't even remember my friends' names," he said.

"I can remember their names, I just can't remember which one is which."

"You know everyone likes you," Phil said, wildly misunderstanding the cause of her unease.

"I like them too, I just don't like being around them."

"It feels like you draw these lines around yourself, and you won't let me or anyone else in. I want everyone to get to know the real you."

"Why? Why should anyone have to know the real me but me?"

"Because *I'd* like to know the real you," Phil said, a response that simultaneously touched Mona for its inept sweetness and alarmed her, because, after all, if Phil didn't know the real Mona—then who?

"How much would you say this matters to you?" Dr. Billy asked Phil.

"Well . . ." he said.

Mona understood: Phil just needed a win. Sometimes in marriage it mattered more *that* you won than *what* you won; sometimes in marriage you just needed a victory to look yourself in the eye while you were flossing in the morning. Earlier that year, Phil had been offered a job in Bethesda at the National Institutes of Health. The thought of leaving New York and the Rabble and moving to suburban Maryland had horrified Mona. Mona, never admitting even to herself either her intentions or her strategy, pursued a course of constant passive aggression. "Of course you should go if you want," she said. "Maybe we could do things long-distance for a while and see what happens." Mona knew that suffering the loss still smarted, not because he particularly wanted to take the job—

the salary was only okay and Phil was equally reluctant to leave the city—but because *he* wanted to be the one who decided, for *his* reasons. Now Phil needed a few points on the marital scoreboard.

Mona looked over at Dr. Billy. The look in his eyes—kind of red-rimmed and sad and nervous—persuaded Mona to reach out and hold Phil's big hand, a gesture that wasn't technically promising to go to Ultimate Thanksgiving with him, but very close.

———

FOR HER PART, Mona was upset about *Twelfth Night*, Mona's third *Twelfth* in fourteen years: she had been Viola, she had been Olivia, and now, in another sign that Time had devoured, was devouring, and would continue to devour, she was Maria.

Clara Huskins had directed the show. Back when Mona was just starting at 107 Avenue C, Clara had been one of Milton's protégées. The pattern over the last four-plus decades was that every few years, Milton would find some promising young director, generally female, announce that she was the second coming of Peter Brook, make her his new director-in-residence, hint broadly that she would take over the whole shebang just as soon as he retired, pay her peanuts, string her out for years, criticize her relentlessly, praise her sporadically but lavishly, drive her to the ragged edge of incipient insanity, and then denounce her as an ingrate and a traitor when she got tired of the game and moved on. Everyone in the profession knew this, and still Milton had found, year after year, brilliant young directors to take up residencies, a testament to Milton's uncanny ability to look women in the eye and say with absolute sincerity the words, "I need you." Mona could remember many a night with Clara, Clara's eyes teary, Clara talking about becoming an accountant. Her father was an accountant and it was a damn good, stress-free, productive life. She had finally quit Milton and 107 Avenue C, two years past her breaking point, and Mona didn't know if she had ever spoken with Milton again.

Now she was back at 107. Theater-world considered Clara's return some kind of galaxy-brain move on the new artistic director's part, to mend fences and make statements and be inclusive, especially now that Clara, in her exuberant post-Milton phase, had gone on to direct *The Fault in Our Stars* on Broadway for Disney, for which tourists regularly splurged four digits.

Mona loved Clara Huskins, but oh God, she hated her show. She had been bored since day one of rehearsals. Clara had the entire show blocked out before they even began, which some directors did but Mona loathed. "I'd like you to come *sashaying* in stage left," Clara said. "Do I have to?" Mona said. "Just *try*," said Clara. From that moment on, Mona had been bored all through rehearsals, Clara's rehearsal room everything Milton's rehearsal room *wasn't*: efficient, stress-free, professional, collegiate, cordial, respectful, even fun.

Then Clara's show was boring too, at least from Mona's point of view, although audiences seemed to love it, grooving on the rowdy songs and Roaring Twenties gangster costumes, the more adventurous of them going down the slide Clara had installed from balcony to stage, until at the end everyone stood up and sang along to the chorus Clara had Feste teach them. But Mona knew that the audiences were wrong, as they often were. *Twelfth Night* was a cavalcade of cruelty, grief, and loss, not some Elizabethan meet-cute rom-com. Mona was dreading the run of the show, which looked to be a great success.

Phil saw the show for the first time last night, and in the Uber on the way home, before they could talk, he said, "Hold on. I've got to call Patty back."

Patty was the nurse at the hospital. Now they zoomed up the FDR, traffic fluid, his voice seeming to drop a half octave as he took Mrs. Wong off IV Lasix and put her on oral, then reduced her DVT prophylaxis to standard heparin dosing. Mona snuggled up to him when he said to keep Mr. Cohen on the IV vancomycin but to add levofloxacin PO for a possible atelectasis. Phil said they needed to bring in a liver doc in the a.m. for a consult on Mrs. Tommasino.

When he hung up, Mona leaned on his chest for a moment. Then, hesitantly, she asked, "Was I okay tonight?"

"You were great," he said, his voice now returned to its normal timbre.

"Really?" she said.

"I loved it."

"Was I funny?"

"Everyone was laughing."

"What about you?"

Phil looked out the window a moment. Finally he said, "Do you *want* the truth?"

"Of course I do," she lied.

"I didn't always get what you were doing up there. This was such a goofy show. And you just seemed a little out of step."

Scholars of Mona and Phil's marriage will now recall the Great Fights of 2002, 2007, and 2011, the Peace Conference of 2013, and, just a couple of years back, the Very Serious Discussion. The casus belli in every case was Phil's insistence on giving Mona notes. All of those conversations and this one too went something like this: "What exactly are you trying to tell me, Phil? Are you telling me I was awful? Do I come to the hospital and tell *you* how to scrub in?" "I wouldn't mind if it made me better at what I was doing." "And killing what little confidence I have is going to make me *better* at what I was doing?" "I was just trying to say that you seemed happier doing other things than how you seemed tonight." "So I was supposed to play 'happy'? That was my role? Maria is 'happy'?" "Why are you so *angry* at me?" said Phil, genuinely perplexed. *Because I hate throwing a Frisbee,* Mona didn't say. *Because Vikram is coming, and I'd like to have an excuse at least to consider sleeping with him,* Mona didn't say. *Because sometimes the only time I feel anything with you is when we're fighting,* Mona certainly didn't say. Instead Mona said, "I don't want notes from you. I tell you this and I tell you this and I tell you this and *still* you want to tell me what I should do when I stand onstage. I need there to be one sphere of my life for which I, just me, am responsible. Where I am the grown-up. That is my work." "I'm not giving you notes. I'm just telling you what I thought." "All I need from you is confidence. I've got a director and an audience and critics to tell me I'm terrible. I know I'm terrible. I just want you to give me courage." "So you want me to lie. Sorry. I'm not good at lying."

What more was there to say? Phil *wasn't* good at lying, one of the very qualities of Phil that had made him so attractive as a mate. Still, it drove Mona bonkers that Phil couldn't lie to her with sufficient skill that she did not immediately understand that she was being lied to.

She had gone to bed last night furious. She might have clubbed him to death with the bedside lamp if she'd been able to muster the energy. Mona thought that everything was a disaster: her performance, her marriage, her life. Phil lay on his side of the bed watching college basketball highlights on his phone.

"Why are you so angry?" he finally said.

"Do we have to discuss it again?" Mona said.

"I just want you to be happy," Phil said. She did not understand how Phil could fail to understand the cruelty in such a remark, how slippery and manipulative it was. Phil did not want *her* to be happy; Phil wanted a happy wife. There was a difference. "I just think you could—" he continued.

"No no no no no no no," Mona said.

Phil put his phone down, stunned. There was a place of hot emotion in his wife that did not exist in himself. It was like a sixth sense that he did not possess: he did not understand it, he could not interpret it. Whenever he touched it, he was at once frightened and hurt and aroused.

"I don't understand what's got you so stirred up," he said.

"Exactly."

She turned off her light. She lay in the dark room a moment.

"I'm too tired," she finally said. "You and Aaron should go to that thing tomorrow without me."

A few minutes later, still lying in the dark, still angry, she heard Bruce and Sheila let themselves in with their spare key.

5

Bruce was staring at Mona, like those creepy posters of Uncle Sam. No matter where she went in the kitchen, his eyes followed. She took Phil's note, crumpled it into a small ball, and tossed it into the garbage. Bruce watched the garbage pail open, watched the little yellow projectile tumble through the air, watched the lid of the garbage pail close. He watched Mona rub her nose. He opened his mouth, Mona stared at him, he paused.

Then he attacked.

There had been a time when Bruce had been a conversationalist if the occasion required it, as someone of a certain age might once, before the knees were totally gone, have rallied a tennis ball on weekends. His best subjects had been theater, shows, Chinese politics (about which he was strangely knowledgeable), actors, modern art, and, believe it or not, tax reform. His work as a corporate lawyer took him to London frequently, so he knew all the latest London shows. Mona never trusted Bruce's Anglophile taste—everything he saw was "extraordinary," "marvelous," or "brilliant," provided the show was pronounced in sufficiently incomprehensible working-class accents—but she took pleasure in his enthusiasm, and he deferred to her expertise ("Of course I don't know the play the way you do . . .") in a way that she found appropriate and flattering. All of this came to an end maybe five years back, roughly around the time of his retirement, when arthritis of Bruce's conversational joints set in and he became interested exclusively in what he called "the authorship question."

Bruce's latest trick was to corner her and argue both sides of the "question" while Mona mutely stared on. "So I found myself thinking about what you were saying," he began, apropos of absolutely nothing that Mona had ever said. "And what you say has its merits," he conceded. "But I've done a little more research," he transitioned, the word "research" in this case nothing like scholarly endeavor but referring instead to the days spent on Facebook with his fellow obsessives, then to some wormhole he had fallen into on Reddit. "And I think that there's something here you should consider," he concluded, the word "conclude" not entirely *le mot juste*, as the words from "and" to "consider" were actually prelude, not conclusion, to a disquisition that could endure the better part of sanity; but neither was the word "conclude" wholly irrelevant, as the phrase *concluded* Mona's active involvement in the conversation. Now she was fixed like a butterfly to a corkboard, unable to escape, unwilling to reply for fear of coaxing him into yet more speech, as Bruce began slowly, methodically to expose the latest fruits of his investigations.

For his part, Bruce was convinced that he and Mona had been locked for years now in thrilling intellectual combat, a battle of wits and minds in which he gave as good as he got; that Mona enjoyed this debate as much as he did; and that his views on the authorship of the plays of William Shakespeare were not utterly insane. On each of these points, Bruce was wrong.

There had been every variety of argument over the years between them on the subject. Back in the day, they had traded emails into which were embedded dozens of links that neither party ever clicked. When Mona had not heard from Bruce on the subject for several months, Mona thought gratefully that Bruce's interest in the subject had finally died. Then, like a subterranean forest fire, the brawl re-exploded into incandescent life, after Bruce watched a

YouTube video on the subject, then, in the way of YouTube, many other videos as well, somehow all affirming his deranged point of view. This had led to a series of conversations so rancorous that two years back Mona had shouted at Bruce at his own eightieth birthday party, "Would you shut the fuck up about it? Would you just do my mental health that small favor?" Phil hustled her out of his parents' presence and said, "I know it's hard but he's old and he's got his ideas, could you just bear with him?" So Mona apologized, Bruce hugged her—and then recommenced his speech, like a good actor interrupted by a heckler, from the very syllable where he had been interrupted.

But this Thanksgiving Day, the drugs, finally kicking in, did wonders for Mona. Ol' Bad Coffee was galloping around the corral like Secretariat. He hadn't felt so good since he was a foal. The painkillers produced in Mona a wave of ease and joy, her self-absorption abated, and she tolerated Bruce, she tolerated Sheila, she tolerated all of struggling humanity. How great it was to have the family together! Just to live was such a privilege! "That's so interesting," she said to Bruce, awarding herself a shiny medal for Goodness. "I can tell you've been doing your reading." What Mona appreciated most about the opiate's warm glow was that, released from the pain of her own preoccupations, she could consider the preoccupations of others. Mona never wanted to be sober again. It wasn't Sheila and Bruce's fault that they were Sheila and Bruce, after all, any more than it was her fault that she was Mona; they had rebelled against their Sheilaness and Bruceosity for as long as human beings possibly could. She had known Bruce long enough now to remember a time when her sister called him the Stone-Cold Silver Fox, because for a guy his age, he was pretty hot, you know? Mona remembered what an air of authority Sheila exuded when she was still working. She had been one of New York's leading book publicists. It was as if at the end of a long show they had finally taken off their costumes to stand in front of their audiences and be revealed in all their tedious glory.

Bruce's antique eyes glowed. Mona could tell: he was *alive.*

"The evidence! the cover-up!" he cried. "Fraud! Impostor! Phony!"

Mona listened to Bruce prattle and began to chop onions and celery. She took pride in her ability to dice an onion. When she had played the Scottish Lady for Milton, he had insisted that Mona learn to chop an onion with the easy dexterity of a trained chef. The entire audience had been rubbing their eyes all through the show while Mona whacked away. She handed cutting boards and knives to Sheila and Bruce also, and they began to chop too, happy like dogs and children to have an important job. Mona was amazed as always how kindness and serenity, albeit drug-induced, could calm a room; how much easier everyone was when their hands were occupied.

Bruce was peaceful now, concentrated on cutting onions and not his fingers. He was settled down into an easy groove of paranoid discourse, his pleasant baritone no more than background noise.

Mona's thoughts drifted here and there. Bruce said something about Prospero and the Earl of Oxford and she thought about old men. That's where she'd be headed next, she supposed. There were so many of them, after all. Shakespeare had been fascinated by the old farts. Still, there was something sad about the thought that with Cleopatra she was coming to the end of the line of his great women. She had played male roles (her Richard II had made quite a splash, once upon a time) but Mona wasn't a man, and the women had spoken to something intimate in her life, maturing side by side with her since adolescence: Juliet, Rosalind, Imogen, Portia, Margaret,

Kate, even the Scottish Lady. They were so splendid, those women, right through Cleopatra. And then—Gertrude. *That's something to look forward to*, said no actress in the history of the stage. *What a great Gertrude*, said no spectator ever. Rather than play Gertrude, Elena Wills, Milton's last Cleopatra, had retired from the stage and moved to Vermont.

Bruce interrupted himself. "Sweetheart, when was the last time you sharpened your knives?"

"Phil does it," Mona said.

"He sure didn't get to this one," he said. "I'll tell you what I'm going to do. I'm going to sharpen your knives for you."

Bruce's happiness, already significant, increased: there was something in Bruce that abhorred a dull knife, but loved discussing dull knives. He was about to ask a second time where Mona kept her whetstone when Mona said, "Did you ever see Vikram Gupta play Master Shallow?"

Mona had no idea why she said that, but it worked: Bruce's knife hovered mid-onion. He had calmed enough to be distracted, and for a moment the old Bruce flashed out.

"Oh my, that was something," he said. "I never saw anything like it."

Vikram had played Master Shallow at what? Thirty? No older than that. He'd played Hotspur in Part One and Milton put him back as old Shallow for Part Two: first the embodiment of fiery youth, then the embodiment of doddering senility, all without makeup or costumes. But he made you believe. God only knows *how* he did it. You couldn't argue with genius, though. There were things you could do with talent and technique, and then there were *other* things that you could only do with genius. Mona didn't have genius. She knew that and accepted it. Acting for her was crossing a broad chasm on a narrow rope bridge. Every step was planned, considered, second-guessed; the purpose of all that was to permit her the spontaneity of sprinting. She was a classic outside-in actress. She stood onstage with a large bag of effects, tricks, poses, postures, mannerisms, artifices, and wiles which she employed to manipulate both her own emotions and the emotions of her audiences. From time to time she approached something like the truth, but always indirectly and at a distance, never with that sparkling leap across the chasm of disbelief that Vikram managed with such feline grace. For Mona it was always a fight.

———————

MONA TOOK THE CHESTNUTS out of the fridge and found the pine nuts in the cupboard. She had decided to attempt her father's Lebanese stuffing for the turkey. The recipe for the dish had long been lost; every year she tried to make it from memory and failed. She knew with certainty only that it required toasted pine nuts. She poured a large handful into a frying pan and stirred them, saying "Uh-huh" from time to time in response to no particular prompt from her in-laws.

Mona wasn't sure that Phil really understood the nature of her quondam affair with Vikram. This was before she met him. The official line on her relationship with Vikram was that they had "been together" for, "I dunno, a couple months, maybe?" back in the nineties, but "it didn't really work" and was "kind of boring" because the only thing Vikram ever wanted to do was "talk about himself." It took all of Mona's art and skill to say these words with the appropriate lack of affect.

The truth was that playing Ophelia to Vikram's Hamlet had

been the defining erotic experience of her twenties. Every night from the wings she watched as he said the first line of his first soliloquy, "O, that this too too solid flesh would melt." Then, on his next line, "Oh God! God!" he'd collapse. Mona had never seen an actor cry like that before, eyes streaming and snot—real honest-to-God *snot*—pouring from his nose, all without ever missing a beat of the line that followed: "How weary, stale, flat and unprofitable seem to me all the uses of this world." Vikram was able to do it every show. Mona told her sister about the snot. Zahra said, "Gross." But it wasn't gross at all. Mona thought it was the sexiest thing she had ever seen.

It was Milton, still in charge at 107 Avenue C at the time, who had first proposed that she play Cleopatra opposite his Antony. "Cleopatra?" Mona said. "Do you think so? Really?" Milton persuaded Vikram to fly in from London and workshop the show for three days. It was the first time she had seen Vikram in person since the nineties. By day two she was over the shock of his physical decline, and by day three, she was aware that her marriage would be in serious danger if she did the show. He still had *that* voice, the one Mona would have paid good money to listen to reading the phone book, if phone books still existed to be read. It pierced through any crowd not just with its strength but with its clarity and musicality and absolute unadulterated sexiness.

Vikram was, as Milton supposed, a perfect Antony—dissolute, ruined, middle-aged, magnificent. There was a moment at the table read that made her knees weak, which is a euphemism for another physiological response entirely. Antony and Cleopatra are bickering, as always, when Antony leans over and kisses her. "The nobleness of life is to do thus," he says. Mona could not stop thinking about that. Was *that* the nobleness of life? Was it really? Had she been mistaken all along? Sometimes at night in the weeks after the workshop Mona dreamed of falling in love. Oh, those dreams! They tormented her! Mona would have preferred the worst nightmare to those sweet, sweet dreams of love. Those dreams revealed that there was in her, latent and unused, a capacity still for passion.

On the last day of the workshop, either Vikram or Antony— Mona did not know which—invited her or Cleopatra to walk him back to his hotel. Mona could see that when the show went into rehearsals and then performance, walking back to his hotel would be a habit for the two of them. It was on her way home, after all. They would linger at the hotel entrance, reluctant to say good night. Eventually he would invite her in for a drink at the hotel bar, where Mona would feel like an adult woman having a drink with Vikram Gupta at the hotel bar. Later he would whisper in her ear: "Now, for the love of Love and her soft hours, / Let's not confound the time with conference harsh. / There's not a minute of our lives should stretch / Without some pleasure now." Only a certain kind of man can say that kind of lush rubbish and carry it off, but Antony *was* that kind of man. So was Vikram. *Not a minute of our lives should stretch without some pleasure now*: this was like cruel mockery of Phil, whose minutes were a series of obligations met and mastered. Phil scheduled Saturday morning visits with elderly aunts wasting away in old-age homes in remote corners of the city. On his day off, he bitch-slapped the taxes into submission. Every year, Phil spent a sunny fall weekend organizing the storage space they rented in the Bronx to hold his medical records and Mona's boxes of memorabilia.

When the casting for *Antony and Cleopatra* was proposed, she took Phil aside and said, "I won't do it if it makes you feel uncomfortable."

"But it's Cleopatra," Phil said. "Of course you have to do it."

The fact that Phil said this—the generosity of the thought!—made Mona love him for his goodness, even as his presumption that she could not be tempted (or that Vikram would not wish to tempt her) infuriated her. How dumb he was to take her for granted! The thing of it was, Phil should have understood that Mona was vulnerable. You shouldn't *need* to tell your husband that *now* was the moment to be inflamed with jealousy. You shouldn't *need* to explain to him why. That was the whole point of marriage—that there was someone in your life you could count on to be paying attention.

Had Phil displayed such an alarming, even offensive lack of jealousy precisely because he was unfaithful himself?

Mona was so startled by the question that she opened the refrigerator for no reason at all, just to feel the cool air on her face. She pretended to rummage in the vegetable drawer for garlic.

She wondered: Had he asked her to attend Ultimate, and asked her again, and asked her yet again, just because he did not want her to go, his asseverations to the contrary clear proof of his guilt? That's what Mona would have done if she were cheating on Phil. He had found her Maria boring because he found *her* boring. He was probably off in the woods right now fooling around with that chick who sent out the organizing emails, Melanie McDowell. Mona remembered the stupid grin on Phil's face when he told her that he had kissed her once in high school, when they both had braces. Now she had three kids and chased down Frisbees like a Labrador, and probably sank to her knees behind an elm whenever Phil offered her career advice.

These jealous thoughts produced in Mona an inundation of physical desire for her husband. She pulled her head out of the crisper and went back to the cutting board. The jealousy broke through the dam of Mona's opiate-induced numbness and crested across the flat

plains of matrimonial boredom. She thought of Melanie McDowell's excitement; her own excitement mounted. She thought about
the scratchy leaves and brambles under Melanie McDowell's ass as
Phil roughly rode her deep in a forest clearing. She thought of Phil
coming home and, not saying a word, bending her over the bathroom sink. She thought about sucking on his fingers. She thought of
Phil kneading her ass and twisting her nipples, her own fingernails
sinking deeply into his thighs . . .

The problem with the opiates was that the very moment you
thought to yourself that you were feeling fine, you started to feel
less fine. The pleasure abated inevitably into irritability. You were
either up or down, life reduced to a bright biochemical binary.
This was something she always forgot on the way out to Happiness and recalled on the way back home. An hour of happiness was
never enough.

There was this thing Bruce did and had done since forever, this
way of saying, "You see, Mona," and leaning over into her space.
Mona took a step back and Bruce advanced.

"I'm sorry?" she said, thinking idly about plunging the knife with
which she was dicing the onion into the soft, spongy space between
Bruce's fifth and sixth left intercostal and gently wiggling it.

"I said, the so-called 'scholarly community' is starting to understand the evidence," Bruce said. "People can't deny forever what's
right in front of their eyes."

"No, they certainly can't," she said, the erotic fantasy that just
seconds ago had held her entranced now entirely disappeared, like
the letters *D-E-S-I-R-E* traced one by one onto the surface of a
still pond.

6

Before Mona saw the cornflower-blue eyes open, or heard her sigh, or noticed the rustling of the covers, she felt the energy of the room shift, from old to young.

"Morning, everyone!" Rachel said, her pretty pixie head emerging from under the duvet like a sleek seal poking out of the sea foam.

Bruce and Sheila turned around, both of them surprised by the sleepy voice. They looked with amazement at this impossibly bright-faced little person in pale blue pajamas.

"Did you sleep well?" asked Sheila.

"Of course she slept well," Bruce said. "Just look at her! Everyone at that age sleeps well."

Rachel let out a little sigh. "Except I had the strangest dream."

"You're not going to make us listen to it, are you?" said Mona, walking around from the kitchen and hugging her. Rachel smelled like the citrus body lotion that Mona sent her for her birthday.

Mona felt a visceral tenderness for her niece that she felt for no one else, maybe not even her own child. Aaron had disappointed Mona by accompanying his father to Ultimate, an event he had always led her to believe he hated as much as she did. Mona wasn't sure if Phil had somehow suborned Aaron into attending, thinking to sabotage Mona's domestic strike; or if Aaron had some subtle masculine agenda of his own. In any case, it felt like further proof that he was slipping away from her. That Aaron was no longer five or seven or eleven was another of Mona's myriad sorrows. He had just recently grown taller than her. Every now and again Aaron could still thrill her, wrapping his too-long arms around her in one of those spontaneous childish embraces that caused Mona to melt away to nothingness. But those moments were fewer and fewer. Mona could look at pictures of him on her phone in his various phases of childhood and find herself in tears. At least Rachel was still Rachel, in every way her sister's daughter. Mona loved her perfect little shape and form, her unlined face, her short clean hair—Rachel was the cleanest creature Mona had ever met. Mona could almost see if she squinted Rachel's silver-gray aura gleaming around her, matching the freshly polished stainless steel of Mona's refrigerator door.

"Mom was driving too fast," Rachel said.

Dreams about her sister were the only exception to Mona's rule that the dreams of others were always boring. Mona believed/didn't believe that in these dreams it was/was not possible to communicate with the other side, the slash indicating Mona's precise place of certainty/uncertainty on the question. She thought about the slash all the time. Mona still held a smidgen of hope that Zahra might come back, if not exactly in the way things were before, then in some other way: she even went once to a Meet Up in Astoria of people who had had near-death experiences. It had been a remarkable night of theater. Mona had been convinced for a few days thereafter that Zahra's soul was very near. But then disbelief set in again. The question of whatever happened to her sister, whom she had loved and whom she missed, who had been and now who wasn't, plagued Mona: her sister came to her regularly at night unhappy and frightened, complaining that her credit card no longer worked, which just might be/was probably not an accurate dispatch from the afterlife/Mona's subconscious.

"Was it the kind of dream where you knew she was—" Mona

still couldn't quite say the word "dead." "Or was it the kind where she was still here and it was just a normal dream?"

"It was the kind where she was alive and I didn't know she was dead and we were fighting the whole time."

Dreams about Zahra were so precious—it seemed a terrible waste of a rare opportunity to spend one fighting.

"Were you scared?"

"Not exactly," Rachel said. "I just thought we were going to get a ticket."

For a moment Mona felt her sister's presence. Zahra drove too fast and was always trying to do many things as she drove: apply mascara, answer a telephone call, drink from a cup of hot tea, and yell at the Subaru that cut her off in traffic. Once Mona had yanked the steering wheel from her sister's hands as she plunged across lanes of traffic toward a ravine.

Rachel lowered her head on her aunt's shoulder. Mona could feel the small head on her shoulder, lifting and dipping with each breath. This was Rachel's way of saying that she was prepared to make peace, that the events of the summer were, if not forgotten, then tabled.

It was hardly Bruce's fault that he sneezed, and still less his fault that he sneezed again—and who could really blame him for the third sneeze either?—but with those three intrusive blasts the spell was broken. Mona did blame him. She glared at him irritably. Rachel sat up, and pulled her knees close to her chest.

"Do we have coffee?" she said.

———————

MONA HAD KNOWN RACHEL all her life, of course, but she only really started spending time with her in the summer after her junior year in high school, when Rachel asked Mona to bring her in as an intern at 107 Avenue C, not because of some deep passion for theater, but to give a shine to her college applications. Rachel had worked with the admin staff on reorganizing the company's website, and Milton had even offered her a nonspeaking role in his new *Dream*, as a member of Titania's entourage. Rachel didn't have much talent for acting but could be counted on to remember her entrances and exits, and she had a quality of unambitious, un-smirking invisibility that Milton was always looking for in his spear-holders, something surprisingly hard to find in a city of young actors eager to steal a stage. Soon Rachel, with her bright, adult manner, was integrated as a mascot into the Rabble, invited to after-show house parties, or just to hang out in the dressing room. That summer, Rachel got drunk for what Mona supposed was the first time in her life at an after-party. Mona had been distracted while Rachel knocked back tequila shots. Nothing really changed in Rachel's affect except that she turned a kind of curious green. Then she went to the bathroom and with very little drama barfed, Mona holding her hair back and feeling like she was finally doing some good work as an aunt. She promised never to mention the incident to her mother, which was a moot point, because Rachel mentioned it to Zahra herself, and the two of them laughed about it, which somehow felt to Mona for reasons she could not justify like a violation of *her* privacy.

That same quality of easy calm, which Mona found at once mysterious and unlike every other member of her family, showed itself again a few months later when Zahra had been dying. Then Rachel had known, almost instinctively, in a way that Mona certainly didn't, how to tend her. There had been an incident when Zahra, all doped up, had peed in the bed. Mona had tried to change the sheets without making Zahra stand up but found the geometry of the procedure difficult, even getting frustrated with her sister. But Rachel had said, "I'll do it," and smoothly rolled her mother to one side of the bed, stripped the dirty linen from the other side, and in one smooth motion rolled Zahra back onto the fresh sheets.

After Zahra died, Mona put up a temporary wall in the living room, and Rachel came to live with them for the remainder of her senior year. The alternative had been dropping out of Stuyvesant and moving to Duluth, where Vadim was teaching playwriting. Established in the household, she proved a strange and independent creature, already adult and fully formed: Rachel set her alarm and left in the morning before anyone else was awake, she stayed on top of her schoolwork, she kept her little room neat and empty. She was a vegetarian and cooked separately for herself. Mona kept waiting for the moment when the two of them would cry it out over Zahra, but it never really happened. The closest to an outburst Rachel ever got was when, helping Mona in the kitchen, she remarked that she really wished she had learned her mom's recipe for tiramisù. "She was always trying to teach me," Rachel said. "I know the recipe," Mona said, and instantly felt like a world-class tool, because obviously it wasn't about how you warm the whites before folding them into the mascarpone. The only sign that Rachel noticed Mona's gaffe was a little grimace, her smooth face otherwise as inexpressive as an eggshell.

———

"WE ALL MISS YOU IN THE GROUP!" Sheila said.

"I miss you all too," Rachel said.

To Mona's surprise, Rachel and Sheila had developed an unlikely friendship during the year Rachel lived in the temporary bedroom.

They had no bond of blood between them but both saw themselves as victims of the patriarchy, Sheila complaining of the injustice implicitly, in the way she rolled her eyes as her husband yammered unceasingly on, Rachel explicitly. Rachel had been the only person in the universe to take seriously the dynamics of Sheila's relationship with Nora Weiner and the rest of the Gang, even doing what Mona had refused to do: she had attended a session of the book club via Zoom, where Sheila had introduced Rachel as her "almost-granddaughter." So far as Mona knew, Sheila didn't realize that Rachel had live-tweeted the event, inventing nicknames for each of the participants and quoting their thoughts on Elena Ferrante or Karl Ove Knausgaard with painful accuracy. Every time Sheila said something, Rachel gave commentary: "And Sheila scores!" or, "Swish! In your face, Nora W.!"

Mona ground the coffee beans while Sheila and Rachel talked. Rachel even remembered the names of the other members of the Gang. She asked after them one by one, and Sheila answered, the answers inevitably expressed as the conjunction of a malady and a factoid about a grandchild. ("Oh, she's feeling much better after the hip surgery. And you know her granddaughter Sarah? She's getting gay married!") Mona loved the obliterating noise of the coffee grinder, how all conversation stopped for a moment when she pressed the little button. She timed it to coincide with Bruce opening his mouth, perfusing the kitchen with the rich oily smell of whatever expensive coffee Whole Foods had persuaded her to buy. Mona had just set the coffee to drip when Sheila shrieked, no exaggeration that word, but a heart-stopping, overwrought cry: "Oh no, sweetie, oh no."

Mona's glance went to Sheila first and then followed Sheila's eyes to Rachel's forearm, which Sheila cradled tenderly in her hands as if it had been mauled by a tiger.

"Let me see," Mona said. Obediently, as if expecting to be

scolded, Rachel showed Mona the inseam of her forearm where in neat cursive script had been tattooed the words *Simply the thing I am.* Centered under the words was a rose, neat and tightly folded, no larger than a fingernail.

Sheila's group could have interpreted that tattoo for weeks. There were levels and sublevels of meaning. When Rachel had been fourteen, she and her mother had fought, viciously, over a tattoo of a rose that Rachel proposed to affix to her ankle. "I will not let you permanently disfigure your body with a rose," Zahra said. "Putting a rose on your body is like saying, *I haven't got a thought in my little head. I'm going to choose the most stereotyped image of femininity because I cannot think of something more clever or original.*" That fight had been one of the grand fights of Rachel's adolescence, spilling over into a mauling examination of everything in Zahra's life, from the hypocrisy of Zahra's own ankle tattoo (a spiral of lace, long regretted) to the general disorder of the apartment they shared (Zahra had been a terrible slob), to Zahra's stalking (and that was the correct word, unfortunately) of Rachel's father Vadim, who Rachel insisted had fled the apartment and the relationship because Zahra was an insupportable bitch. This was not long after Zahra was first diagnosed. So all of that was in the tattoo. Mona understood that.

But then there were the words themselves, from *All's Well.* A captain named Parolles had been demoted from his rank, and as sometimes happens in Shakespeare and in life, he had found in his humiliation the inspiration for a moment of wisdom:

> ... Captain I'll be no more;
> But I will eat and drink, and sleep as soft
> As Captain shall: Simply the thing I am
> Shall make me live.

Mona had been prompted to quote those lines because Rachel had been devastated by her failure to win a place at Yale, an ambition that Mona found inexplicable but which had completely consumed Rachel for years. They were some of her very most favorite lines in all of Shakespeare, and reciting them to Rachel had felt like a very intimate thing. Mona was surprised that Rachel had listened, taken the lines, turned them around, thought about them some more.

Simply the thing I am / Shall make me live. Mona was deeply opposed to tattoos in every way, shape, or form—a permanent ugly transformation of the body was everything an actress didn't want—but as a credo in life, this one, she thought, wasn't bad.

"Do you want milk in your coffee?" she asked.

"Do you have almond milk?" Rachel said.

"And just what's wrong with cow's milk?" Bruce said. "Since when is the milk of a cow no longer acceptable?"

"I think I have some almond milk," Mona said.

Bruce said, "I tried that almond milk. It doesn't taste much like almonds and it sure doesn't taste like milk."

"We had almond milk in Italy," Sheila said. "Where they stole your wallet. You liked it."

"That was in Italy."

"Almonds taste different in Italy?" Mona said.

"I was different in Italy," Bruce said. He looked around the room with happy, puppyish eyes. "Oh, what a treat it is to have three such beautiful women at breakfast."

Mona was unexpectedly touched by his remark. She felt guilty about the coffee grinder. "Thank you," she said.

"I thank *you*, lovely lady."

———————

MONA WONDERED whether she and Rachel might be able to pass the entirety of the holiday weekend without ever discussing their fight, the only significant fight Mona ever had with her niece.

At the end of the summer, the plan had been for Phil to accompany Mona and Rachel to her first semester at Amherst, but Phil had an emergency at the hospital: the nurses' union was threatening a wildcat strike at midnight, and Phil was one of the lead negotiators.

"I could just take the train," Rachel said.

"Don't be ridiculous," Mona said. "With all your suitcases and everything? Phil's going to stay here and I'll drive you. It'll be fun."

Rachel had a worried, doubtful look on her face as they headed north. Mona was, notoriously, not a great driver. She had learned to drive late in life—one of the few people to get a driver's license *after* moving to Manhattan, at Phil's insistence—and only drove on rare occasions. The presence of other vehicles on the road disturbed her. She had a particular distaste for merging on or off the freeway, and once settled on the freeway, didn't like to change lanes, preferring to sit behind an eighteen-wheeler for mile after mile rather than attempt to swing around his side.

They'd just cleared the city traffic when the car got very silent. Mona had no idea what to talk to Rachel about. She had a notion that Rachel considered her essentially a silly person, and alone with her niece she became intensely self-conscious. What would be perfect, Mona thought, is if Rachel were suddenly to burst into sobs. Then Mona could say, "What's the matter, honey?" and Rachel could say there had been a boy and there had been summer and now it was over and Rachel would cry and Mona would tell her about her own summer loves, and Mona would tell Rachel about Zahra's summer loves, and Rachel would say, "I didn't know that about Mom," and Mona would say, "Your mom had a bit of a history, shall we say?" and then they would talk about Zahra and maybe even Zahra's abortion when she was seventeen and what it was like being Hafez's daughter and maybe that's why Zahra was attracted to someone like Vadim, someone soft and thoughtful but with no center or real ambition. And maybe, Mona fantasized, the car would get a flat and just to show her niece what a bad-ass she was, Mona would change the flat with no problems because that was something she could do. Phil had insisted that she learn. You just needed the doohickey from the trunk. Then maybe the right kind of song would come on the radio or Rachel's phone or whatever people used nowadays, like Billy Joel maybe? The kind of cheesy thing you only listen to on a road trip? and they'd sing together, perfect song after perfect song, the late-summer afternoon on the open road expanding and dilating like an artery.

That would have been just perfect.

What happened instead was that an hour out, traffic lousy, hunkered down in the exhaust of some northbound brontosaurus, the sky gray, Mona's head already hurting, Rachel just said, "So how's Milton?"

And Mona just said, "Rachel, did you talk to the *Times* about him?"

And Rachel just said, "Yeah, they called me and I told them what happened."

Mona stared straight ahead. So Phil had been right all along, she thought: it was Phil who had first proposed when the article in the *Times* came out that Rachel had been Anonymous Source Number Three, one of the "eleven women who have come forward to describe a pattern of sexual abuse, emotional cruelty, and violations of trust by a man they considered a mentor and friend."

"Rachel?" Mona said. "No way."

But then Phil read the incriminating paragraphs out loud:

> One woman who requested anonymity said that Mr. Katz routinely created sexual provocations in the rehearsal room.
>
> She recalled an incident when, although she was in a nonspeaking role in the performance, Mr. Katz insisted in rehearsal that she loudly imitate a woman having an orgasm. On another occasion, she said, he asked the woman a series of intrusive questions about her sexual life.
>
> On still another occasion, she said, at the conclusion of a performance, Mr. Katz hugged her backstage without an invitation. "He kissed me, and because I was frightened to make any noise, I had to kiss him back," she said. "After that, he was always waiting for me."
>
> Shortly after that experience, the young woman left the company altogether.

"I'd bet anything that's Rachel," Phil said.

"That could be any single woman in the company over the last fifty years," Mona said. "I bet there's three hundred women who could say the same thing. He's kissed me more than you have."

But the seeds of doubt had been planted. Mona remembered that there had in fact been a moment when Rachel had complained that Milton kissed her when she came offstage. As for the orgasm, Milton sooner or later asked almost everyone in the company—men and women alike—to throw one out on the table. She hadn't been in the rehearsal room when Rachel had been asked to orgasm, but it was one of Milton's regular warm-ups. "It *should* be embarrassing," he always said. "The embarrassment is where the good stuff lives." Still, Mona wasn't sure. Mona always had the impression that Rachel liked Milton. Milton had written an enthusiastic letter of recommendation for Rachel's college application, and when Rachel was admitted to college, she insisted on going down to 107 Avenue C to visit him. She had even brought him a stuffed animal, a little woolly mammoth.

Now Mona held the wheel tightly, not daring to glance over at Rachel. It was Rachel's tone of voice—insouciant, ironic, matter-of-fact—as much as her actions that infuriated Mona.

"Well," Mona finally said.

"I'm sorry," Rachel said.

"Why are you sorry? You're a big girl. You made your decision."

"Please."

"Please what?"

"Please just don't be angry with me."

"I'm not angry," Mona lied.

Rachel said, "I knew I shouldn't have talked to you about it."

"You already talked to the whole wide world. The least you can do is talk to me too."

A mile or so passed in silence. Mona wished that she wasn't driving. Trying to have this conversation and stay alive was brain-breaking. She began to hate the truck and its Neanderthal driver.

"I didn't *know* what was going to happen," Rachel said. "The reporter was nice and she wanted to talk about what it was like to be a young woman at the company. She didn't tell me that the whole story was going to be like Milton Katz was a monster and molests women blah-blah-blah, and I didn't know that Milton was going to—that they were going to get rid of him."

"How could you *not* know what was going to happen?" Mona said.

"I just didn't."

"Did you even think about it at all? Or did you just decide, 'Hey, today is Tuesday, let's destroy Milton'?"

"I thought about it," Rachel said.

"Not very hard."

"I even called Sheila."

Mona took a quick sideways glance. Rachel was hugging her knees and leaning up against the window, trying to create as much space as possible between her and Mona.

"Sheila?" Mona said. "Like Sheila and Bruce?"

"She's not as dumb as you think she is."

"No one could be as dumb as I think Sheila is."

Rachel didn't say anything.

Mona said, "You called *Sheila* in Florida and you didn't come to me?"

"Because you wouldn't have listened! You would have told me I was being silly."

"You were being silly!"

"My mother always said there was nothing in the world worse than trying to argue with you. You just don't ever want to listen."

Mona was no longer just angry with Rachel; she was angry with Zahra too, who inspired in Mona a deeper anger than Rachel ever could.

"Don't you dare," she said through gritted teeth. "Don't you *dare* say that your mother would be on your side. Zahra was the most loyal person I ever met and she would be ashamed of you."

Just as soon as Mona said the words, she regretted them. Neither Rachel nor Mona spoke for a long time. Mona decided to pass the truck. She started to pull into the left lane, only to be frightened by loud insistent honking: she had forgotten to check the mirror. She swung back into her own lane.

"I'm sorry," Mona said. "That was a terrible thing to say."

Rachel had begun to cry. "No, it's true," she said.

Mona had never seen Rachel cry before. Mona felt monstrous. They drove ten minutes or so in silence. "So this is fun," Mona finally said, and Rachel giggled slightly through her tears.

"I was just an intern, okay? I was just there for the college applications. I wasn't trying to make art or bare my soul or find my frigging Lady Macbeth. And he'd find some way to be alone with me and ask me these intimate questions, looking all deep in my eyes, like if I ever had a boyfriend. And he wouldn't take no for answer. I'd make up some excuse to get away and the next day Milton would find me after a show or whatever and want to kiss me because I'd been so terrific at standing onstage and not looking bored."

"And that bothered you that much?"

"Wouldn't it bother you?"

"I mean—" Mona said. Mona wanted to say that she loved Milton, despite his faults, and had a huge reservoir of patience for the man, built up over decades; that Milton asked inappropriate questions but that was the reason, when confronted in the rehearsal room with hard problems, he gave inappropriate solutions, because his conduct in *every* sphere of life was unconstrained by respect for propriety. Before she could find the words, Rachel interrupted her.

"He was sleazy and gross and totally inappropriate. And everyone in the company under the age of forty thought that."

They arrived at Amherst with their physical bodies intact, their emotional bodies bruised. There had been no resolution to the argument. The best that could be said was that neither wanted to continue it. The way Rachel looked at Mona as they unloaded her bags suggested to Mona some complete incomprehension on Rachel's part of the way things were between men and women; but Mona had the strange insight that Rachel was thinking the very same thing, that Mona simply had no idea how things were between men and women.

———

NOW THERE WAS A BURST OF FURIOUS COOKING. Everyone helped. The turkey, absurd and pasty-skinned, was brought out of the refrigerator and patted dry, the stuffing, now ready, inserted into the appropriate cavity. Mona hated turkey. Every year she threatened to order in Peking duck for everyone, and every year here she was again, reaming out a late bird's butt. Green beans were trimmed, potatoes and carrots peeled, nutmeg grated, pots rustled, water boiled, salad spun. Mona reckoned that she had made well over twenty Thanksgiving meals over the years, and she knew intimately the whole process of preparing this elaborate meal that no one would particularly enjoy. At least there would be leftovers: Mona loved the great drama of freezing and defrosting things, good food turning hard and gray, then coming back on demand to color and vivacity, a process that always reminded Mona of the lovely ending of *The Winter's Tale*, when the statue of Hermione comes to life.

Mona spent five minutes looking for the hand blender, which had to be here somewhere, it's not like a hand blender was just going to sprout wings and fly south for the winter. Barney jumped up on the couch into the warm spot Rachel had left behind. Mona bumped into Bruce, and Sheila got in her way. Then Sheila bumped into Rachel and Bruce just stood in front of the open refrigerator door as if hypnotized. Sheila said, "Excuse me, please." Mona said, "Every-one out. Too many cooks in the kitchen," and the others retired to the living room, where they stared at their phones. Mona thought of going downstairs to get her own phone, still locked in the mailbox, but the silence in her brain was pleasant. If Mona breathed just the right way, holding her breath at the top, exhaling really slowly, and then holding her breath again at the bottom, she could still feel a little high. Bruce was going through his Facebook feed, systematically liking all the posts by his ideological allies, or inserting the angry, red-faced emoticon next to those he disagreed with, "disagreed" not quite the right word, the appropriate word expressing rather his desire to slap his enemies silly, like buzzing mosquitoes in the night. He was muttering slightly to himself as he did so. Sheila was sending greetings to the Gang, all of them dispersed to their own Thanksgiving feasts. They all communicated through a group text that Nora Weiner's grandson set up for them. Rachel was scrolling through her Instagram feed, her eyes glazed and spooky.

Mona was pleased that things were easy with Rachel, easier even than she had dared to hope. When Mona came home from Amherst, Phil had correctly advised her to make peace as quickly as possible. "Don't let it fester," he said. Mona recognized Phil's wisdom and sent her a large box of beauty supplies from a trendy Nolita boutique for her birthday. Now Mona interpreted Rachel's smell— like limes, rosemary, and chamomile—as a sign that Rachel was equally eager to drop the fight.

Mona understood also that Sheila's advice to Rachel had been an attack on her husband from an oblique angle, that Milton had been collateral damage in a marital war enduring now over half a century. Bruce remained a deep and true believer in the legend of Milton. Bruce's affection for Milton had been in the day equal parts touching and weird. Mona once heard Bruce say, "I could never do what Milton does, but thank goodness he does it." Mona never understood just what Bruce thought Milton did. Milton had intimated for years, never saying so outright, certainly never actually believing it, that he shared Bruce's sentiments on the authorship question, that only political necessity required him to keep quiet. When Bruce brought the subject up, Milton would put his finger to his lips, sweep his eyes from side to side, and say, "The walls have ears, my friend."

Bruce had just retired from the board when the revolution came for Milton. When Milton's departure from the company was announced, Bruce canceled his season tickets as well as his wife's and sent a letter to the editors of the *Times* that was never published, in which he denounced "the corrupt logic of abandoning an artistic legend, a genius of our time, on account of the hysterical complaints of a bevy of would-be starlets." There had been a period of a month or two when Bruce had wandered off the authorship question to denounce the current board and management of the company, the intolerant temper of the times, and the waste of a great man's talent. Then the two subjects—Milton's fall and the rise of the great fraud Shakespeare—had fused into a single threnody of discontent. To bewail the one was to bewail the other. They were both symptomatic of the corruption endemic to the earth.

Mona had to pee. She asked Sheila to stir the stuffing, and asked Bruce to peel two more yams. She told Rachel she could make another pot of coffee if anyone wanted—the good beans were in the fridge.

7

Mona went to the bathroom, peed, lay on her bed, and got stoned. The pot was meant as a kind of perk-me-up to the opiates, whose influence had diminished to the vanishing point. Smoking pot had been transformed by the introduction of the vape into her life. Her lungs had always been sensitive and she never thought it was a great idea to coat them or her pharynx in clouds of noxious smoke. Her voice was her life, after all. But somehow she had convinced herself that vaping pot—nothing but wholesome hot steam, after all—might actually be a positive good. In recent months, the vape was making its way between her lips more and more frequently.

Mona's thoughts drifted back to her conversation with Rachel on the car trip up to Amherst. It wasn't the first time she had replayed the argument in her mind, replacing the angry insults with calm, measured phrases.

Mona wanted to say that, for her part, she had never really been bothered by the hugging. Milton was a hugger, a toucher, a kisser, a caresser; a stroker of women's hair, a sniffer of perfumes, a rubber of necks and thighs, a holder of hands, a cuddler, a squeezer of shoulders. That's who he was. Milton in the elevator would wrap an arm around you. If he hadn't seen you in a day, he'd hug you—hell, if he hadn't seen you in a couple of hours, he might hug—and no little delicate-hands-on-shoulder-butts-out-wide hugs either. These were body-to-body embraces, from toe to forehead, his big body smooshed up right against yours, protuberance on protuberance, fold on fold. In any case, it was true: Milton had a voracious desire for physical contact. If you were tight, he'd knead his thumbs into your neck and shoulders. If you were frightened, his hugs were an encouragement; if you had flopped, a consolation. Mona knew that the touching bothered the younger women in the company, and sometimes it bothered her too.

But there was a whole category of Milton-related offenses that Mona just labeled "old hippie," which is what Milton basically was: an old hippie doing guerrilla Shakespeare in a squat in the East Village, who'd somehow leaped high into the ranks of the Establishment by doing the same thing year after year after year. "He was a throwback, a relic," Mona thought in Rachel's direction, saying the things she hadn't had the wherewithal to say the summer before. "People used to be like that because the people a generation before Milton *weren't* like that. Milton's parents were born under the czar, believe it or not, and they probably hugged Milton precisely twice in his life. It's like you're telling this untrained golden retriever that he's not supposed to jump up and slobber on you when he sees you." "He didn't do it to men," Rachel said. Mona preferred these arguments in her head to their real-life counterparts, because she always had a ready response. "First, he did do it to men. He hugged men and massaged their necks and lay hands on them also. And the straight guys used to be more visibly uncomfortable with that than women, and they used to be mocked for it, about having hang-ups about being touched by a man. Times used to be different. When your generation takes over, you'll get to set the rules, and then the younger generation will rebel against you. But it's not fair to set the elders out on the ice floe just because they committed the sin of aging."

Mona was very happy with how calmly and easily she had won the argument. Rachel-in-Mona's-mind had a kind of abashed look, as if she realized that she really hadn't been right about this all this time. "Well, maybe you've got a point," imaginary Rachel admitted, which Mona thought was very gracious.

Mona was just about to get up and go back to the kitchen when make-believe Rachel started fighting all over again.

"But he *was* a predator," she said.

"Sharks are predators," Mona said. "So are lions. Milton was something different. The thing is, honey, there wasn't another Milton on offer. He didn't come in lots of different models and you could just pick the Milton that you wanted. The same set of compulsions, drives, neuroticisms, and eccentricities that allowed Milton to do something that no one else could have done made him a man who did things no one else would do. If you go around taming the wild Miltons of this world, you'll end up in a very tame world—and I'm not sure that's the world I want to live in. The Rabble *was* Milton, and without Milton it wouldn't have existed. Without Milton none of it would have happened."

———

MONA SUDDENLY WAS AWARE that either her thoughts or the room were spinning. She had bought the cannabis oil because her guy had promised her that it was a "connecting" blend. He had insisted that under its influence, she'd put together "chains of thought and inspiration." What it did was knock her solidly on her ass. She lay on the bed and looked at the ceiling.

The thing about being very stoned was that it forced you to think about things your unstoned brain was able to avoid thinking about.

Mona's unstoned brain refused to think about Cleopatra. Mona's newly stoned brain headed straight toward the subject.

Mona curled up on the blanket and felt very small. She regretted getting stoned and regretted becoming an actress and regretted accepting the role and regretted the fact that she couldn't embrace the challenge courageously and gratefully like a decent human being, understanding that failure was an inherent part of making art and that the moral greatness lay in the courage, not the accomplishment.

It was the imminence of it all, the verging on now-ness, the very un-theoretical fact of what was about to happen. Advance ticket sales were good. The whole machinery of the company was springing into motion to crush her. She had an appointment with Liz Wheeler, the costume designer, just next week. Terrence, the new artistic director, was leaving her voice mails: "Just checking in!" he chided. "Just circling back!" he threatened. "Just closing the loop!" he reproached. Mary Ngoro, the hoity-toity dramaturge Terrence had poached from the RSC, had sent her an email inviting her to get in touch if she wanted to go over any lines, which email just reeked with passive-aggressive menace.

The only other role in Shakespeare as total and complete and omnivorous as Cleopatra was Hamlet. But Hamlet was *easy* compared to Cleopatra. The trade secret was that Hamlet was actually not that tough. A lot of lines, the big soliloquies, a way-deep dive into the abyss of the soul—but actors loved the role because no matter what you brought into it, if you made it to the end and could keep a straight face, you came out covered in glory. If you were funny, the role was funny, and if you were deep, the role was deep, and if you were sexy, so was he; and if you were none of those things, audiences loved you because you were an antihero. It was an utterly miraculous part: you just had to bring yourself to the stage.

But Mona had never actually seen a great Cleopatra. She had seen great moments of Cleopatra, but she had never seen an actress master the role from end to end: actresses who got the sexy missed the funny; actresses who got the funny didn't get the imperial; and those who were imperial weren't sexy *or* funny. "Age cannot wither her, nor custom stale / Her infinite variety." How on earth do you play *that?* But Mona knew what it meant. It meant Cleopatra had to find every laugh, push the audience away, pull them back, play with them like they were puppets on a string, radiate desire, satisfy the desire, incite the desire again, ache with tender love, long for death, play power games with the most powerful men on earth, laugh with her girlfriends, lose her marbles totally, fear death, and then die with heartbreaking courage and nobility. Holy shit, the arias in that part were hard! Just the *breath* you needed! This was not beginner-level Shakespeare. The audience had to believe that Antony would abandon everything—wife, honor, power, life itself—for this woman. Then, after Antony was off, downing a cold beer in the dressing room, the actress who played Cleopatra had to take the stage without him and keep an audience already up past eleven right with her while she killed herself. Those were either the greatest or the most excruciating thirty minutes in theater.

There was a line in the play that filled Mona with nervous horror. She didn't like to think about it much because it made her so anxious. Every actress who played Cleopatra had to come to terms with it, and quite frankly, most of them couldn't handle it. It came in Act Three, just after intermission, when Caesar offers Cleopatra her kingdom and independence, provided she betray Antony. Antony, as uncertain of Cleopatra's response as he was uncertain of the quality of her love, says to her: "To the boy Caesar send this grizzled head, / And he will fill thy wishes to the brim / With principalities," to which Cleopatra replies, "That head, my lord?" In the space of those four words, Cleopatra considers—and the audience sees Cleopatra considering—for the very first time the possibility of a world without that grizzled head; in the space of that four-syllable love poem Cleopatra realizes that that grizzled head is of all things most precious to her in the world. It was a moment of sheer magic if you said it right, and if you didn't, that's when the audience started squirming. Mona didn't know if she had that note in her. Those four words were a candle that needed to shine straight down to the very depths of your soul.

———

IT TOOK MONA A MOMENT to realize that the voices from the other side of the door were Bruce and Rachel arguing.

"I *like* him," Bruce said. "I've known guys like him all my life, I know just what he's about."

Bruce was the only person in Mona's orbit who admitted that he had voted for Donald Trump, whom he saw as an ally in his battle over the authorship question. Not that Donald Trump cared who wrote the plays attributed to William Shakespeare, mind you. Not even Bruce thought that. But Bruce knew just where Donald Trump *would* stand on the issue if he were to take a stand. Donald Trump would not be afraid of the Stratfordians, of their snootiness and their endless bullying. Bruce was sick of living in a country where you weren't allowed to think what you wanted to think. Bruce had done his research, and he had thought a lot about the question, and he was tired of people like Hillary Clinton making fun of him because he'd arrived at his own conclusions.

"Just the thought of living in Donald Trump's America makes

me want to throw myself out the window," Rachel said, with a little laugh.

Rachel might have consciously intended the laugh as a calming gesture, a way of acknowledging her disagreement with Bruce while still maintaining a façade of civility. But Mona could hear in that laugh through the bedroom door what was obvious to Bruce as well: that Rachel did not take him seriously. Rachel's laughter struck Bruce precisely in the place he was most vulnerable: his fear that in old age he'd become an object of ridicule in the eyes of the female members of his entourage.

"Make sure that window's high enough!" Bruce said.

Sheila had been observing the fight from the kitchen counter. Now she began to worry that she would be embarrassed, somehow, in front of Rachel, which was like being embarrassed in front of a much younger version of herself.

"Bruce!" she said. "Not again. That's enough."

Bruce in private responded well to a sharp rebuke from his wife, but rarely in front of others.

"All of you people can go jump out of a window!" Bruce said, his voice cracking. Bruce's inability to control his voice, on which he used to rely in moments of crisis to convey a bass note of masculine dominance, frustrated him still further. "Just don't push me out with you!"

"Who's trying to push you out the window?" Rachel said. She wasn't sure what she was fighting for or why; she felt only that it was essential to be heard, that to remain silent would be suffocating. She sensed that her ability to maintain a cool tone in her voice, even as Bruce failed to do so, gave her an advantage. "Just tell me that. That's what I don't understand. Nobody's trying to push people like *you* out of a window. Why are all of you so upset?"

Bruce saw his face in the mirror and paused to consider, ever so fleetingly, his responsibilities as a family elder. In that moment he thought that he could end the argument by chuckling with grandfatherly calm, a tactic he had employed successfully to defuse many a tense negotiation both domestic and professional over the years. The impulse swiftly passed as he ceded to the urgings of the little arsonist who lived in his soul, whose desire to provoke, outrage, and set good things aflame had been suppressed all through a long lifetime of disciplined decency. The man who had voted twice for Jimmy Carter now yielded to what an uncanny instinct for disorder told him was the most provocative line of argument available.

"Tell that to Milton," he said.

"Tell *what* to Milton?" Rachel said.

Mona felt through the door of the bedroom Rachel's rising anxiety, like an animal attacked on one flank, and then unexpectedly on the other. The unlikely union of "Donald Trump" and "Milton Katz" in the same conversation had surprised her. She had been prepared for the one argument; had rehearsed it, had considered it, was even eager for it. But the other conversation she had promised herself to leave dormant. It was not something she was prepared to admit to herself, much less others, but on the subject of Milton she was far less certain that she was in the right. When she had brought the subject up with Mona in the car, she had been looking for moral confirmation: she thought that Mona might say, "Good for you, honey. I wish I had done the same thing." She had been surprised by the ferocity of her aunt's condemnation, centering precisely on that element in her character in which she took the most pride. Rachel had begun to wonder if there was a complexity to the art of moral judgment that she had not suspected. Perhaps arriving at correct judgment would require more sophisticated tools than she at the moment possessed.

Bruce, to his immense surprise, sensed that he had gained an unexpected advantage. His clue might have been the flash of panic in Sheila's eyes as she felt herself being dragged inexorably into the fight. If Bruce cottoned on to her involvement in the Milton business, her marriage would be for a long time a miserable place. Bruce looked away from his wife and back at Rachel. He had long lost interest in "winning" the fight, in any conventional sense of victory; success would come when Rachel was as hot with rage as he was, spluttering and incoherent. "Tell Milton there's no window. Tell the girls who threw Milton out the window that there's no window. Oh, there's a window all right."

With that single word "girls," all of the simmering tensions in the room, like all the simmering tensions at countless family meals across the land, now came to a boil. Mona thought to herself, *Please, Rachel. Not now.* Only Rachel could stop what was coming. But this was asking of Rachel greater maturity than any independent-minded young woman could muster. Mona certainly wouldn't have been capable at her age either.

Mona, lying spread-eagled on the bed, knew that she should stand up, should burst cheerfully through the bedroom door, should say, "Bruce, oh my goodness! I forgot the parsley! Bruce, you're all dressed, could you be a lifesaver?" and in this way save Thanksgiving. But she couldn't. She simply couldn't move. She was too stoned. Mona was in that stage of being stoned where she began to wonder most sincerely if the pot had been laced with hallucinogenic toad drippings.

She wished she had her phone. She needed her phone to self-soothe.

She *had* forgotten the parsley.

It was funny how much flavor parsley really added to things, especially now that everybody used Italian parsley. What a change that was in American life, Italian parsley, and no one talked about it at all.

The silence from the other side of the door was long and painful. Mona had the sensation in the pit of her stomach that accompanies witnessing a fragile vase falling to the floor, the vase bouncing once on the carpet, rising miraculously still intact into the air, only to fall a second time, now onto the stone floor, where it explodes.

Rachel said, "For your information, I was one of the *women* who spoke to the *Times* about Milton."

This declaration, Mona knew, was not actually intended for Bruce; it was not even intended for Mona, eavesdropping through the closed door. If anything, the declaration—the word "confession" here was clearly inappropriate, suggesting as it does some admission and disavowal of sin—was meant for Rachel herself. Rachel's soul felt liberated. She had united the various strands of her personality: niece, student, activist, victim, and witness. She had done the right thing, she decided, and she intended to stand tall in her womanhood no matter the consequences to this Thanksgiving dinner. Rachel was prepared to speak her truth and let the heavens fall.

And with that, somehow, Mona was in action. It came on her all at once: yoga pants, tennis shoes, her down vest. Then she was through the bedroom door. Barney was up on his feet. She said, "C'mon, buddy." She grabbed his leash. He began to bound around in excited circles. They were all in the living room, but Mona barely saw them. "We're just going out to get some parsley," she cried as cheerfully as she could, as if she had heard nothing, as if all was well with the world. "Rachel, will you keep an eye on the stove?" Not waiting for an answer, she was out the door and moving down the hallway, past the Finklers, past the Greenes, past the apartment that was always up on AirBnb. She saw the other, *better* Mona Zahid in the mirror in the elevator. Mona longed to jump through the mirror, grapple herself to the ground, pull her own hair.

Then, finally, after what seemed an interminable delay, the phone was in her hand. She didn't know where to go with it. She couldn't go up to the apartment again, she couldn't face them. Barney looked up at her. She stood in the lobby and waited while her phone rebooted, taking its own sweet time. She looked through the mail in the mailbox. It had been piling up for days. There were bank statements, a ConEd bill, something from T-Mobile. There was a forest of flyers and circulars. Every theater company in New York City had sent her a brochure. She examined them one by one, staring at the bright type and strong colors.

There was also a postcard in the mailbox. Mona's face was on one side, staring at her in homicidal madness. She was Lady M. The company had produced the line of postcards years ago. You could still buy them in the lobby shop. She saw herself, covered in blood, stained with grief and misery, face slack with suffering, and recoiled: she had looked so good back then! Just five years ago and she didn't have *any* of that shit on her neck. That was all new. She looked at the postcard, then at the mirror on the lobby wall. Some turkey-necked stranger looked back at her.

The postcard was from Milton.

On the back, he had written, "My Cleopatra—the role you were meant to play. What I've been waiting for. Call me. I am dying, Egypt, dying: Give me some wine, and let me speak a little. Ever loving, ever yours, ever Milton."

INTERLUDE

ANTONY

                         Thou hast seen these signs—
They are black vesper's pageants.
That which is now a horse, even with a thought—
The rack dislimns, and makes it indistinct,
As water is in water.

Sometimes in those first few weeks after he was fired Milton went up on the roof. He walked up to the ledge and looked over. He looked at the cars parked below, which even from the height of the roof had begun to look small. He looked down at his neighbors with their sacks of groceries and strollers, holding their phones up to their ears as they walked their dogs, all of them so frantic with life, so urgent and anxious. There was no railing on the edge of the roof. He leaned forward, leaned back, leaned forward. He might have done it, but he was haunted by the fear that the last thing he'd hear on the way down would be his phone ringing. In his fantasy it was always Vijay Singh calling. Somehow there was time to answer. "Milton, the donors are on strike," Vijay would say. "Either you come back or 107 is going under." Then *splat*. So Milton leaned back from the ledge and went back in the house. He wandered from bedroom to bedroom, then found himself back up on the roof all over again. He couldn't stop thinking about what he should have said to the board. He couldn't stop thinking about his show. He'd been in technicals for *Henry IV*, both parts, working twelve-hour days. The ten thousand details had been overwhelming. He'd think of a note he had wanted to give, a detail he wanted to change, some staging or blocking he hadn't liked, and then he'd remember that he was out. He was sleeping about two hours a night. Once, late at night, leaning over the ledge, he looked down and saw a fox, running right down the middle of Joralemon Street.

The only relief from the temptation of the roof in those first weeks and months was Karolina. She'd been cleaning the house every Tuesday for decades now. Milton didn't know how many times he'd even seen her in all those years. Maybe half a dozen times. Milton found her one morning in the kitchen, scrubbing the sink and dancing to the music she heard in her earbuds. She was wearing a pair of denim overalls, like a teenager. She had her gray hair in a pair of pigtails, thick like ropes, that bounced as she worked. She jumped when Milton said, "Good morning, Karolina." But then she smiled and Milton said, "I'm making tea. You want some tea?"

Soon they were at the kitchen table, a couple of steaming mugs in front of them. She didn't look at him like he was a monster. He wasn't even sure she knew about the article in the *Times* or what happened over at 107 Avenue C. "Karolina, tell me about yourself," Milton said. "Me? There's not so much to say," she said. "Just tell me something," Milton insisted. So she told him about the beet and potato farm she grew up on, a couple of hours outside Kraków. "We were, how you call, nature people," she said. "You didn't grow up there alone, did you?" So Milton learned about sister one, the good sister, and sister two, the mean one. "Why was she so mean?" Milton asked. "There was one time . . ."

A couple of hours later, Karolina said, "Now Milton, tell me something about you."

The last thing Milton expected at that moment were the tears. Even when Susan died, he didn't cry like this. He hadn't cried like this since he was nine and Sparkie was hit by a car. His shoulders shook as he wept helplessly. Karolina stood up and folded Milton into her large bosom. "Poor Milton," she said. "Poor poor Milton." She wrapped her hands around Milton's head as he sobbed. Milton liked the way she held his head tight and rocked him, and he liked her smell, like patchouli and dish soap. When Milton was done crying, she let him go and sat in her seat again, like this was all a normal thing.

Milton thereafter found himself looking forward to Karolina's Tuesday visits all week long. He thought up questions to ask her about her life; he wanted her to like him. They drank cup after cup of tea in the kitchen together over the boxes of Polish pastries Karolina started bringing with her. Milton sometimes wept, sometimes he didn't. When she left, the clean house felt scary and clean, and he started to worry about the roof again.

This had been going on for six months or so when Karolina told Milton that she would be moving to North Carolina in the fall, where her son lived. Her apartment building in Queens was coming down to make way for luxury condos, and with the landlord's buyout offer, she could afford the down payment on a little house near Raleigh.

"Why don't you take this place instead?" he asked.

The offer surprised Milton just as much as it surprised her. His daughter had long made it clear that she didn't want the townhouse. Ginnie taught philosophy at ASU. She already owned a house and didn't believe it was ethical to own two. She told Milton that if he left it to her, she'd sell it and donate the proceeds to Planned Parenthood. So Milton and Susan had planned on leaving the place to the Rabble, as a guesthouse for visiting artists. The whole complex was supposed be called the "Milton Katz and Susan Robertson House." It was hard to imagine them calling it that nowadays.

"What are you mean, Milton?" Karolina asked.

"This place is big enough for the two of us. You could take the apartment downstairs. Make me one of those casseroles once in a while, keep an eye on me so I don't fall down the stairs, and when I go, the place is yours. It won't be long."

"Milton, don't say like that," Karolina said, looking at the kitchen cabinets, the linoleum floors, and out the kitchen window at the untended garden, where already she imagined neat rows of medicinal herbs.

So Karolina moved into the basement studio with her endless boxes of crap and furniture, with her plants and crystals, her sewing machine and plastic boxes. Her stuff overflowed the basement and she asked Milton if she could use the guest bedroom on the second floor as a crafting studio. "Suit yourself," he said. "Mi casa es su casa."

Milton hadn't realized that the crafting studio was a beachhead to occupancy in the house proper. He had imagined her safely tucked away in the basement, except from time to time when Milton felt like throwing himself off the roof. Instead she was everywhere, always. The side door in the kitchen that led to her downstairs apartment was permanently open. He came down for breakfast and found her perched in the kitchen in a fleece robe. She FaceTimed every member of her family every morning, and so they were in his house too, an entire extended clan, shouting at one another in loud Polish. To avoid seeing her at breakfast, Milton unplugged the coffeepot and took it up to his little office in the attic and made coffee there. That's how she conquered the kitchen. Then she conquered the living room, by reprogramming the television in such a way that every time he hit the power button looking for the baseball, there was nothing but images of mountains, seas, and other peaceful places accompanied by the tinkling of bells. Milton couldn't get rid of the pretty places. He spent an hour smashing the buttons on the remote control, feeling his blood pressure spike, until finally slinking back upstairs in defeat.

Milton now assiduously avoided Karolina. If he saw her, she started talking about her fight with her sister, or her nephew's divorce. Sometimes she offered to rearrange his energy. He regretted his decision to invite her into the house. The only place in the house he didn't feel her vibes was his attic office, where he made his bed on the leather couch. That was okay. Even before he had been obliged to sleep there, he had found it, for reasons only his back knew, more comfortable than his bed. From time to time he went downstairs. Inevitably she would find him. "Milton, we make tea for talking," she would say, her large powerful body between him and his safe place upstairs.

Weeks passed, then months, Milton not realizing how bad things were until one night he dreamed that he was in the ocean. Every summer he and Susan used to rent a house on the Jersey Shore where they'd go on weekends, and Milton would swim an hour or two in the mornings, never along the coastline like a reasonable person, but heading straight out until sometimes land was out of sight and he was all alone. That's the place he was in his dream when the octopus attacked him. He felt the limbs engorged with suckers wrapping around his arms and legs, then the suckers attaching to him as the strong beast pulled him under. He saw the octopus's eyes bulging madly from its head, and he understood that he was in a battle for survival with an alien intelligence, menacing and profound.

After that Milton stayed away from Karolina altogether. He no longer saw her as benign. He understood that she was only waiting for him to die. He didn't leave the attic much now. Karolina put tasteless meals outside his door, which Milton, who could see no alternative, ate at his desk, putting the dirty plates back outside if he remembered. The last time he saw her was a few weeks ago. She opened the door, said, "Milton, I do a little cleaning for you, okay?"

"Leave it," Milton said.

"I'm just one minute," she said, picking up the papers on his desk and dusting.

Time began to slow. She would not leave. He picked up the food on the plate, a handful of boiled meat and cabbage, and threw it at her head. He missed but she got the message. "Milton!" she said sharply. She stood there for a minute and glared at him. Then she stormed out of the room. He locked the door behind her.

That's when Milton realized he was starting to lose it. The sudden uncontrollable upswelling of fear and rage stunned him. The food had been on the plate one moment, then lay strewn across the floor the next.

It had happened to his mother too, at the end. Small strokes, they said. She thought her doctor was trying to poison her. Milton could still remember the medicines the doctors put her on to cure her of her fear of doctors. They pumped her so full of olanzapine that all she could do was drool.

Milton sat on the leather couch trembling. He closed his eyes and tried to calm himself down. It was funny: Milton could barely remember the name of his own daughter these days, but he was still off-book on every line of every play. At least that was still there. Now he thought:

> Sometime we see a cloud that's dragonish,
> A vapor sometime like a bear or lion,
> A towered citadel, a pendent rock,
> A forkèd mountain, or blue promontory
> With trees upon 't that nod unto the world
> And mock our eyes with air. Thou hast seen these
> signs—

They are black vesper's pageants.
That which is now a horse, even with a thought—
The rack dislimns, and makes it indistinct,
As water is in water.

Sixty-five years in Shakespeare and still making discoveries, still finding moments he had never understood. "The rack dislimns." The greatest pun he never heard. "The drifting cloud obliterates," glosses Michael Neill, whose Oxford edition of the play Milton had dog-eared and spine-crumpled on his shelf. But now he knew: the rack was also the rack, the torture device, and when it dis-limbed, off went your arms and legs. The rack dislimns. That was what was happening to Milton. Things were growing indistinct. Black vesper's pageants.

———

KAROLINA CALLED GINNIE, who called Milton.

"How are you holding up, Dad?" she said.

"I want her out of the house."

"She says you won't leave your office. She's worried about you."

"I like it up here."

"She says you threw some food at her."

"I can't live like this, with her spying over my shoulder and listening to my conversations and judging me all the time."

Ginnie said, "I'm grateful she's there. You can fire her if you want, but I'm not doing it. We don't have to go over this again. You know what I think."

Milton did know what Ginnie thought: there wasn't anyone who had ever met Ginnie who did not know what she thought. "Speaker of Truth" might have been stamped on her business cards, and the truth she had delivered to him with no very great squeamishness was that she thought he belonged in assisted living in Arizona. A few weeks back, she had sent him a brochure. "Under the circumstances, maybe it's the best option," she wrote on a Post-it note.

"Not for me," Milton said.

"Well, I'm not doing your dirty work for you," Ginnie said. "You want her out, you get rid of her."

" 'My way of life is fallen into the sere, the yellow leaf, and that which should accompany old age, as honor, love, obedience—' "

Ginnie interrupted. "You can tell yourself whatever story you want, Dad, but at the end of the day she's a nice lady and there aren't a whole lot of other nice ladies out there who want to take care of you."

————————

THE CALMEST TIME IN THE HOUSE was morning, before Karolina was up. Milton was generally up by sunrise. That's when Milton wrote, or tried to. About five years back, an editor over at Knopf, Leo Stein, cornered him at a fundraiser and asked if he wanted to write a memoir. A series of swell boozy lunches at a place not far from 107 followed, the two of them swapping stories of coming up rough in immigrant New York in the fifties, the wild parties and big men they had known over the years, then competing at the end of the meal over who was going to expense it. When Milton had trouble getting going on the memoir, Leo Stein messengered him a yellow notepad. On page one, he wrote, "Start Here," and drew a little arrow to the first line. "Send me ten pages a week," he wrote. Milton was just getting cooking on the project when he saw in the

Times over his hard-boiled egg one rainy February morning that Leo Stein was dead, a heart attack, keeled over right at his desk.

The project was reassigned to another editor. It took her six months to get in touch. Then Milton and his new editor went to lunch, Milton agreeing to drag his ass to Midtown. Milton asked if she wanted to get a bottle of wine and she glanced at her watch. "I wish I could," she said. She couldn't have been older than thirty-five, and the whole time they were sitting there, Milton wanted to tell her to take a deep breath and enjoy, that it wouldn't last forever. She had a slender, nervous face, with high cheekbones and a chiseled jaw, all of it framed pleasingly by shiny dark hair, the kind of face that Milton's mother used to call black Irish. Milton told her a few of the stories from the old days and her eyes glazed over. Milton had never felt more like a living cadaver than he did at that lunch. Whenever he sat down to work on the book thereafter, the thought of his new editor's nervous pale face and the look of barely concealed boredom in her green eyes made him go dry.

Then came the article in the *Times* and exile, and after that, Milton figured, the book was dead. He didn't even bother to check in with his agent or his pretty editor.

Milton had been sitting alone in that upstairs office for a month or so when he found one of Leo Stein's yellow notepads in his desk drawer. Milton looked at the yellow pad. "Start here," Leo Stein said from the grave. Milton wrote:

My old man, he owned half a Greek diner in Hell's Kitchen. The other half was owned by this mean old Greek named Papadopoulos. Long story how a Jew owns half a Greek diner, serving up bacon, ham, and western omelets, but my dad and Papadopoulos made a go of it, working their fingers to the bone. So my dad, when I was twenty-seven and he was sixty-four, my dad has a heart attack and dies. Now I own half a Greek diner, and I want to sell, because I want to start a theater company and put on plays, and this guy Papadopoulos will not buy out my half, will not sell. He made a promise to my dad to get me started in the diner business, and by God, Papadopoulos will keep his promise. Papadopoulos hates my guts. This guy is eighty-five years old, knows about six words of English, three of them being, "Fuck you, sailor." That's all you ever heard out of old Papadopoulos. So a year goes by and this diner, it's ruining my life. It's losing money, I'm working twenty hours a day to keep it going, it needs new plumbing, new electrical, the city tells me it has roaches, the dishwasher is broken, I go to Papadopoulos and say, "Please let's sell this place and I'm going to put on a Merchant of Venice.*" What I want to do is I want to put on a* Merchant *with real Jews. Jews like the Jews I knew all my life. Jews like my dad. And I want to set it in a place like Dekalb Avenue in the Bronx, where I grew up.*

Papadopoulos says, "Fuck you, sailor."

So I go home all depressed, thinking I'll never have the money to have a company of my own, which is all I wanted in the world, a theater company to put on the plays of Shakespeare the way God meant me to put them on. That's when I visit my Uncle Abe's friend Iggy Longman. And Iggy, he's like the devil. He tells you things you don't want to hear. Iggy was in newspaper distribution, which back in those days was a rough trade. He says, "You really want to do this theater mishegas?" And I say, "Iggy, it's all I ever wanted." And he says, "Okay, here's what you gotta do." I say, "Iggy, I can't do that." He says, "Suit yourself. A diner's a good business." So I go into the diner around three in the morning on the coldest night in February. Place is totally empty. And I do what Iggy tells me. Only when I throw the match, I don't realize the alley door is locked. The place goes up like that. Nothing but fire between me and the front door.

And so I ran for it. I got third-degree burns all over my legs. You won't ever see me at the beach or the pool, because no one wants to see what my legs look like.

But that's what I had to do to start this company. Run through a wall of fire. That's how bad you have to want to do something if you want to get it done.

———————

IN THE AFTERNOONS, Milton watched his life on his iPad.

Every Rabble production going back to the seventies had at least one recording, made with a house cam set up near the lighting booth, the recordings ending up in the archives of the New York Public Library over in Lincoln Center. From time to time over the last decade, there had been proposals from the kids who did the website to make the company's extensive archives available to the public, but Milton had always refused. You couldn't film theater, Milton thought: theater was a creation in the moment, a collaboration of spirit between actor, text, and audience. Film might record actors wandering around onstage saying their lines, might capture the coughs or applause of the public, might register costumes, lighting, and props—but the product that ensued was everything but what really mattered.

When Milton found that the new management at 107 had put the whole archive online, he was outraged. He thought about calling his lawyer—he thought he had something somewhere in his contract—but before long, he was spending his afternoons and evenings doing nothing else but watching the old shows. Milton liked to sip scotch as he watched. The alcohol seemed to loosen long-encrusted memories. Some of the shows were better than Milton remembered, and some of them far worse. Milton was struck by the way memory became just another story over time, a few of them true, most of them false. Sometimes Milton, watching these productions in his attic office, would pause the play and drift into the past. He felt like a time traveler. He would start a show and hours would pass as he crawled spider-like along an ever-expanding web of memories: *Coriolanus*, the red-haired Aufidius who stole the show, this rehearsal, that after-party, going home to his daughter, his second wife, the apartment in the West Village, the greengrocer on the corner, the greengrocer's son who died in a car accident, the funeral, the greengrocer in his arms sobbing, visiting his mistress after the funeral, the two of them just so happy to be alive.

So Milton passed his days now in this hazy, dreamful state. He wasn't unhappy. The urge to climb up on the roof was gone. It was a fragile kind of existence. Various years, various Miltons blended together in his soul. Milton sometimes thought about how it used to be. He missed lunch, showing up every afternoon at the Trumilou, where he used to rule like a lord from his table, the one Jean-Pierre kept just for him. Caesar salad, bottle of Sancerre, double espresso, strolling back to the rehearsal room feeling like a god, everything correct with the world. Then he missed the work in the rehearsal room, missed it like a phantom limb, and he missed the evenings in the Irish bar, where the actors, his actors, would surround him like family. But Milton might have made his peace with it all, accepted everything, if Karolina hadn't gone altogether too far.

———————

SHE KNOCKED ON HIS OFFICE DOOR ONE AFTERNOON. He had been watching a very early production of *The Seagull*, and pausing it from time to time to remember his Konstantin, and the strange snowy winter of 1978, the way the snow piled up on the fire escape of the rehearsal room.

He ignored her knock.

"Please to open door, Milton," she said.

"Just come in," he finally said.

She opened the door cautiously and stood in the doorway, her large square body filling the frame.

"Milton, I talk Ginnie yesterday," she said.

"And?"

"I tell Ginnie you are depressing, alone in room, watching iPad. I say, 'How can I help Milton?' Ginnie says you are addict. I say, 'Addict? What you mean, Milton is addict?' Ginnie says you are addict internet, addict depression. She says we need to help you, Milton."

After that, Milton didn't expect that things would stay the same. It was only a question of when Karolina and Ginnie would act. Then one afternoon he went to the Rabble archives. His iPad said, "Safari cannot open the page 'http://www.disorderedrabble.com/' because your iPad is not connected to the internet." Milton read this over and over again. It made no sense to him, like Turkish.

Milton shouted down the stairs, "Karolina, what happened to YouTube?"

She appeared at the bottom of the stairwell.

"Karolina, did you turn YouTube off?"

Karolina's lower lip began to tremble. "Please, Milton. Please. Ginnie says you must leave house. Ginnie says—"

Milton started to shout and curse at her. But he had trouble finding the right words in the right order. "You unnatural hags," he shouted. Then he went back to his study.

For a day or two Milton was panicked. He'd been a rough kid, quick with his fists, his role models in life thugs like Iggy Longman. More than once Milton's mother had predicted that if he didn't reform his ways, he'd end up in prison. Then he pulled a knife on his eleventh-grade gym teacher and spent three months upstate in a juvenile reformatory. Even the reformatory hadn't calmed him down. They put him in the hole two weeks for fighting. Milton didn't have a clock down in the hole or natural lighting, just a bare lightbulb that never went out and a single goddamn fly buzzing incessantly around Milton's head. Milton tried everything he could to measure out time sitting there alone in the hole: he counted out his heartbeats and his breath, he paced and did push-ups, he tried to see how many times in a row he could whack off. He didn't know how long he'd been in there when he realized that time had stopped altogether: the whole world had frozen in a moment and only Milton was still in motion. All Milton wanted was to be frozen also. Years later Milton would put on a *Richard II*. Richard was in his prison cell at the end of the play, and he thinks, "I wasted time, and now doth time waste me." That's how it felt to be in the hole.

Milton pulled his address book out of his desk drawer and paged through it. Quarto, Folio, Second Folio, Third Folio: the address book had passed over the decades from generation to generation, copied over every ten or fifteen years from old book to new. Milton usually asked one of his assistants to do the copying, and to check, if she could, that the addresses were still valid. "Address?" his assistant had written in the margin when she couldn't find new contact information. *If only I knew*, thought Milton. The dead outnumbered the living. There were people in there who'd been dead for decades, people who wouldn't take his calls if he were dead and calling from the Great Beyond with important news. He turned the pages. There were old girlfriends in the book, women who'd been so beautiful once they could stop a beating heart; they were grandmothers now. He stopped at *P*. He wished he could call Joe Papp. He and Joe had been rivals for a while, Joe over at the Public soaking up the fame and fortune, Milton liking everything about the Public except the work they did. Then the rivalry died out and the two of them were friends. He had Mayor Lindsay's name in his address book too and Alan Howard's and Peter Hall's. What an actor Alan was. Last time he saw Peter Hall in London, Peter, loopy with dementia, hadn't known who he was. There was hardly a name in the book Milton could look at and not feel something.

Milton found a postcard in his top desk drawer. He had a big stack of them there. He used to send them out by the dozen. If he saw a show and liked it, he'd send a few lines. He liked to thank people: he'd send a card thanking the caterer at a fundraiser, or the union rep who solved his Equity problems at the last minute. He carefully wrote Mona's name on the postcard. Her address was in his book, and he copied it out. He thought about what to write for a day or so, then wrote a small paragraph.

The next morning, Milton heard the brassy voice play its long-awaited solo, "I go out now shopping, Milton," then he heard the door slam. When Milton got to the front door he was frightened. He hadn't left the house in months and he had no idea what was waiting for him out there. But the clean, cool air was pleasant, and the sharp wind calming, and he was charmed by the little children riding by on their scooters. Milton looked at the clouds. They were like faces of fat men, like a white tropical beach on dark blue sea-sky. High above a jet left a long contrail that Milton watched dissolve away.

Milton found the mailbox right where it was supposed to be, on the corner. Some things never changed. When he was a kid he loved to drop the mail in the box. His mother always asked him, "Miltie, do you want to mail letters with me?" Then the two of them would walk hand in hand down the street to the mailbox, Miltie pulling the little slot that opened with a gratifying *thwunk*, then feeling the same sense of satisfaction and loss as he dropped the postcard into the void.

ACT TWO

PORTIA

You see me, Lord Bassanio, where I stand,
Such as I am.

1

Never mind the content of the postcard. That was disturbing also, if true. But Milton had played this particular card before. More than once, he had announced his imminent demise and been proven wrong. Milton was the wolf who cried, "Me!" There had been the heart attack, of course, a few months after the end of his affair with Vanessa, when Milton collapsed to his knees right in the rehearsal room of *Titus Andronicus*, his arms widespread, a look of beatific deliverance on his face, wondering eyes upturned as if the ceiling had dissolved and flights of buxom angels, slow-beating their silvery wings, were welcoming him hither. A few years later, there was his cancer scare. Mona had started prepping her memorial speech back then, only to have Milton pop back up into vibrancy, the whole thing turning out to be that rarest of all things, a mistaken diagnosis. Mona had preemptively mourned Milton enough times over the years that the bedrock of her belief was that the man was functionally immortal.

But the fact of that postcard—the notion of Milton with his thick sausage fingers writing words on paper—that was stunning. It was a physical link. His signature was his usual scrawling loops, indecipherable but for the dramatic, oversize *M* and the spiky, protuberant *K*. "I am dying," he had written.

Then Mona looked at her phone. The battery was deep in red. She had forgotten to charge it. She started to look at her emails and stopped herself. She wanted to stay for just one more minute in the space of her thoughts. It seemed disrespectful to Milton and his imminent death not to give him a few moments of silent attention. She turned the phone back off and slipped it into her pocket.

She began to walk toward parsley, Barney sauntering beside her. Barney took an unending delight in the city—its rich smells, its diverting sounds, its bright colors—admirably indifferent to the commotion that might have freaked a country dog. He could even handle Midtown, which Mona really couldn't say of herself. Had he been able to formulate such a thought and express it in words, Barney might have said that the secret to his happiness was *purpose*. He had one; it made all the difference. He had once found almost an entire pizza on the sidewalk, coated with cheese and sausage, and had managed to eat the whole thing before Mona, who was distracted by her phone, noticed. Now his dream was to repeat the best minute of his life. He knew that such a thing would not happen by accident. It required work and commitment.

Mona had a vision of the day to come. Mona knew that in a few hours, Phil and Aaron would come back, Phil talking about how beautiful it was out there "in the country," using precisely the same exuberantly tree-positive verbiage he had employed the year before and the year before that, Aaron heading straight to his bedroom. Phil would have pies in hand from Dora's, a pie place out in the country, where customers were obliged to reserve Thanksgiving pies a month in advance, an act of diligence Phil never failed to perform. Mona would soon be hiding in the bedroom, staring at those large, empty apartments on her phone. Phil, reeking of autumn and trees and Melanie McDowell, would come into the bedroom and nag her to spend just a few minutes with his family. The apartment would be too warm. A little later, Phil's brother Harry would show up with his family, Susanna in front, asserting her matriarchal dominance, Charlie skulking four steps behind. Aaron would be coaxed out of his room to salute his cousin. Having Charlie and Aaron in the same apartment was inevitably stressful. They were nominally friends, but Mona saw no signs of warmth between them: their only social activity was competitive bragging, chiefly about performances on standardized tests, also about the number of subscribers on their Dystopia channels. Both were passionate about activities the other found contemptible: Charlie's channel featured nothing but him performing stupid tricks on his skateboard, Aaron played jazz piano on his. These holidays used to be better when Harry smoked pot, but he had quit a few years back, when Charlie turned twelve and Harry decided it set a bad example for the boy to see his father eating bag after bag of Doritos. Mona couldn't say that he was wrong, exactly, but she missed their talks out on the fire escape. Also Zahra used to come to Thanksgiving back then. Now Mona made a clique of her own. The thought of being in that apartment all day with all those other people who were nothing like Mona but also as close to her as any humans on the planet made Mona feel so sad and lonely she thought it would be a good idea to crawl into a hole and die.

It took a couple of blocks for Mona to settle into a rhythm. She was always better in motion. She loved late autumn and its light, the way the walls and trees turned amber and gold. It was unseasonably warm. The sun was on her face and a little breeze was picking up leaves and shuffling them around, which made Barney curious and hopeful. He liked leaves. On the day he found the pizza, there had been leaves. If a leaf strayed near him, he'd pick it up with his snout and carry it a few steps, enjoying the bitter taste of sap and its cool, rough texture on his tongue.

———————

ONE OF NEW YORK's celebrated urban hawks flying serenely over-
head and watching Mona and her beagle wander the streets and
avenues of the Upper West Side on her way to Whole Foods might
have thought her itinerary made perfect sense, because hawks were
used to watching mice and squirrels, and mice and squirrels rarely
walk in straight lines, and neither did Mona. She zigged and zagged
all over the place, to avoid the people in the neighborhood with
whom she had once bickered, or to whom she might potentially
have to apologize.

There was, for example, a four-block no-go zone around this
guy Matt Cohen's apartment. He had been a parent at Aaron's day
care back when Aaron still went to day care, who asked her to read
the script of a play he was working on. "I'd be honored," Mona said.
Only the play was so bad that Mona didn't know what to say to
him. A decade now had passed, and those blocks were still radio-
active. The thing about Manhattan was that if you wanted to see
someone on purpose, you had to make an appointment for coffee
six months in advance. Then one of you would cancel. But if you
wanted to avoid someone—well, best of luck. Then three blocks
down Amsterdam on the east side, there was the dry cleaner. Mona
had been one hundred percent in the wrong on this one. She had
accused the dry cleaner of losing her favorite blouse, and then had
discovered it a week later in her closet. It was the kind of freak-
out, frankly, that somebody might have filmed nowadays and put
on TikTok. She had been planning on going back and saying sorry
now for three years, but until she got up the right combination of
motivation and nerve, she needed to cross at the light.

Then Mona was standing outside Whole Foods trying to

remember what she was supposed to buy in there. She had dashed out of the house to buy *something*—was it toilet paper? sparkling water? Why was her memory so lousy nowadays? An eggplant? She thought it was funny that you could remember that you had forgotten something, like looking at a hole in your own brain. If you could remember that you couldn't remember something, why couldn't you remember it? Barney had a look on his face like he could remember what she had forgotten, but he didn't know how to talk.

Milton still didn't know that Zahra had died.

That's what she had forgotten.

She had gone five minutes without thinking of either of them, five whole minutes in which she had forgotten that she needed to tell him about Zahra. It had seemed very important to Mona for a long time now to tell Milton about Zahra and she hadn't been able to do it. Not that Milton and Zahra had been particularly close. Mona figured they had seen each other no more than a dozen times over the years: in Mona's dressing room after a show, both of them looking proud, or at Mona's apartment, on one of the few occasions over the years when she decided to host a dinner party, and once or twice when Mona dragged her sister to Milton's Brooklyn townhouse for a fundraiser. But they had been intimates nevertheless, each hearing innumerable stories about the other, both of them instinctively liking one another. Zahra had died just a month or so after the article in the *Times*, and Mona had thought, *Milton should probably know.* But she hadn't quite been able to find the energy to do all of the necessary explaining and talking and consoling and being consoled that communicating with Milton would require under the circumstances.

Now she stood in front of Whole Foods and wondered how much

time she had left. She fingered the card in her pocket. Not very long from now she would wake up one morning and there would be a little notice in the *Times*, "Milton Katz, Disgraced Director and Producer, Dead at 80." Mona would sit there a minute staring at the phone, as if there were a loophole in the story, and then the guilt and regret would close in around her. Mona decided, right there and then, to go and visit him. There was nothing stopping them. She and Barney were going to go on foot to Brooklyn Heights. Mona turned her phone back on again. Phil still hadn't called her to apologize. By now he and Melanie McDowell were stroking one another's hair and talking about how goddamn sad it was that they had wasted the years since high school. They could have had a lifetime together. She sent a text to Rachel, "Will you & Sheila take care of turkey? Baste & rotate, treat with love. Back later. I'm going out for a while."

2

Mona planned Milton's memorial service as she walked, a thought-groove she first slid into when Milton kept nearly dying but then had really gotten into in a serious way in those weird months just after he was sent to Siberia and nobody in the company could think or talk of anything else. Mona had planned his funeral daily back then, the way young girls plan weddings, when she was out running or making dinner or just lying in Savasana after yoga, when she wasn't supposed to be thinking of anything at all.

But would there even be a memorial service for Milton? The notion that the company would allow its founder's death to pass unmarked was almost inconceivable: for how many decades had the Rabble been synonymous with Milton? Yet she could see the memorial service dividing the company in two, and an article in the *Times*—yet another one!—and comments on blogs, and polemics on social media, nothing civil, nothing kind, until finally Terrence, in the interests of maintaining peace and with his uncanny weasel instinct toward unseemly compromise, would propose a *seminar* or something, maybe over at the New School—a dissection of Milton's life and legacy, with bland speeches by neutered academics and balanced testimony from the Philes and the Phobes alike, the afternoon event an opportunity to pry his life open, peer inside, and judge him fairly.

No, thank you, Mona thought.

But a proper memorial service—*that* she would attend. This was a thought that made her smile. Something simple. Joyous. Undignified. (*They would collectively roast and eat Milton's corpse. Had Mona heard that? thought that? dreamed it?*) She imagined actors giving (very) brief speeches, or telling stories about Milton, or appreciations of Milton, and there would be sonnets, and monologues, and what Milton would most appreciate, scenes performed extempore or practiced and perfect until the audience believed that they were impromptu. She would wear her black pantsuit to Milton's thing, the one that was ostensibly professional but hugged her ass in a way that was secretly sexy and maybe just a little magical. There would be a lectern, stage left, and Milton's mystical carpet, stage center. The actors would all stand together and as if pushing something very heavy would unroll the carpet together. Then maybe, as the evening went on, scripts passed out just like that. An evening like one of Milton's best rehearsals, or the parties at his house afterwards. That was the proper tribute to Milton, to re-create those brilliant séances: *An Evening of Play in Honor of the Life of Milton Katz.*

SHE ALWAYS BEGAN HER EULOGY the same way: "And so, after all those years, he had me come in."

It was long ago, in the days before Terrence and his new age of egalitarianism and the open Equity casting call, and auditions for the company then were by invitation only, the whole thing like winning one of Willy Wonka's Golden Tickets. There was no apparent rhyme or reason to his invitations. One year they said Milton wanted clowns and every clown in New York perked up. The next year clowns were out. Some years no one was invited at all. If the audition went well, you might have a place at 107 Avenue

C for a year, you might stay for two, you might stay for twenty—it all depended on Milton.

And then there were the cases like Mona, plucked out of the blue, invited who-knows-why, who on that very blessed morning when her agent, Useless Tommy, called to say—mirabile dictu!—that Milton (Milton!) Katz would be very pleased to see her (Mona!) present a monologue or two of her choice, had been sitting in a sunbeam making a list in her spiral-bound notebook of Life Options B–Z. So far the list included law school, vet school, getting a real estate license, opening a café, moving to Austin, event planning, becoming a yoga teacher, and learning to code. The list did not include "More of the Same."

She was almost thirty and Saturn was returning and Mona's career, as the internalized voice of her father never ceased to emphasize, had to that point not been a great success, at least if you judged success by conventional measures like paying the rent or making great art or happiness. She had come out of Juilliard with a reputation as a topflight classical actress. That got her as much work as she could handle on the festival circuit, spending the summers in Utah or Santa Barbara at Equity minimum. That had been fun, playing great roles and sleeping with her castmates afterwards, but second-rate shows in second-rate towns for eighth-rate money was looking less glam to Mona as a plan for her thirties. The winters were just so hard. She would come back to New York in September at the end of the season and audition all the time and tutor the SAT between jobs. There had been moments when it all seemed about to come together: she had played Nerissa at the Public, then Hermia in a short-lived Broadway production of the *Dream*—not quite leads, but there she was, on the appropriate stages making the appropriate noises. There had been a brief flurry of excitement when she booked Imogen on the Guthrie main stage a few years back, the kind of big role in a big theater that you figured was going to snow-ball into the next big thing and then the thing after that, but despite good reviews and kind houses, the whole thing went nowhere after the last curtain call and she was right back to square one.

She was sick to death of auditions, callbacks, rumors, cattle calls, and disappointment. She had no health insurance, no car, and she struggled every month to find eight hundred and twenty-five dol-lars to pay her third of the rent in the three-bedroom she shared with strangers an hour on the train from Manhattan. Above all, Mona was sick of being a cliché. The scarlet *L*, which stood for "Loser Starving Wannabe Actress," was stamped upon her brow. It glowed like neon when she admitted her profession to civilians. "Have you been in anything I've seen?" they asked. They asked, "Do you have a day job?" to which Mona replied that she played bassoon in the New York Philharmonic. It was amazing how many people did not realize that this was a joke.

Then came Useless Tommy's call and the dancing around the room and the celebratory drinks with her sister, and only when she was lying in her bed that night did she appreciate that this was it, pretty much, for her career as an actress, because if this didn't come through, she didn't think she was going to keep on going. Maybe she'd coast along on inertia and pride for a few more months or a year, but basically, she'd had enough.

"And I barfed my oatmeal up right there in the ladies' bathroom in Grand Central. Then I brushed my teeth and ate a banana."

Milton made Mona wait with the taste of barf and banana on her breath in the audition room for over an hour. It was like any rehearsal room Mona had ever been in, with scuffed hardwood floors and a half dozen molded plastic chairs arranged around the walls. There was a window, open slightly, that looked out onto Avenue C. Mona wondered if she should close it so that she wouldn't have to compete with street noise for Milton's attention, but there was a bad smell in the room and she didn't want to compete with that either. She hadn't known where to put her stuff, her purse and her winter coat, so she'd piled them on a chair. She had gone through a dozen outfits the night before with her sister. Zahra had rejected everything Mona had in her closet. "God, you dress like somebody's grandmother," Zahra said, looking with repulsion at the heap of blouses, skirts, and dresses on the bed. "And not one of those sexy grandmothers either." Finally Zahra had an inspiration, dragging Mona in a taxi to her apartment, where she put her in a Cavalli dress ("I *knew* I had something," she said) that Mona had to admit made her feel at least a little like an Italian movie star from the 1950s.

Mona wondered if she had prepared sufficiently for the audition—but then, how could she have prepared more? She had been given no assignment, no specific part to work up. Milton's secretary, calling Mona to schedule the appointment, had told her she'd be better off just getting a good night's sleep. Not much consolation there, sister: every night at three for a month she had been awake, staring at the ceiling, flipping on the lights, and running monologues.

Now she sat in the audition room as the minutes ticked by wondering if time had stopped altogether or whether she was in the wrong room when the door opened and a man who looked sorta, kinda like Milton Katz walked in.

Mona had always imagined that the real Milton Katz went about surrounded by an entourage of aides, like the president or the pope. But this Milton Katz was alone. Mona didn't trust her words to express her thoughts but believed that if she summoned to mind a precise recollection of Milton as he was then, she could transmit the image telepathically to her audience. He was in his early fifties and handsome, with rugged, roughly symmetrical features, large, dark eyes, and a lot of hair: curly dark on top with streaks of gray over the ears, then a thick gray-black thatch of beard. He was wearing a jean jacket and a white T-shirt. The look in his eyes was startlingly intelligent and bluntly erotic. Mona imitated Milton looking Mona up and down, then raising an eyebrow just very, very slightly. It was meant as a compliment. There was in the gesture a hint of flirtation and surprise. It didn't feel sleazy at the time. It felt exciting and funny. Then he was shaking her hand and charging into the audition room and looking for his glasses, which were hanging from a chain around his neck, and saying, "This is great. I'm a big fan."

This was so unanticipated that Mona said, "Of what?"

"Of you, of course!"

"I know so much about your work, Mr. Katz, and—"

"Call me Milton."

Then Milton explained to her that this wasn't an audition exactly. "We don't do that shit," he said. She had the chops, from what he had seen of her work, to take a place in this company, or any company anywhere. The only people he brought into this room were people whose work he already admired. She could take over a stage, no doubt about that. That Imogen! But auditions (Milton air-quoted the word) around here were different. There wasn't some role that he was going to give to another actress if he didn't give it to her. In any case, he didn't believe in competitive (quote-unquote) auditions. Asking artists to compete was barbaric. Sometimes great actors, big talents, weren't right for the company, and sometimes it happened, he said, that an actor didn't like him, and that was okay also. Sometimes it happened that it wasn't a fit now, but it might be a few years down the line. The important thing was *to have a good time*. They were in the room *right now* and this was acting and it counted *every bit* as much as press night in the theater downstairs. It *all* mattered. The insights were as valid and the places they could go just as meaningful and intense. He just wanted to see what she had going on.

———

BARNEY WAS MOVING HIS BOWELS. His sable ears were back and his eyes, which tended toward the beady under the best of circumstances, bulged.

They were out front of the vegan Tamil taco stand, the owner standing forlornly in the doorway of his trailer. Even on Thanksgiving he arrived early and put on a pot of lentils to boil, then began the tedious process of preparing tortillas, all for a clientele who would never arrive. The Thai green curry burrito stand two blocks down Central Park West was always jammed, customers lined up even on the most ferocious winter days. But vegan Tamil tacos met no one's needs. Now he watched Mona's dog defecate in front of his stall, in which he had invested his wife's dowry, and he watched Mona reach into her pocket for a little plastic bag, and he watched Mona scoop up the feces with her hand, her *right* hand, only the thinnest sheath of plastic between her and the corruption, and he thought to himself what a strange and repulsive place he found himself in, and how sad it was to be so far from home.

And Mona for her part felt the warm feces through the plastic and wondered if she really was as lucky as she suddenly felt. Her pocket was always a land of surprises to her. Rummaging for the plastic bag, she had found just now her vape, a tube of lip gloss, ten dollars, and—God was good!—four pills just the right size and shape as to be from Zahra's bottle. She must have left them there and forgotten them. She threw the bag of dog shit in the garbage and held the pills in her naked right hand, lifted them to her mouth, and dry swallowed them, one after the other.

———————

"SO WHADDYA GOT FOR ME?" Milton said.

Mona had long ago learned what every professional actor must learn: how to perform despite fear. The fear never got better; it was always there every time she approached the stage. But you learned over time to creep around the fear, not to listen to it, to understand that while the fear was full of lies, it was also full of energy. She took her anxiety and made it anger and gave that anger to Lady Percy.

Mona's first monologue was from Henry Four, the second part. This had been Mona's standard audition piece for a couple of years now. Lady Percy was Hotspur's widow, berating her father-in-law for abandoning her husband on the battlefield, consigning him to death. Now she was trying to persuade her father-in-law not to begin another futile and destructive war. She blinked her eyes and Northumberland stood in front of her; she saw him standing in front of a mirror, shaving his fleshy, self-satisfied face. Sometimes she gave him a walrus mustache, other times one of those fussy goatees. The important thing was to see him clearly. What infuriated her chiefly was the refusal to stop shaving and look her—his daughter-in-law! his son's widow!—in the eye. She allowed herself a moment, just one, of pure rage:

O yet, for ~~fuck's~~ God's sake, go not to these wars.

The time was, father, that you broke your word,

When you were more endeared to it than now—

Mona knew that generating that kind of emotion with no pre-amble was extremely difficult to do, like a standing backflip; her ability to flash from neutral to explosive, to fill every corner of a room with her presence, was something a director would look for. She had trained on the monologue by shouting "Look at me!" on every breath. Now the shout was silent. But Lady Mona knew that if Northumberland did so much as look at her, she would burst into tears, and she wanted that less than anything; it would humiliate her. Milton famously liked his Shakespeare cool. The *words* con-veyed the sentiment. So Mona played the speech not as an exercise in excess—many an actress could rant and cry—but as a depiction of a woman struggling to modulate the intensity of her emotions. This was much harder and more subtle.

Somewhere in the speech Milton reached for his reading glasses, hanging on a chain around his neck. His hand pawed at the air. All the while he looked at her face like a prospector separating pyrite from gold.

Mona imagined Northumberland carefully tweezing his nose hairs, picking out the boogers. "Look at me!" she shouted. *"Who then persuaded you to stay at home?"* Mona sometimes had a dream: she was fighting for her life, and her arms were rubbery, feathery, fragile things. That's how it was fighting with Northumberland: her blows never landed. Only at the end of the speech did Mona's intensity abate, when Northumberland turned around and *his* eyes, not hers, were wet with tears. She said,

Never

    O never

        do his ghost the wrong
To hold your honor more precise and nice
With others than with him.

          Let them alone!
The Marshal and the Archbishop are strong.
Had my sweet Harry had but half their numbers,
Today might I, hanging on Hotspur's neck,
Have talked of Monmouth's grave.

Mona thought about hanging on Hotspur's neck, and the way he smelled, like sweat and limes, the roughness of his stubble, the soldierly solidity of the man. Mona thought about her dog in the vet's office, lying limp on the steel table, his eyes glassy. Mona couldn't always generate real tears on command, but the accumulated stress of the audition and the excitement of being in a room with Milton Katz and the barfing and the lack of sleep made them come easy, and still she tamped them down, struggling to maintain control.

There was a moment of silence in the audition room when Mona was finished. She wiped her cheek. Then Milton applauded, which almost never happened in a normal audition. But Milton applauded subway buskers and street performers and renowned artists with equal, grateful fervor. He understood how hard it was to stand onstage.

MILTON KEPT ASKING FOR MORE and Mona kept giving. She had never been in an audition like this before. The other auditions, even the ones she had passed, had lasted no more than five minutes and ended with a curt "We'll be in touch." Those directors had been looking for triangles to slot into a triangle-shaped role: if Mona was a good triangle, she'd get the job. But Mona felt like Milton was seeing her for the strange, irregular shape she was. Playing for Milton felt like a conversation in which she lowered, word by word and phrase by phrase, her defenses. It was not something he said—he stayed almost silent—but rather in the way he watched her, his head crooked at a curious angle. He was just so interested.

Mona imagined herself telling her sister Zahra, "It's not what I expected. He was so *there*. How many times has he heard those speeches? But he looked at me like he had never heard it before."

Mona wanted to stand in front of Milton and play for him forever. The civilians always asked, "How do you remember all those lines?" Mona never knew what to say to that. The trick wasn't remembering the lines; anyone could do that if you just worked hard enough. Memory was a muscle that strengthened through effort. The art, however, was in standing on a stage and *forgetting* the words so you could invent them as you said them. Playing for Milton made Mona feel like the words were new; they were just the words that the moment called for, Shakespeare's words arising from the same place as her own words, and as she spoke them, Mona balanced in the moment, neither anticipating the word to come nor looking back at the word just past, the new word coming into her mouth just as it was needed, at once surprising and inevitable.

Mona put all that excitement into her next piece, the death of Falstaff: "He parted ev'n just between twelve and one, ev'n at the turning o' th' tide; for after I saw him fumble with the sheets, and play with flowers, and smile upon his finger's end, I knew there was but one way."

Again Milton applauded and again Mona was happy. She pulled piece after piece out of her collection. She was showing him all her tricks and range. She played comic and tragic and expository. She had dozens of pieces in her repertoire and it felt like he wanted to see them all. It was all so free and easy that Mona was surprised when Milton's features rearranged themselves into something serious. They'd been working for an hour.

He said, "You've got a good, good instrument. You've been well trained. You speak clearly, I understand every word, and you're a fine verse-speaker. You fill a room. You've definitely got what a lot of people are looking for. But what we do here is—in my experience it's very different from what they do at other companies."

Milton paused the way a man does when he gathers his strength to break your heart. So that was it. She had scaled the mountain only to be turned back by storms at the summit. She saw ahead of her as if signposted the earnest commiserations of her friends, the long spell of depression, more auditions, more temporary jobs, more disappointment, the gentle roll and tide of life, and finally telling her grandchildren with a weary sigh, many years from now, that there had been a time, once, when she had lived in New York and aspired to be an actress.

Milton continued, "In my experience, very few actors are prepared to do what we do here. A lot of actors who come into this room tell me they want to do our kind of work, but very few actors, when the time comes, are actually interested. It is very hard. It is not always fun. Our work goes very deep, deeper than is comfortable, and I have a sense that you are keeping something back from me. That's the place that interests me. I need more."

Mona later thought that should be on his epitaph:

ACT TWO

Here Lies
Milton Katz

Lousy Husband
Crummy Father
Artist

He needed more.

Then she sighed for her audience the way that Milton sighed in the audition room.

"My father was a difficult man also," he said. "I have this feeling, something about your father, that's what's holding you back."

There it was! Boom! Mona was being Miltonized! She had heard so many stories: the expertly thrown psychic darts, the whispered suggestion, the uncanny prompt.

"Believe me, I know difficult fathers. So I know how deep it goes, that desire to please Pop. And how scary it can be to try. I think there is another place your work can go. But I'm not sure that you *want* to go there. I'd like to see you work here again today, but this time without worrying about your father."

"Again?" Mona said, not knowing how to do anything without worrying about the man about whom she had been worrying roughly since birth.

───────

MONA AND BARNEY CUT INTO THE PARK and disappeared. Mona had a secret belief, secret because it was nutty, that she was invisible whenever she set foot in the park. She didn't know why this invisibility thing happened, but she was grateful.

Had Phil been out here running four times a week, as she did, he would have been the mayor of Central Park. "Hey buddy! How's the knee?" he would have shouted to the gray-haired guy in sweats chugging along. "Looking good, Marla!" he would have cried to Donald Trump's ex. He would have gathered up interesting biographical facts about each and every runner in the park: "Did you know that guy used to be a Marine Corps sniper? Seventy-seven confirmed kills." Mona liked to tell people about the time when she and Phil were first dating, and they went for a walk in the park. Phil stopped to point out some birds to a pair of Swedish tourists. "Those little guys migrate all the way from South America," he said. Soon they were all having breakfast together in a diner. That was something Mona very much loved about Phil, that he was in no way frightened of human interaction. Phil had a fully paid-up membership card for Planet Earth.

Mona, on the other hand, suspected since childhood that she had been abandoned on this planet by aliens. Enters, stage left, one Hafez Zahid, in the role of Mona's father. Why did the people on Planet Mona leave her in the care of Hafez Zahid? Who knows? Mona would eventually learn, finally, after a lot of suffering, that the real cause of disputation *in re: Hafez v. Humanity* was as inaccessible to reason as a tsunami. Why did she understand and love Juliet? Not only because she loved Romeo, but because her father was Capulet. There was a moment in her first high school show when Capulet of Verona disappeared and in his stead Hafez of Home was berating her: "God's bread, it makes me mad," her father shouted, and every time, hearing those words, Mona collapsed. This was the moment in the production that made Mr. Ellenbogen tell Mona, "Young lady, you have a very special talent. I've never seen a student actress nail that role before."

Mona's Juliet was a performance so unabashedly sexy, so infused with hormonal lust and obsessive desire, that a rumor ran through school that strange fathers had started showing up in the auditorium to watch her. Hafez walked out of the show somewhere in the middle of Act Three. When Mona came home from her performance that evening, she found the entire contents of her bedroom had been deposited on the sidewalk, posters ripped down from the wall, stuffed animals thrown in the bushes, clothes tossed on the lawn. Even her bed was in the gutter. Mona slept on Mr. Ellenbogen's couch for four days, until the end of the play's run.

———————

MONA THOUGHT ABOUT HER FATHER'S FACE—the thick black hair, the mustache streaked with gray, those sad, melancholy eyes, forever angry and confused and disappointed—looking down at her from the second-floor window as she stood on the front lawn amid the detritus of her bedroom. Then she looked at Milton looking at her. He wanted a kind of attention she had never given a man before. Mona was aware that something would happen in the next minute that would divide her life into before and after.

And here is what made Mona a great stage actress: she always knew where her audience was. No one could teach you this. You had to go and find your audience, you had to meet them on *their* ground, and only then could you lead them where you wanted them to go. The technique, the memorization, the verse-speaking, the body work, the voice training—all that was only in service to that goal. Mona knew, in that instant, that Milton was a hungry audience. He wanted an actress who could make him feel her love.

And if she could do that, not in some crude sexual way but in the more intimate way that really mattered, Milton, for his part, would bring her to places she would never find on her own, the high country where the air was thin and the views expansive and very few people ever had the chance to wander. What infuriated Mona years later, when the article in the *Times* came out, and the denunciations and the screeds were posted on the internet, was that Milton had been so totally clear with everyone who wandered into the audition room about the terms of the deal.

Mona was still walking her dog in Central Park on a brisk Thanksgiving morning on her way to Milton's house and still in the audition room with Milton and still standing onstage at Milton's memorial service.

"Milton Katz didn't care about other people," she finally said. "At least not like other people care about people. I will say that straight out. He was going to use you. He was going to chew you up and spit you out. But if you were a young actor, Milton Katz was the audience you wanted. Playing in front of Milton was like playing in front of an audience of a thousand—that's how much intensity he brought to listening. When you played for Milton, a whole theater laughed and cried. *All* of Milton was in the rehearsal room, every time. If acting was what mattered to you more than anything else in the world, Milton was the best audience in the world."

The Philes would applaud and the Phobes would sulk and then Mona intended to deliver the monologue with which her tumultuous twenty-year relationship with Milton began. The runners on the Loop might even have noticed Mona shouting out the lines as she walked. Some of them, the ones alert to minor celebrity, might have gone home and said, "Do you know who I saw today?" But when Mona thought Shakespeare, she *had* to speak it. The words between the ears were flat; it was boring on the page; it all came alive on the breath.

––––––––

MONA HAD ANOTHER SPEECH UP HER SLEEVE, but it was still kind of raw. She thought it might be the most beautiful and painful declaration of love in all of Shakespeare. She'd never really nailed it, to tell the truth. It scared her silly. Still, she decided to give it a shot, and she did it the way they had always told her at drama school not to do auditions. The advice at drama school was never to audition into the eyes of a referee: it made people uncomfortable, and personalized what was supposed to be a professional encounter. But Mona did this speech straight at Milton.

The first line was a bitch. It took all her courage and then some to say it. Finally, after holding the pause, she said,

> You see me, Lord Bassanio, where I stand,
> Such as I am.

Only it wasn't to Lord Bassanio, that doofus, that Portia was talking: it was to Milton. Mona loved this sentence, with its succession of slow, simple monosyllables, as much as any in all of Shakespeare. That first line, if you said it right and if you meant it, was jumping out of the plane and hoping the parachute opened. Either it was everything or it was nothing; either it was complete and total exposure or it was worthless. Mona the actress was a pose intended to hide Portia the woman from the world. So you got rid of the actress, and Mona, just Mona, Mona such as she was, was onstage.

The mourners leaned forward, aware but not knowing why, that they were witness to a moment of intimate revelation.

> Though for myself alone,
> I would not be ambitious in my wish
> To wish myself much better,
>
> yet for *you*—

> I would be trebled twenty times myself,
> A thousand times more fair,
> ten thousand times more rich,

> That only to stand high in your account.

Mona had seen actresses play these lines ironically. Lucky, plucky them! But Mona was sincere. She opened her arms wide, the better to reveal that in her own best estimation of her worth, she simply wasn't good enough. Inadequacy like waves washed over her. There were so many reasons not to love her. She thought of the claustrophobic limits of her talent, her breath in the morning, how fat she was in middle school and in her mind still was, the ugliness she saw in the mirror, her tendency toward casual cruelty, the pools of indifference and spite that she knew were gathered in the recesses of her soul—she thought of all these things and allowed herself a long wallow in the mud of self-hatred. So abrupt was Portia's reckoning (Mona's reckoning) that she did something Shakespearean heroines did only rarely: she fumbled for words.

But the full sum of me

Is sum of something—

{a pause, panicked, drying on the line, the audience worried}

which, to-term-in-gross,

Is

an unlessoned girl

unschooled

unpracticed—

{unlovable}

And only here did Mona, who had been doing the entire speech for Milton on a single lungful of stale audition room air, take her first breath. With that breath a flicker of happiness, as welcome as it was unexpected, surprised her. This was Shakespeare's gift. If you said the lines and played the meter and breathed where he told you to breathe and said the words as best you understood them, the breath would lead you and you would feel things. The words would master you even as you mastered them, and you would become an empty vehicle by which that brain which first quilled them out in a flea-infested London attic reached those eager brains sitting in front of you. Then an audience of a thousand or an audience of just Milton Katz would breathe with you, hold their breath when you held yours, and they would feel things too. There was nothing else in the world that mattered half so much to Mona as the experience of standing onstage saying these words.

Only now with that breath did Mona allow herself a little ironic smile accompanied by a slight curvature of the eyebrow. Maybe, just maybe, she was going to be fine.

—Happy in this, she is not yet *so* old
But she *may* learn;

> {*a sip of breath, Milton half chuckling, the happiness finding him too*}

happier in this,
She is not bred so dull but she *can* learn;

> {*a gulp of breath believe me I can learn*}

Happiest of all, in that her gentle spirit
Commits itself to yours to be *directed*,

> {*eyes on Milton*}

As from her lord,
    her governor,
       her king.

> {*full exhale*}

Mona knew Portia's sentiments were hardly fashionable nowadays—to some, they were even objectionable—but that was how she had felt that first day in the audition room with Milton; and some part of her, giving the speech to Milton's bright-eyed ghost at his memorial service, felt that way still today. The truth of the matter, Mona thought, was that Milton wasn't a complicated man. Milton had wanted from her what he wanted out of everyone: complete and total surrender.

And Milton had been right: not everyone was prepared to give him what he wanted.

Mona came out of the park into the rich, fertile plains of donor country. Here there was townhouse after penthouse after mansion that she had visited over the years, each the site of a different fundraiser, gala, open evening, or fête organized by some socially ambitious, artistically sensitive Upper East Side matron.

Milton roped every member of the Rabble into attending a fundraiser at least once a year, an obligation that Mona, like the rest of the Rabble, dreaded but that Milton seemed genuinely to enjoy. These evenings always began with a staged scene or monologue from members of the company but would inevitably end up with an informal play reading by the whole group. These spur-of-the-moment performances had happened so many times over the years that it was understood that they would happen again, but nevertheless provoked the same ripple of nervous energy when Milton said, "Shakespeare isn't just a spectator sport. Should we do a scene or two? All of us?" Then guests and hosts alike would swing the furniture and folding chairs around to form a circle; Milton would sometimes call the catering staff over and include them also. Milton brought the same joyful attention to these readings as he brought to the rehearsal room. No matter that half the "actors" stumbled over the words or ostentatiously flubbed their entrances: he treated them as brave simply for giving it a go, rewarding them with belly laughs on comic lines, sentimental sighs in tender moments, and always the same rapt, unwavering attention.

Sometimes, Mona remembered, she used to drift away during these performances to pilfer little things from the houses she visited, sneaking off to steal the good soap from the various bathrooms, or a book from the bookshelves—nothing valuable, just a paperback or a volume of poetry, which she would read on the long subway rides to and from 107 Avenue C.

Mona wondered how many of the donors would attend Milton's funeral.

She walked past the Met, closed for the holiday. She imagined the statues and portraits climbing down from their pedestals and frames, then retiring to the museum's dressing rooms, where they took off their heavy costumes and clammy makeup, made themselves cups of tea, and settled in, as the actors inevitably did, for a good long gossip. She took a hit off her vape as she walked, exhaled a pungent steamy cloud, and shivered. The weather changed so quickly at this time of year: a cold wind had brought low clouds down from the north. She was high now, but not glad. The first round of her sister's pills had been bright, clear bursts of happiness, spontaneous and fragile like youth in their joy. But the second round made her sluggish and anesthetized, almost melancholy, as sometimes happened with the opiates, and the vape made her feel worse. She went east on 81st Street, then turned right on Madison. She went past the shell of a French restaurant, a FOR LEASE sign in the window. She been there once with Phil, the night she told him she was pregnant. The owner himself, hearing the news, had brought her dessert. For years she had thought that they should go back with Aaron. She kept walking. A sign commanded: LEFT LANE MUST TURN LEFT. She turned left and, a block later, right. She passed The Shade Store. She saw a truck: SIGNATURE INTERIOR DEMOLITION. She began to walk faster, the blocks dark in shadows and the intersections full of crosstown light, her pupils rhythmically dilating and constricting.

The Sweet Hereafter, over on Second, was gone also, replaced by a spinning gym. She used to come here with Zahra. Shopping with Zahra before shows had been a crucial part of Mona's preparation: the two meeting somewhere for lunch, endless talking about Vadim, then Zahra, the queen of thrift store shopping, finding Mona something—maybe a pair of shoes, maybe a dress, maybe nothing more than a shade of nail polish—that made Mona feel like the woman who could make the character come alive. This was not the costume Mona would eventually wear onstage—that was the costume designer's job. This was something more personal, something that Mona could wear to the first day of rehearsals and feel some flash of confidence that her character might eventually emerge. Zahra had been dressing Mona in this way since the time the girls "played television" in the living room, Zahra ransacking the closets and trunks so Mona could star in private performances of *Alf* and *Three's Company*.

Zahra had been a Cleopatra too. Mona was sure—genetics and oncology be damned!—that it was Vadim's affair that had provoked the tumor: her liver had been too angry to stop reproducing. But nobody was supposed to have been *dying* of cancer here. Christ, no. Vadim was supposed to have come rushing to her side, where she lay all fey and helpless. Somehow it had all just got out of hand—and if all that wasn't some *Look-at-me, I'm Cleopatra!* shit, Mona didn't know what was.

———

MONA STOOD AT THE COUNTER OF THE STARBUCKS thinking about what she should say. She was supposed to order something. She knew that. She had been walking block after block in a cotton-mouthed fug, a hint of a headache coming on, looking for something she could eat that didn't sound nauseating or wouldn't require too much talking or more than the ten dollars she had in her pocket. She had come into the shop with a firm intention. Now the words were like little flies buzzing around her brain.

"I can order?" said the woman behind Mona in a Slavic accent. She was on her phone and agitated. Mona didn't know if the voice that said, "What am I, invisible?" was in Mona's head or if she actually said it. The woman with the Slavic accent stepped past Mona and ordered a Grande Caffè Mocha with soy milk, triple shot, not too hot, extra foam. She continued to talk loudly on her phone as she paid.

Then Mona stepped back up to the counter all over again. She tried as hard as she could to remember how to order.

Finally she said, "I'll have a pumpkin cream cheese muffin, a double latte, and a large water, no ice, for my dog."

"Name?"

"Zahra. Z-A-H-R-A."

Mona always gave "Zahra" as her Starbucks name when Zahra was alive. Then she'd text her a picture of her name on the cup. That had been one of their things.

Mona sat at the big common table, waiting for her coffee and nibbling at her muffin. Barney lay on the floor beside her, slurping his water, more water ending up on the floor than his tongue. Mona watched the barista and silently criticized her technique. A few years back, as a favor to Vadim, she had played a barista in a site-specific show he put on out in a Starbucks in Greenpoint. Audiences ordered their coffees and drinks as the actors (playing employees who aspired to be actors) talked about life working at

Starbucks. The play was a meditation on middle age, on failed dreams and making do with what life gives you, on the alienation that every New Yorker over the age of forty feels every time they set foot in a Starbucks, instead of buying their takeout coffee from a Greek diner with a crusty counterman who calls you his *kardia mou*. The *Times* made the show a Critic's Pick. Vadim had been working on a follow-up, *Whole Food Fight*, when Zahra died.

She had not known, she thought, that it was all so fragile, that something as solid as New York could slip away so easily.

Mona looked up at the woman with the Slavic accent who had cut in line in front of her. Somehow she already had her coffee in her hand. Now she was shouting into her phone. Mona couldn't understand a word and yet she understood everything. She was singing a mighty aria of rage and sorrow and betrayal. You couldn't act for a living and not notice that most people were going through their lives acting, and acting badly, from the minute they woke up to the minute they went to sleep. There was a falsity that ran through everything. But when people stopped acting—you couldn't look away. No one in that Starbucks, busy as it was, could take their eyes off her. Cleopatra was howling love pain. The other customers were so shocked they didn't even think to film her. "When you sued staying, *then* was the time for words. No going *then*." *This* was how theater was supposed to feel, this sense of *I-can't-believe-she's-really-doing-this-right-here*. The woman was Mona's age and she looked as if she belonged atop a troika pulled by frenzied horses across the frozen steppe, pursued by wolves, whip in one hand, phone in the other. "Eternity was in our lips and eyes, / Bliss in our brows' bent; none our parts so poor / But was a race of heaven." *You tell him, girl!* Mona thought. Life surged through her phone and into her and outward to fill the coffee shop. Mona wondered, looking at her, when her sense of shame would kick in. But she only shouted louder. "I would I had thy inches!" she bellowed. "Thou shouldst know there were a heart in Egypt!" Then came her glorious exit: this queen—no, this *empress*—took her Grande Caffè Mocha with soy milk, triple shot, not too hot, extra foam, and threw it against the wall. She actually did it. People shrieked. It was all Mona could do to keep herself from applauding.

"Zahra!" the woman behind the counter cried.

"Zahra!" she repeated after a minute.

Then, finally, "We got a Zahra in the house?"

4

Mona was still thinking about that Cleopatra—how alive she had made that Starbucks, how free she had been, how beautiful; not just thinking about her, but *absorbing* her, playing the scene in her mind so that she could reproduce it on demand; the blocks passing now, Mona hardly aware of them, Barney trotting patiently beside her, Mona repeating to herself over and over again, *Eternity was in our lips and eyes, / Bliss in our brows' bent*, when she looked up and realized she was standing directly across the street from Vanessa Levin's building on East 71st Street.

Now Mona sat cross-legged on the bench in front of Vanessa's building, surprised by the power of her own subconscious mind. Dr. Billy's office was ten full blocks away from here, and each and every visit she had taken an Uber to and from his front door, even when the weather was springlike and Phil had wanted to walk through the park, just to avoid running into Vanessa by accident.

Mona tilted her head back. She closed her eyes while Barney sniffed at a splotch of urine under the bench. He was fascinated. One dog, two dogs, many dogs had passed here, he understood. They had peed on the same spot. Barney licked the pavement slowly. The urine told a story: a female in her hormonal prime had announced herself; a dominant male, aroused by the rich scent, had responded. Then other dogs passed by, their urine like the comments and footnotes of rival Talmudic scholars. Barney lifted his paw and peed on the spot himself.

IT WAS A FINE SPRING MORNING, tulips on sale out front of every bodega, when Vanessa Levin first presented herself at 107 Avenue C for the Meet'n'Greet for *Measure*, pink-cheeked as a tulip herself, still so young that she announced proudly to the first person she met in the rehearsal room, the one they called Burbage, that she had taken the subway that very morning by herself for the very first time.

Mona said, "That's so brave!"

"I couldn't sleep last night I was so scared," she said.

Everyone in the room was sneaking glances at Vanessa. Milton found her, the story went, playing Stella in an all-female production of *Streetcar* at Bard. They said that she was the granddaughter of a donor, the whole trip deference to the power of his checkbook, Milton agreeing to go watch Bob Levin's granddaughter and give the family his honest take on her talent. But Milton lost all interest in the money when he saw her. She had been planning on drama school in the fall, but Milton invited her, no audition, to join the company instead. "*An actor acts.* That's all an actor needs: a script, a stage, and an audience."

"Because of the subway?" Mona asked.

"Because of everything!"

Mona had expected to hate Vanessa. But she liked her. You couldn't help but like her. She was so young, so nervous, so excited. She had deliciously pale, creamy skin. Mona told her little stories about the company members they met. "Do you see the tall guy with sunglasses? That's Sivokram. He's taken some kind of vow of silence. Outside the rehearsal room he won't say a word. I don't know where Milton found him. And that's Anne Carman. She's my work mom. Just don't loan her money. She never pays anyone back. She's famous for it. There are three Toms in the company—there's Old Tom, Young Tom, and Party Tom. There's also I think a Tom in admin? I don't really know him. Old Tom has seen it all, and I mean *everything.* He once lived in Laurence Olivier's spare bedroom. Just stay away from Party Tom, if you want my advice. Did I tell you about Anne Carman and money?"

So Mona was babbling and all the while she was studying Vanessa, trying to figure out just what made her the other, *better* Mona Zahid, as if Vanessa vs. Mona were some zero-sum game in which every quality attributed to Vanessa was deducted from Mona's side of the ledger: If Vanessa was pretty, then Mona was ugly; if Vanessa was charming, then Mona was charmless; if Vanessa was talented, then Mona was—

Now Mona had her fingertips very lightly on Vanessa's arm. "This is Vanessa," Mona told the others. "She's our Isabella."

"So you're the one!" Neil Fox said, stepping forward. "Will you kiss me?"

Vanessa took a step back.

He said, "It's a tradition."

"We all need a kiss," Mona said. "From the newest cast member. It's a thing we do. For luck."

"Vanessa's giving away kisses," Neil said. "Anyone who needs one, line up."

The room rang with brittle laughter.

One of Milton's assistants said, "For all the kisses I've given away, someone here should've won the lottery."

"It only works if you're a virgin," said one of the sound techs.

Milton walked in the door.

"Do I really have to kiss *all* of you?" Vanessa said, blushing, who some twenty years later would recount the event and its sequelae to the *Times* in not-inaccurate detail:

> During rehearsals and other occasions, Ms. Levin and other women complained, the company regularly engaged in sexual provocations, including hazing rituals in which the entire company and support staff would kiss and grope new female members of the company. This behavior was encouraged by Mr. Katz, who would often take part himself.

ON THE DAY that Vanessa walked into Burbage, Mona had been in the company a couple of years, and the moment had long passed when a few kisses could faze her. Things happened at 107 Avenue C. That was the kind of place it was. You either adjusted or you left. Mona adjusted. From the day she arrived for her first rehearsal, Mona spent more time by far at 107 Avenue C than she did in her rented room in Brooklyn. From one day to the next she stopped seeing her friends. They called her up and left messages that she didn't have time to answer and invited her to drinks that she was too tired to attend until finally they stopped calling altogether. Once Mona ran into Jillian D'Amato, with whom she'd been semi-besties at Juilliard. Jillian asked, "So is it as culty as they say down there?" Mona said, "I don't know. They keep me too busy to think about it."

Jillian had laughed at the joke but it was pretty much the truth. Every morning there was voice, movement, or speech call at nine. Rehearsals started at ten, when one of the actors would lead warm-ups: stretching; passing around energy balls; singing the national anthems of imaginary, highly patriotic Eastern European nations; the orgy in an old-age home.

But the day really started when Milton, as ever on his own schedule, moving like a stately ocean liner into berth, showed up fifteen, twenty minutes late for rehearsal. Mona inevitably thought of two things when he eventually arrived. The first was that old Carly Simon song, the one about Warren Beatty: "You walked into the party, like you were walking onto a yacht." For years of her life Mona had that tune in her head, driving her crazy. The other was the moment where Hamlet greets the players: "You are welcome, masters; welcome all. I am glad to see thee well. Welcome, good friends." Mona never saw a Hamlet say those lines with such patrician grace as Milton when he walked in the rehearsal room. It didn't matter if you were the lead or the last spear-holder or an understudy who would never put a toe on the stage: Milton would come into the rehearsal room, hug you, shake your hand, caress your cheek. Milton sometimes called his actors "shipmates."

People would later ask Mona: How does Milton get those performances out of his actors? Well, Mona said, beats me. It wasn't like there was a Miltonosophy of Acting or something. All there was, was work, hard work, fun work, nasty work. That, Mona later thought, was the Milton method: doing the lines, playing the scenes, doing it again, trying it differently, experimenting, fighting about it, thinking it through, rethinking it, crying, taking a break, coming back to it from a different angle, doing it over. Milton might watch a scene, say, "Pretty good. Should we do it again?" and then repeat for three, even four days in a row. There was always more to discover, always more to unlock. You took a scene, a moment, a beat, a line, a word, and you said, "What if?" Then you what-iffed the what-if, and you did that again. That's what Milton meant by "experimental" theater. The truth no one wanted to hear about Milton Katz's rehearsal room was that there was no secret sauce you daubed on acting to make it better; the method was there was no method. You came up with ideas, you tried out the ideas, and you abandoned them because they didn't work; then you tried out more ideas. What if you end-stopped that line? What if you put in a caesura? What if you cried? What if you didn't? What if you painted your toenails when you played the scene? Sometimes Milton got right up onstage with his actors as they rehearsed, whispering the words sotto voce, tapping out the beat with his pencil: "Da-DUM, da-DUM, da-da-DUM," he said. "That's how I want to hear it." Mona had memories of Milton ape-like, low to the ground. He would crawl up right behind you. Nostrils flared. Eyes wide. Once he told Vikram that Hamlet should have body odor. "What if you don't wash the day of the show? The front row should smell you. Then you can shower when you're offstage in Act Four. Come out for the graveyard scene smelling clean." Then he decided he wanted Gertrude well per-fumed, and Claudius in cheap cologne. Once there was an actress who was sensitive about her weight. He had his company surround her and chant "Fatty!" That actress was Mona. He got the face he wanted—which was also the face that Mona, seeing herself in the mirror, knew that she wanted.

Early in his career Milton used to do complicated sets and cloth-ing, but by the time Mona joined the Rabble there were just the racks of clothes onstage, the box of props, the wooden swords hang-ing from a hook, and the wigs neatly lined up on wig stands. Mil-ton wasn't interested in realism: the ethos of his theater was that through discipline and art and inspiration and maybe some luck, you could stand onstage in your own body and escape—not just that body, not just the color of your skin, not just gender, not just class, not just the limits of your character or the moral capacities of your soul—*but everything.* That was what Milton's theater was famous for, what people bought the tickets to see. Shortly after Mona joined the company, Milton put on *Romeo and Juliet* set in a nursing home. That show taught Mona as much as anything Milton did in the rehearsal room itself. Every actor on that stage was over the age of eighty, and for a brief but magical moment mid-show one forgot that fact: you saw only the young lovers and felt only young passion, but all the more moving for the inevitable return of the young souls to the old bodies when the curtain went down. That is what great acting can achieve. Mona saw the show four nights in a row, sobbing each time at the end, thrilled to be a member of a company like this.

After rehearsals Milton and the company, whoever didn't have a show that night, would head down to the Leprechaun and drink shots of Jameson's. Then Milton would rant. He had that Bronx accent and his tenor voice cut through the bar like a foghorn, the kind of voice that made the other drinkers swivel and look over.

"Fuck the Method," Milton said. "Fuck Lee Strasberg. The Actors Studio didn't produce one actor who can play Shakespeare except maybe by accident, by ignoring everything Lee Strasberg ever said. You don't play Shakespeare by standing onstage remembering the time when you were four and your favorite dolly got ruined in the washing machine. It just won't work. It doesn't matter what you feel inside. Shakespeare is about the *words.* You have to understand the *words* and you have to say them *fast* and you have to say them *on meter.* That's all."

Not that Milton was consistent on this point, mind you. Many a time and oft had Mona heard the equal and opposite rant, Milton capable not only of doubling back and attacking his own opinions, but of doing so the very same day, even over the very same shot of

Jameson's: "I do not care how much classical training you have had, how brilliantly you speak the speech, how fine your diction—if you haven't learned that there are places you can go with this art that are primal and powerful and awesome, and that it all comes out of something deep, deep inside of you, from a place that's irrational and half-insane that can't be reckoned with, reasoned with, or denied—if you haven't learned that and you want to be an actor, you are what we called in my day an imbecile."

Mona realized later that it wasn't the content of Milton's speeches that mattered so intensely to her but the intensity of desire he expressed: Milton cared more about the thing she loved than anyone else she had ever met cared about anything. Just being around someone who was sincere was wonderful because so few people were. Mona and Milton were alone at the bar, the others having drifted off to their beds, when Milton said, "It's such a privilege to spend our days with these people." The people in question were *Shakespeare's* people, who were entirely real in Milton's mind. They were vibrant with longing for corporeal existence. "They're so goddamn big. They live *more* in these plays than you or I ever will. They feel so intensely. They speak so beautifully. And we catch these people at a time in their life when they are more vivid and more alive than they have ever been. Or you and I will ever be." Sometimes it seemed to Mona that nobody cared about anything except Milton and Shakespeare: those two were the anti-nihilists, charter members of Team Stay Awake Past Midnight. That's why he was always in so much trouble with Equity: he couldn't imagine that actors wouldn't want to spend fifteen hours a day in the rehearsal room with him running scenes. Small children at home? Call Grandma. She's old and has nothing better to do. Milton's creed? "Either forbear, quit presently the chapel, or resolve you for more amazement." Plenty of nights saw Mona sleeping on the floor of Burbage, disgusting as that place was, because she'd been in the rehearsal room with Milton and company long past midnight running lines, and there just wasn't enough time to get back out to Brooklyn, sleep, and get back into town. *Of course* it had been no way to run a professional theater company. This had not been a healthy, safe, inclusive, nurturing space for anyone—not even for Milton, who had finished that run of craziness grasping at his chest on the floor of Burbage, gaping at the angels.

———

MONA FOR HER PART welcomed the phone calls in the night. They started up a couple of months after Mona joined the Rabble.

"Were you sleeping?"

"What time is it?"

"It's too late. Forget I called. It's not important."

"No, wait. I'm waking up."

Mona couldn't remember after all the years every late-night conversation with Milton one by one. It picked up from one night to the next seamlessly. Sometimes she drifted off while Milton was talking, and she'd wake up the next morning to find the receiver on the floor. If she saw Milton at 107 the next day, it was like the conversations never happened.

"Don't you have a wife, Milton?" she asked him once. "Is she okay with you calling other women in the middle of the night?"

"She tolerates me."

"Do you love her?"

You could ask questions like that in the middle of the night when you were talking in the dark. In the twenty-odd years Mona knew him, Mona never saw Milton offended.

"If I woke Susan up at three in the morning to tell her I got my aura manipulated in Chinatown this afternoon, she'd tell me to go to hell."

"You got your aura manipulated in Chinatown?"

"I do it every six months. Wen Ho puts you in a chair in a dark room, he waves his hands around you, you sit there, it takes about twenty minutes, he never touches you, just waves his hands around you, and when you stand up, you feel a decade younger."

"I don't want to feel a decade younger," Mona said. "I hated being a teenager and never want to go back. So what does he look like?"

"Who?" Milton said.

"Wen Ho."

"He's just a little Chinese guy. Maybe fifty or sixty. Gray all over like he's never seen the sun. Maybe they keep him in a cage in the basement and let him out to do auras. Reeks of cigarette smoke. Doesn't speak a word of English. But he's the real deal. You feel he's wrenching around in your guts and you walk out feeling like a million bucks."

The phone calls could last for hours, slats of streetlight across the ceiling, cut in strips by the venetian blinds. Were the calls erotic? Mona never had the sense that Milton was on the other end of the line, breathing heavily. That would have ruined the mood of everything. But there was something inherently sexy about being in bed in your underwear at three in the morning talking to Milton's disembodied voice.

"Don't you sleep at night, Milton?" she asked.

"Nights are hard for me. Always have been. Even when I was a kid."

"So you just call up people and make sure they're exhausted tomorrow too?"

"I wanted to hear your voice."

Under ordinary circumstances, such a statement would have meant so much. But coming from Milton in the middle of the night, maybe it meant only that he'd been awake and bored. Or maybe it meant so much after all. Mona was never sure. Mona didn't really want to be sure one way or the other way. She didn't want to be Milton's latest mistress and she didn't want to be in love with Milton, but she didn't want to rule it out either. She *liked* the middle place.

Mona never knew where these conversations with Milton would go. Mona once mentioned, apropos of who-knows-what, that she'd been chubby as a kid.

Then the questions started. So how did food work in your house? (What do you mean?) Well, who cooked? (My mom, most of the time, my dad on special occasions.) Who was the better cook? (My dad. He didn't know how to make a lot of stuff, but what he made always tasted good.) Why? What did he do to make it taste good? (Probably added a lot more oil and salt, also my mom was always trying out recipes for, I don't know, fish head terrine or something. My mom had this idea that our life would be better if we ate more "fancy" food.) Where are your folks from? (My father is from Lebanon. He came here because of the war. He was supposed to go to medical school but had a nervous breakdown, dropped out of school, and became a pharmacist. Then my mom is a little of everything, some Puerto Rican and some Italian and some Jewish and who-the-hell-knows what else.) Who did the shopping? (My mom, she'd tear through the supermarket at the speed of light. You have never seen a human being move as fast as my mother did in a supermarket.) Did you have meals together? (Pretty much every night.

They both believed in it. I have no idea why, since most meals ended up in a huge fight, but that was their definition of good parenting.) Who sat at the table? (Mother, father, Zahra, and me.) So you sat over here and your mom was over there, and your sister was over there? (Pretty much.) Okay, I get it now. Did you talk about the food? Or was it just there on the table and you guys chowing down? (Milton, you're not getting it. My dad was a *lunatic*. He talked, we ate. Every night. Year after year.) What did he talk about? (About this inheritance he had, mainly. His dad in the old country died and they had an apartment building in the capital, it was supposed to be worth a lot of money. And he was convinced that his brothers were trying to steal it by poisoning him. I swear, that was the only thing I ever heard my dad talk about for years. I did not know that this was crazy when I was a kid. I just thought uncles went around poisoning your dad to get their inheritance. And what you have to imagine, every single time my father talked about it he got so worked up he started to foam at the mouth. No exaggeration. Right there over dinner, little specks of foam in the corner of his mouth.) What did your dad do for a living? (Pharmacist, I just told you.) Oh, that's right. And your mom? (Office manager.) What did your mom do when he went on like that? (Most of the time she just sat there. I remember once she put her head on the table and started banging it. It was really scary if you're just a kid. She was just banging her head on the table and saying, "Why oh why oh why am I here?") What did your sister do? (She took me into the living room and had me dress up and we played television.) Did you guys have dessert? (Sometimes. My dad had a real sweet tooth. Or he'd take us out for ice cream.) So what about birthdays—

It was years after that conversation that Mona played the banquet scene. Milton re-created the emotional texture of her childhood dinners down to the minutest detail. "You sit here and you sit here and you sit here," he said, and Mona understood. She looked at Milton and his face became a mirror and what was reflected back at Mona was Mona. "My lord is often thus and hath been from his youth," Mona told her banquet guests. "If much you note him, you shall offend him and extend his passion." The *Times* would later describe Mona's voice as "suffused with heartbreaking fragility."

MILTON'S *MERCHANT*—the third of his career—was well into repertory by the time Mona joined the Rabble, but when the original Nerissa dropped out to originate a David Mamet role on Broadway, Milton offered the part to Mona for a five-week European tour: twenty-six shows, eight cities.

A couple of weeks into the tour, there was an incident, when Mehmet Erdin, who played Antonio, seduced a young French actress who attended the afternoon master class he was co-teaching at the Comédie-Française. The affair lasted the Paris run, and when the show transferred to Brussels, Mehmet's lover took the TGV up and the affair continued. But when she showed up to surprise him in Amsterdam, she found him walking through a hotel lobby hand in hand with a Dutch woman. It was not clear how the fight started, but the French woman (Mona never learned her name) soon ended up sprawled on her back in the lobby. The police were called, and Mehmet questioned. His understudy went on that night. Eventually Patty Rylans, the unflappable stage manager and tour wrangler, worked her usual magic: she persuaded the French woman not to press charges, consoled the Dutch woman, found a new hotel for

Mehmet, who had been asked by management to vacate his room, and avoided a scandal in the press.

Now half of the cast, Mona included, would not speak to Mehmet. She had not been in the hotel lobby herself, but Party Tom was, and he told Mona that Mehmet had pushed the young French actress to the ground. He had been the aggressor. She had been in tears. The other half of the cast felt that Mehmet was somehow the victim of the story: that he had been stalked and assaulted by an obsessed lover. The cast now fought nonstop offstage, and although they were professionals, always able to put on a show, the tension distracted from the performances, which, even before the incident, had been, if not disastrous, then pedestrian, with reviews mixed, and not unjustly. Mona was not the only member of the cast who thought the show was low in energy and lacked cohesion. The notoriously difficult fifth act, coming as it did after the high drama of the trial scene, felt terribly long. In Geneva, Mehmet accused Party Tom of deliberately sabotaging his performance, by spitting in a glass of wine Mehmet was supposed to sip from in the first act. The accusation was true.

It was into this atmosphere of intense, unpleasant disunity that Milton arrived. The trip was long planned, but he realized immediately that action needed to be taken to save the tour. He fired Mehmet on the spot and sent him back to New York, asking his understudy to step up, then asking Mona to double parts to cover the gap in coverage. Then they began to rehearse again, essentially putting a new show on its feet in a matter of days.

Mona had never seen Milton more effective as a director or more compelling as a leader. He gave a speech: "Listen, folks. We're putting on *Merchant* in Hamburg, Berlin, and Munich. We're going to have full houses of Germans to hear our show. We have to do this right." He took them aside one by one and walked them through their parts, not discussing the Mehmet affair directly but making clear that from the frictions of the incident a new, better production could be thrown together on the fly. A sense of unexpected excitement came into the cast, and the first show, in Hamburg, to a sold-out house, had all the tension and promise of a premiere. It was by far the best performance of the run. Somehow the fifth-act problem had resolved itself, and the final minutes of the show were magical and enchanted—Mona thought Shakespeare never wrote more beautiful verse than that fifth act—and a complicated, subtle indictment of the hatred of Venice at the same time. The audience gave them a long standing ovation. The cast insisted Milton also take a bow. Dressed in jeans, work boots, and black tie, he held Mona's hand and whispered in her ear, "This is the good stuff."

There was a party after the show, organized by their Hamburg hosts. Everyone was giddy. There is nothing like success to make rancor slough away. Everyone drank a little too much champagne. Back at the hotel, Milton asked, "Who wants one more?" Then Milton, Mona, and a few others sat at the hotel bar drinking schnapps as Milton told stories about the old days. This certainly wasn't the first time in company history that an actor had slunk home in disgrace, or the first time that a distraught lover had shown up at an actor's hotel. "There was this time . . ." Milton said, beginning a story whose upshot involved him, Old Tom, and Peter O'Toole leaving their London hotel in wigs.

Then Mona and Milton were in the elevator and Milton kissed her. Mona would later wonder whether Milton had planned the kiss or whether the moment in the elevator was the spontaneous product of post-performance exuberance, the freedom of being far from home, and the late-night drinks. Mona would later read that he kissed Vanessa Levin "forcefully" and think, *yes*, that is how Milton kissed, forcefully and a little clumsily and perhaps even ridiculously, and although it was forcible, it certainly wasn't a kiss you couldn't push away, saying "Milton!" if a kiss from Milton wasn't what you wanted. Mona didn't push him away, but she didn't respond either. She wished that she could push some button, stop time, and think about the kiss. Mona knew that if she wasn't so drunk she definitely wouldn't go to bed with Milton, but she wasn't sure that *that* Mona represented adequately the interests of *this* Mona. She closed her eyes. His mouth tasted of liquor and a cigar he had smoked at the bar. He put his hand on her cheek as he kissed her in a way that *this* Mona decided she liked. The elevator arrived on the seventh floor and he followed her down the hall.

———————

CONTRACTS EXPIRED ON JULY 1. Sometime in April, you met with Milton. It didn't matter that you had slept with him or that he still called you three times a week at three in the morning; that was just night talk. It didn't matter that the *Times* had called your Ophelia "the most electrifying reinterpretation of the role that this critic has seen in a generation." Still, there was a week of sleepless nights and high anxiety preceding the meeting because you had no idea whatsoever what was going to happen when you walked into Milton's office to talk about your contract. You could be Milton's little old mother and he might put on his hound-dog look and say, "I think we're going in a different direction next year, Mom." Then Mom would have to try as hard as she could to look professional and tell Milton that it'd had been a pleasure working together, and she hoped he'd keep her in mind for future work. Or Milton might give Mom a dog's run of parts, full of doubling and fast costume changes and understudies, after which meeting old Mrs. Katz would go home and stare in the mirror and wonder whether this was what she really wanted out of twelve months of no sleep and constant worry.

But sometimes Milton could surprise you, seeing you in places you didn't see yourself. That's how it was when Milton looked at Mona and said, "So do you have an Isabella in there?"

Mona really didn't know if she had an Isabella in there or not. Milton had announced just a few weeks back that he was putting on a *Measure* in the fall, a show that Milton added to the calendar at the last moment because it just seemed topical, with all the Bill Clinton & Monica Lewinsky stuff in the news. Selena Hayes, the in-house PR geek, had added some press release blah-blah-blah about "this play's unusual relevance in a time of sexual repression and conflict," but the show was on the calendar because Milton, like every normal American, was obsessed with the blow job. "Starr's an Angelo, that's what he is. A modern-day Angelo, come to life and stalking the president. Bill Clinton is our Claudio. They're going to condemn him to death for being a lusty fuck. Every woman in the country thought to herself when she voted that she wouldn't mind fucking this president, and this Lewinsky had the courage to show him her ass and wiggle it around and now they're going to crucify him?"

Did that make Monica Lewinsky Isabella? Had Isabella been Monica Lewinsky, Mona could have played the role in her sleep. Monica Lewinsky was a part she could sink her teeth into. The two even looked a little alike.

But Monica Lewinsky wasn't an Isabella. Isabella *wasn't* showing anyone her thong in the Oval Office. Isabella just wanted to be left alone. Mona had taken a crack at Isabella in drama school when she'd been assigned the part for a scene study. There was a moment at the top of the show that Mona couldn't quite get to click, and after that nothing else clicked either. It was just a beat, but it was everything about the character. Isabella was a novice nun. When the audience sees her for the first time, she's talking to an older nun, the tired old sister (as Mona imagined it) staring wistfully out the large window of the cloister at that world she had forsaken.

ISABELLA

And have you nuns no farther privileges?

NUN

Are not these large enough?

ISABELLA

Yes, truly. I speak not as desiring more,
But rather wishing a more strict restraint
Upon the sisterhood.

This wasn't Monica Lewinsky talking. A more strict restraint upon the sisterhood? That was the *last* thing Mona *or* Monica wanted. Mona and Monica loved being women in the world; they loved kisses in closets, sparkling earrings, and skirts that were two inches too short. They loved second dates and did-he-really-say-what-I-thought-he-said? and maybe-yes and maybe-no. They liked the way men's hair felt in their fists if they gripped it tightly, the feel of stubble scraping their chins, and the way men looked at them stupidly. No, Mona couldn't really put herself into the mind of a young girl who was just burning with desire to be locked down. A more strict restraint? All Mona had ever wanted was less restraint. She was a feminist, after all.

But there was something about Isabella that attracted Mona too. Her brother Claudio has been sentenced to death, condemned by the puritanical judge, Angelo, for the crime of impregnating his girlfriend out of wedlock. The plot springs into motion when Angelo is overcome by the same human weaknesses he sought to scourge from others and offers to free Claudio should Isabella sleep with him. But Isabella refuses:

> Th' impression of keen whips I'd wear as rubies
> And strip myself to death, as to a bed
> That longing have been sick for, ere I'd yield
> My body up to shame.

Mona had heard it said by morons that there was no subtext in Shakespeare. But Mona had never heard anyone say "No" and so clearly mean something else. Mona thought that might just be the sexiest sentence she ever heard. You couldn't say that sentence without making it come out like one long orgasmic pant. Mona wondered whether Isabella herself knew how sexy she was. That sentence got Mona thinking that Isabella wasn't such a dull bird as she might have imagined.

Mona didn't say all that to Milton. You could talk yourself out of any inspiration in about a minute. It was better not to think about it too much, even—you could play a role in your brain before you set foot in Burbage, and then show up with nothing left. It was better just to sit on your ideas.

"Why me?" she said.

"She's you."

"Isabella?"

"The way you'll play it."

"So let's give it a whirl," Mona said.

Mona walked out of Milton's office and looked down. She was surprised that her shoes were touching the ground. In theory, of course, the Rabble was a company of equals. But Mona by about week two of her tenure at 107 Avenue C knew that this wasn't really true. The truth was that there was an aristocracy within the company: the cream *did* rise to the top; the actors who regularly played leads pretty much *were* the best. A subtle glow emanated from the pores and souls of the aristocrats, and their feet seemed to hover just slightly over the nasty-ass rugs of Burbage.

———

AT 107 AVENUE C, casting was usually about a year out from first rehearsals, and all through that almost-year, Mona lived in intimate contact with Isabella, to the extent that Zahra pretty much lost interest in talking with her, because every conversation, no matter where it began, ended up with Mona saying something like, "It's just that Isabella is so smart, but she's so strange, I don't know if I can do it."

Then, six weeks before first rehearsal, Milton called Mona back into his office.

"Listen, kiddo," he said. "I've been thinking things over and you might be right. I'm not sure Isabella's as natural a fit for you as I was thinking. I'm thinking you might double Mistress Overdone and Mariana."

"Mistress Overdone and Mariana," Mona said slowly.

"You know what I think about you, how much I respect your

craft. But sometimes in this business, you know, you have to serve the play. That's got to be the priority. Nothing comes before the play."

Milton's door opened. One of Milton's assistants stuck her head in. "Milton?" she said. "Caitlin Koch needs a callback at two. Not two-oh-five. She says it's urgent that you talk today at two precisely if you want the birds."

"Thanks, sweetheart," Milton said.

Then, to Mona, "As I was saying, this isn't about your work. You've got the—"

"Who's playing the role?"

Mona had never seen the expression—at once evasive and excited, guilty and proud—on Milton's face before.

"There's this new girl. I know this is last-minute, but trust me, she's going to take your breath away."

Stepping out into the bright light of Avenue C, Mona felt faint. She crouched down on her heels and let her head flop forward. Two men carrying a couch, neither man breaking stride or glancing at her, walked past her speaking in rapid-fire Spanish, their indifference like a kindness. A woman pushing a stroller was talking on her phone, making an appointment for tomorrow at eight, if the office was open. Mona looked up to see a toddler staring at her.

She barely made it home. She sat right down on the floor of her living room as if she'd been hit in the belly with a brick, her heart beating fast, waves of anxiety crashing over her, her skin prickly with nervous sweat. How fast a nervous breakdown could hit surprised her, because she'd never had a nervous breakdown before. No other professional check, no breakup, no grief had ever hit her with such intensity. Mona said to herself, *So this is what it's like to have a nervous breakdown.*

And some part of Mona, because she was an actress down to the marrow, was watching herself have a nervous breakdown, because it was all so different from what she expected, and if she needed to break down sometime onstage, now she'd know how to play it.

Mona hadn't realized, for example, that having a nervous break-down was so exhausting. It took all her energy to feel so awful. Ophelia was just *so* tired. She had played the part all wrong. All Ophelia wanted was to lie around Elsinore and be left the fuck alone. As it happened, Mona had June and July off, the annual break the actors in the company called the Bridge, and as it happened the breakdown hit the last week of May, so she really had time to wallow. You either had your Bridge midwinter or midsummer, when the company did three shows a week instead of six. The Bridge was supposed to be filled with personal projects and side gigs and festival work—you were supposed to come back to 107 Avenue C fresh like cool cotton—but Mona canceled her summer schedule, telling producers in Vermont and Minnesota that she had hepatitis, and instead passed her Bridge lying on her bed in an old T-shirt, feeling like if she opened the window to let the air circulate there was a good chance she might just jump out of it. She waited by the phone at night for Milton to call. He hadn't called in months. He had lost interest in her altogether. He had used her and replaced her. Her entire value in his eyes had been one drunken night in Hamburg. Mona was absolutely infuriated because he was a lying sack of warmed-over shit. Then she knew that he was absolutely right; she was a talentless impostor who had no business playing this role or any other.

Mona dwelled on a conversation, from a few months back. Another actress in the company about Mona's age, Carrie Hollis, took her aside at the closing party for *Julius Caesar.* Mona had understudied her Portia, who stabs herself in the leg because her husband won't tell her the truth. They were all a little drunk and Carrie Hollis said, "Do you trust Milton?" And Mona said, "Sure, don't you?" And Carrie Hollis said, "Don't trust him. I don't think he likes you." Then they were a little drunker, and Mona asked, "Why doesn't he like me?" And Carrie Hollis said, "It's just that he said you have been very disappointing. He had such high hopes for you." "But he told me he liked me." "See? That's why I don't trust Milton." The only thing about the story that didn't correlate to quote-unquote *reality* was that Carrie Hollis never said any of that. Mona interpreted it all from the way she said, "So are you liking it around here?"

Mona asked Anne Carman if she could come over. Anne had known Milton for decades, playing for him off and on since the early days at 107 Avenue C. Mona came to her often, asking advice on roles, the two of them often sharing a bottle of wine after rehearsals. Now she found her on a stiflingly hot night in her little apartment in an unfashionable neighborhood in Queens.

When Mona was done complaining, Anne said, "Can I give you a little wise counsel?"

"I guess."

Anne got up and went into the kitchen and rummaged around the unwashed dishes. She came back to the dining room table with two glasses and a bottle of whiskey. She poured out small shots for both of them.

"Mona, don't fall in love with Milton."

"I'm *not* in love with Milton."

"Yes you are. Maybe not in love like you want to be the next Mrs. Katz and have a flock of little Katzlings, but make no mistake, darling, you're head over heels in love."

Mona took a sip of her whiskey.

Anne said, "It's a special kind of love actors have for Milton. It's the love you feel when someone finally, finally, *finally* sees you, after so much time being invisible. We're very vulnerable to that as actors, because that's our greatest fear—that nobody can see us. And when Milton sees you, really sees you, you feel like you have this power you never had before."

She poured a little more whiskey into Mona's glass.

"But Mona, don't make Milton into this thing that he's not. I've known Milton since before you were born. I've seen actors come into this company every single year thinking that Milton is this omniscient God whose judgments are absolute and divine. And he's not. He gets it wrong sometimes. If you want to survive in this business, you have to have an internal standard of excellence to which you aspire. You can't live for Milton's love. Because he's careless with people. And if you don't understand that, then Milton will break your heart over and over again."

Mona went home and lay on the bed again, the fan swirling the stale air. The only time the phone rang in all those long hot nights was a wrong number, and still she was so grateful for the distraction that she almost cried. The idea plagued her: *Milton had it within his power to make her happy and he chose not to do so.* Mona said that sentence, just once, to Zahra, who said, "Get a grip."

"I know, it's silly, it's just that—"

"Just what?"

"I just need to know."

"Know what? Know what, exactly?"

It was Zahra who eventually hauled Mona into Dr. Dortzbach's office, saying, "I don't know what to do with you." Dr. Dortzbach was the first and best of Mona's therapists, who had attended to

Mona's psychological needs in a fern-filled, sun-splashed office in Chelsea. She had a practice that specialized in actors, writers, and other creatives who found themselves sobbing in their bathtubs for hours on end.

There in Dr. Dortzbach's office, Mona recounted painful facts, admitting, for example, that she had taken to following Milton home. More than once, she had waited for him half a block down Avenue C, then trailed him as he left work. It was one of the few activities that motivated her to get out of bed. She had even thought up costumes to disguise herself. There were two voices in Mona's head. One told her that she was totally crazy. But the other voice told her that she had the right to know. She was giving her life to Milton. By now Mona's imagination had overwhelmed her completely. She needed to know who this new actress was who had replaced her—the other, *better* Mona Zahid. Was he heading to her place after work? But Milton only went home. She watched Milton trudging up the street from the subway, then a light on the first floor when he walked in the front door, then a light on the second floor. She heard the sound of jazz on warm evenings from an open window.

So Mona told this story to Dr. Dortzbach, expecting her to rise up, point a bony finger at Mona, denounce her as a perverted, psychopathic stalker, and insist she leave her office.

Instead Dr. Dortzbach said, "So who is this man to you? And why do you let him have that kind of power over you?" her voice so kindly and concerned that Mona burst into tears.

IT WAS HAFEZ—OF ALL PEOPLE!—who brought her out of her crisis all those years ago. After Mona's mother died Hafez bought an RV. Nowadays if you wanted to reach him, you had to leave a message for him with Uncle Ali in Philadelphia. He *might* get back to you. But every few months a box of watercolor paintings, sunsets mainly, also some flowers and trees, also some rocks, arrived at Mona's door, sometimes thirty or forty paintings at a time. Mona shoved them under her bed. On every painting there was a place name, and by this Mona knew that her father had been drifting across the country, from the Florida Keys to Sitka, Alaska.

Then, one morning in late July, the doorbell rang and Hafez was standing in front of her, and just like that, Mona smiled spontaneously for the first time in who-knows-how-long. Zahra had left a message with Uncle Ali that Mona was in trouble. Mona had never thought she could be so happy to see her daddy. She was two inches taller than him, but somehow she felt like she was six and looking up at him when he picked her up from school. He folded her into his short arms and rubbed her hair. As soon as she smelled his cologne she started to sniffle.

Hafez spent two weeks in her apartment, sitting on her couch and watching the news and muttering to himself in outrage: "In the Oval Office! Right in the Oval Office! That girl's father should walk up to him and punch him in the face!"

"Daddy, Monica was attracted to him, he was attracted to her. It was their private business. I'm not Hillary Clinton and neither are you. That's *their* business."

"It's my business! I pay his salary! I pay my taxes!"

"That's what makes me angry too. We're paying our taxes so that he can do his job and instead he has to deal with *this*."

"In the Oval Office! Right in the Oval Office . . . !"

Facts, arguments, reasons, opinions were like arrows launched at Hafez's solid steel sides. Nothing short of nuclear annihilation would destroy her father. He had survived the death of his mother at six, a childhood of beatings, the loss of his country, a civil war, the death of his first wife at twenty-five, the abandonment of his childhood dream of being a doctor, the loss of his second wife and a lifetime of persistent mental illness—and he still kept going, driving around the country like some post-apocalyptic hero, painting his sunsets and ranting about the president and thinking from time to time about his daughters.

After dinner Hafez would listen to one of his recordings of Maria Callas. All this was a throwback to childhood, where nightly Hafez would put recordings of Maria Callas on the record player and it was expected on pain of detonation that the entire family remain quiet as he listened and sighed and sometimes sobbed. The CDs in the spiral-bound folder had been records then, but otherwise nothing had changed. Mona took pleasure in watching her father's face as he listened.

One night, Hafez told Mona a story about Callas. He must have read it in one of the biographies he had studied, but the way he told the story was more or less as if he had been there himself.

It happened at La Scala, he said, and Maria was Medea, one of her great roles. But as it happened Maria was not "on voice" that night. This was something, Hafez implied, that happened. No one can expect greatness every night from what was only a human pharynx, larynx, and epiglottis. That was the wonder of La Divina, Hafez implied: that she coaxed immortality from mortality.

"They begin to boo her," Hafez said. "Maria hears the hissing. Some part of her feels like crying. But then. Medea must sing the word '*Crudel!*' to Jason. You cruel man! The orchestra plays fortissimo—two beats! Then everyone waits. But she is quiet. No one knows what is going to happen. Because she does not come in, does not sing her line. She is looking at the audience, just looking, staring. What is she saying? She is saying, *This is my stage! This is La Scala! If you boo me, if you hate me, I hate you more!*

"Then, only then, does she sings her line, '*Crudel!*' directly to the audience.

"And the audience is quiet, totally, totally quiet. Everyone is quiet. Three thousand people, all of them dominated by this little lady. Then she sings again to the audience, shaking her fist: '*Ho dato tutto a te.*' *I gave everything to you.* And they are hers. She has beaten them down."

Later, when Mona explained the business with Isabella and Milton and Vanessa, it was all Mona could do to keep Hafez from heading over to 107 Avenue C and ambushing Milton as he walked out of the Leprechaun, punching *him* in the face.

She said, "Daddy, he's my boss. Daddy, it's just a role. Daddy, if you want to help me, help me learn my lines. The Meet'n'Greet is just next week."

5

The obvious answer to Dr. Dortzbach's question—"So who is this man to you? And why do you let him have that kind of power over you?"—was that Mona had a strained and difficult relationship with her own father, and had created in Milton an idealized substitute, whose approval and affection were of paramount value to her.

Mona sat in the late-fall sunshine outside Vanessa Levin's house and wondered why she had been so resistant to that thought, which seemed to her now both true and slightly banal.

Of course she'd been after a daddy—just like Vanessa back then, both of them agreeing to sleep with Milton, and worship Milton, to substitute for inadequate paternal love, just like so many other women in Milton's complicated little harem over the years. And not just Milton's harem: Cleopatra went through one powerful older Roman general after another. Mona married Phil. Sheila married Bruce. None of it was so mysterious or subtle at all, or so terrible for that matter: at the end of the long day, a good daddy was a good thing to have.

Phil had a friend who had a friend at the *Times* who told her that it was Vanessa Levin's on-the-record testimony that got the article to run. The stories of Anonymous Sources One through Eleven were just ornaments and trills, embellishments, and counterplot to Vanessa's detailed retelling of how Milton had seduced her, abused her, squeezed out her talent like a lemon, then punished her when she attempted to break free.

Mona read the article so many times after it was published that she had more or less memorized it:

> Vanessa Levin was minutes away from stepping onstage in her professional debut in an Off Broadway production of *Measure for Measure* when she learned that her grandfather had suffered a massive heart attack. The 22-year-old actress asked Milton Katz, the show's then 57-year-old director and the founder of the acclaimed Disorder'd Rabble theater company, whether she should still go on. In response, he pushed her against a makeup mirror and forcefully kissed her, she said in a recent interview.

That's how the article (and the affair) began—the lede, Mona thought it was called, that all-important lure that hooked the unwilling reader by the gills and dragged them upward to the light. *Chapeau* to Angie Steinmetz, Mona thought, whose name was on the byline and whom a cursory Google search revealed was all of thirty-two years old! So young and so talented! Who wouldn't want to read on after that? It was a perfect tasty combination of prurience and outrage. Mona particularly enjoyed that "forcefully," which suggested—what, exactly? A little tongue? Maybe a hand between the thighs? How much more effective it was to leave the precise terms of the offense undefined! And if that wasn't bad enough, there was the photo that accompanied the article. It must have been taken when Vanessa was about twelve, in what Mona figured could only have been a middle school production of *Peter Pan*. The girl in the photo was prepubescent, no taller than four foot ten, flat-chested and stick-legged, smiling from ear to ear, as innocent as a spring lamb. It was that picture, as much as anything, Mona figured, that destroyed Milton.

———————

MONA SAW HERSELF in the plate-glass window of the door of Vanessa Levin's building. What would Vanessa think if she were to walk out the door right now, phone in hand, busy with her own last-minute Thanksgiving errand? Would she squeal and hug her? Or would she see Mona and run back inside, sending out the big Irish bruiser of a doorman to confront her. "Can I help you, ma'am?"

Mona had once been on good enough terms with the doormen downstairs that they knew her by face, not even bothering to call up when she arrived. From that first Meet'n'Greet, where Vanessa trailed after Mona like a duckling, they had been friends. At lunch, Mona had asked Vanessa if she wanted to have a bite before the afternoon table read, and the two of them walked over to the Cuban place, where they had rice and beans. A week into rehearsals, Vanessa learned that Mona was riding the subway upwards of an hour to get home after rehearsals, and she invited her to sleep on her couch if rehearsals ran late. When Vanessa went back to Connecticut to visit her grandfather, which she often did, she would ask Mona to cat-sit.

When Vanessa left the company, Mona didn't see her again for almost a decade. She understood, from Party Tom, that she had moved to Tel Aviv, where she had found a job as the assistant artistic director in a theater working with poor Arab children. Mona looked up the theater on the web and found a little picture of Vanessa smiling, just a little rounder than she remembered her, a splotch of red on her cheek. A few years later she was married to the artistic director, and then a few years after that she was divorced.

Then Vanessa found Mona on Facebook. By then Mona had established herself as a lead in the company. She had played Rosalind, she had played Richard II and Cassius, she'd played Hermione and Helena and Margaret. Mona had become a better actress with each passing year. Her breath deepened and her range expanded. Those were the years, she later thought, in which she really learned to act.

Mona knew that Rachel would have disapproved of her decision to stay in the company—but would she have had those experiences had she left? Would she have become the thing she was? The best and brightest point of being a bunch of years old was that you could see things just a little more clearly. What Mona could see now, which she couldn't see at that first session in Dr. Dortzbach's office, was that the whole setup down at 107 Avenue C—the alpha primate striding the halls dispensing privilege, fear, and inspiration; the females grooming themselves and displaying the splendor of their bright red asses—was just about guaranteed to create emotions of great intensity, and wounds that remained livid decades later. It was a psychological world they had *all* created together, Milton *and* his women, a place unfit for any purpose, Mona reckoned, but one: putting on plays. For which purpose it basically worked: whatever the twisted psychological dynamics of the place, they had put on a hell of a lot of good plays together.

All through those years, Mona thought about Vanessa only occasionally. The friend request on Facebook had surprised and pleased her—but why? Mona remembered the two of them sitting side by side on Vanessa's couch in her apartment after rehearsals, talking sometimes late into the night until they fell asleep on the couch. There was no reason now they couldn't be Facebook friends, couldn't trade recipes and political takes, couldn't post pictures of their pets in adorable poses or of themselves in pretty new dresses on date nights with their men. Now Vanessa was working at the Public. There were photos of Vanessa out for drinks in the Village with her coworkers, their faces white in the glare of an aggressive flash as they smiled for the cameras. It was Mona's impression that Vanessa was a little thicker, a little rounder in every photo. Then, to Mona's surprise, appearing without preamble or warning, Vanessa was in a hospital gown, her face flushed, hair disordered, a newborn baby boy in her arms. "Congrats!!!!!!!!!" Mona wrote. She added a string of emoticons: a couple of baby bottles, a heart. Mona assiduously liked the photos over the years that followed because babies, obviously, then toddlers. From time to time Mona or Vanessa would write on one or the other's wall, "We really have to get together again!" or "It's been too long!"

Barney looked up at Mona and with his mature, understanding eyes told her that it was time to visit Milton, that she shouldn't put it off any longer. But Mona ignored him. She was not so high that she was going to take advice from a dog. *Why shouldn't I call Vanessa?* she thought indignantly. They could talk about old times. Showing up at Vanessa's house out of the blue wasn't the sort of thing Mona ordinarily did, but it was the sort of spontaneous thing she wished that she could do. Zahra would have gone. Mona hadn't seen Vanessa in so long—but at her age, wasn't that always the case? You miss out on a decade here, a decade there. The time flies by. You catch up.

Mona's phone had only 2 percent battery but it was enough. She looked up Vanessa's name and there was the little phone icon and *why not just try?* Then the phone was ringing and the soft pretty voice on the other end said, "Hello?"

"Vanessa?" Mona said. "It's Mona!"

"Mona?"

"Zahid!"

"Oh!"

Mona said, "I've only got two percent battery but I'm just downstairs and I thought, why not?"

"You're just downstairs? Downstairs where?"

"Of your building? On Seventy-First? You're still here, aren't you?"

"What are you doing here?"

"I was just, I was just walking the dog and he thought . . . I mean, I thought . . . that if you weren't busy you might want a glass of wine. Or a margarita. On Thanksgiving."

Vanessa laughed. "Come on up, Mona. It's been a long time."

ACT THREE

CLEOPATRA

Give me my robe, put on my crown; I have
Immortal longings in me.

1

A burst of festive noise startled Barney. He tilted his ears back and began to nose the hostess suspiciously, sniffing his way up her leg.

"I didn't know you were having a party," Mona said. "It's Thanksgiving and I just showed up. Of course you're busy. I'm so sorry. I should go."

"*Everyone* just shows up here on Thanksgiving," Vanessa said. "It's my thing. Didn't you see it on Facebook? I invite everyone. We do a potluck—it's all vegetarian—and you brought your dog! Is he good with people?"

"He's a sweetheart," Mona said, which was not the truth. The truth was that Barney was suspicious, jealous, and judgmental. He had been known to growl at or even bite other dogs if Mona so much as rubbed their heads. "I should've brought a bottle of wine at least. Or some cauliflower. I'm just so high I wasn't thinking clearly."

Vanessa laughed. "Still Mona."

"Still me, I think."

All of this was so different from how Mona had expected things to be. Vanessa, despite her leading role in Milton's deposition, did not post on Facebook about him or about her time at 107 Avenue C, with one exception: three weeks or so after Milton left 107 for the last time, she posted a picture of herself at a performance of *Uncle Vanya*. (Mona wasn't in the show.) She wrote, "First time in the house in twenty years!" There followed in the comments the usual argument, vituperation, and invective, as well as a stream of congratulations from her admirers on her courage. Mona had been so stressed by the conversation that she took a Xanax and muted Vanessa for thirty days. When her name reappeared in her feed, it was only to show pictures of her and her son feeding the goats in the Central Park Zoo. Mona wasn't sure what Vanessa said about Milton in her absence, but she didn't suppose it was admiring. From this incident Mona had it in mind that she and Vanessa were on the outs somehow, that Vanessa, to the extent that she thought of Mona, thought of her as hostile, the two of them not just members of different factions of the Milton-wars, but possessors of entirely different worldviews. But Vanessa seemed happy to see her, genuinely convivial, as if Mona's unexpected arrival at her apartment, disheveled, stoned, leading a disapproving beagle on a leash, was exactly the thing that would make her Thanksgiving Day delightful.

"You look great," Mona said, not entirely untruthfully and not entirely truthfully either: Vanessa nowadays looked like the strong, fleshy farmer's wife, the one who goes after the mouse with a rolling pin. The weight was distributed around her in a way that suggested luxurious excess.

"So do you!" Vanessa said. "Come on in! You have to come meet everyone."

Mona might have turned on her heel and fled, if Vanessa hadn't taken her by the forearm. Vanessa touched her fingers to the mezuzah on her door, then brought her fingers to her mouth. Mona didn't have a choice. She took a breath, held it a beat, and walked into the party, the act of crossing the threshold a piece of performance art entitled *Beautiful Woman Walks into a Party* #7. As a warm-up, Milton used to have everyone in the company walk into a party as a beautiful woman, from Vanessa, who was in fact a beautiful young woman at the time, to Old Tom, well past eighty. It was Old Tom who taught Mona how to play the scene: "Imagine, baby, that you are walking into a room on fire. Feel the heat. So you are frightened. Then it takes you a moment, just a moment, to realize that you are fireproof. That's the joy."

Mona shook out her hair, straightened her back, and walked into the flames. She looked around the little apartment. It had seemed like such a grand affair back when Mona used to crash on Vanessa's couch after rehearsals. Then Vanessa was the only person Mona knew who owned her own apartment, at the age of twenty-two. Now Mona saw it for what it was: a one-bedroom that in a normal city might have been a studio, with an open-plan kitchen, the place far too small for all the Thanksgiving partygoers milling about with glasses of wine and tiny paper plates in hand. There were plants everywhere: hanging plants obscuring the window fronting 71st Street, large potted ficuses and ferns, creepers overflowing from ceramic pots perched on ledges and bookshelves.

Mona was already plotting her exit from the party—this thing had been a mistake, she decided, the waves of anxiety mounting higher up the shore—when she saw the ghost of her ex-something standing at the kitchen counter scooping up guacamole with a tortilla chip.

"That man looks just like Will Powers," she said.

"You know Will?" Vanessa said.

"I used to—"

"There he is."

"Kayla Kosterman told me he was dead."

Vanessa looked carefully at Will Powers. Mona could hear the crunch of his tortilla chip across the room.

"I don't think so," she finally said.

"It was a big deal. Everyone was talking about it."

"Who was talking about what?"

"About Will Powers."

Vanessa didn't say anything for a long time.

"You don't mean *Bill Powell*, do you? The lighting tech guy?"

"*No!*" Mona said, momentarily outraged. Then she watched Will Powers wipe a smear of avocado off his face with a napkin and said, "Bill's dead too?"

Vanessa laughed as if Mona had been making an elaborate joke. "You are too funny!" she said. Then she leaned over and hugged Mona and Mona could smell the wine on her breath and her lotion and citrus face cream and the smell of chili. Now that she could smell the alcohol, things made more sense. Mona felt at once that she was less inebriated than everyone else in the room and more; she was inebriated along a different axis. She was anything but tipsy. Her high was deeper, richer, slower, with a melancholic bass note, like a cello solo.

Vanessa said, "You are a woman who looks like she just might need a glass of wine."

"I'm a woman who thinks she just might need the whole bottle."

Vanessa laughed again, her whole body shaking.

Mona felt Barney tug. She disentangled herself from Vanessa and said, "Can I let this guy off his leash? Do you mind?"

"My cat is going to freak and hide in the closet."

Mona would realize, just after she unlatched the dog, that Vanessa in fact had not given her permission.

Vanessa came back in a moment with a glass of white wine.

"Someone brought this," she said. "I think it's supposed to be good? I'm not a wine person. What a surprise to see you! It's been too long!"

The doorbell rang. Vanessa said, "I'll be right back!" From the kitchen Mona heard a joyous voice cry out, "It's hummus!" Mona looked at Will Powers. He had yet to notice her. He was talking to a woman who was laughing and touching his forearm. Mona didn't want to interrupt his conversation. She thought it more appropriate to be immersed in conversation with some other man when he spotted her.

Mona decided she was no worse dressed than anyone in the room, really—when did people stop dressing up for parties? Everyone had come to Vanessa's party as if coming straight from a spin class. Mona had some lip gloss in her pocket. Rachel had given it to her for her birthday, explaining that it was the new kind of lip gloss which caused a minor allergic reaction every time you put it on, so your lips would get plump and sexy. Mona swiped it on and felt her lips burn as if she had just eaten chili peppers. She took out her scrunchie and shook her shoulders. She caught a glimpse in the mirror in the hall of her hair cascading across her shoulders, and thought, *Holy shit.* This was one of the great hair days of her life. Good hair always came when you least expected it. You can plan for good hair and work for it, you could buy product and style, but the hard truth was that hair obeyed its own mysterious laws, like those wonderful nights when Mona went onstage with premonitions of disaster only to form an unexpected bond deeper than love with her audience. These things just happened. She had washed it last night after the show, and the walk in the cool, dry air had set it in a gentle wave, like a movie star from the 1940s. She had the littlest streak of gray. Rachel insisted, not quite convincingly, that it was sexy.

The partygoers were in clusters: the open-plan kitchen people milled around the counter or heated up things on the stove; a couch cluster congregated around a woman in bright red leggings. Near the half-open window, the people who vaped blew steam out onto the street. The strange thing about New York was that you knew everyone at every party, including the people you didn't know. She recognized three or four people in the room, including the late Will Powers, and she knew that the people she didn't know would know somebody she did. These were all theater or theater-adjacent people. Mona was just famous enough that a few people who recognized her looked at her for a moment, wondering if it was gauche to recognize her, but not so famous that they could remember what her name was. She sipped her wine, which, just as Vanessa had promised, was good.

Mona wondered how she would explain to Phil that she had abandoned his parents, her niece, their son, the Chums, and all his family on Thanksgiving Day to attend a party with strangers on the East Side. The thing about Mona and parties, as Phil had explained to Dr. Billy, is that she actually liked them. He'd been to plenty of parties where Mona had a good time. This comment had frustrated Mona because it wasn't as if she could choose which parties she'd like. Taking her to parties was like punishing her because sometimes she wasn't a pain in the ass.

Mona remembered the last time she was out socially. It was an after-party for a Broadway show on which her old drama school buddy Jillian D'Amato had done the set design. There she'd gotten into a nice long conversation with one of the swings, a woman she thought she might actually be friends with, based on their common fondness for beagles and orchids, only to discover later when she followed her on Facebook that she hated her. Mona did not wish to be deluded again. Everyone in the room, she supposed, was making or had made the same calculation: real life was just a proving ground for the far more consequential world of online friendships. You had to live with your online friends, after all, every day for the rest of your life.

Mona wished that she could go up to strangers and talk about her hair; it was not a question of vanity so much as simple fascination: Why today and not yesterday? How could it happen again tomorrow? The thought of Will Powers admiring her hair made her smile, and the act of smiling gave her confidence. She took a step in the direction of the kindly-faced woman in red leggings on the couch. She was holding a ball of energy in her hands. She tossed it lightly in the air and it hovered above her like a bubble blown by a toddler.

The woman said, "So I was dropping off Lily at doggy day care and this woman was on her phone, she was dropping off her bichon frisé, and she goes, 'And can you believe? After eighteen years of marriage Simon finally told her *that*? I mean, how can you not tell your wife *that* for eighteen years?' And I was like, I have to know what Simon told her. So I followed her three blocks up Columbus even though I was going downtown just to hear. She must have thought I was a stalker because she kept looking at me like I wanted to steal her purse. Then she got into a taxi, and now I have no idea what Simon never told his wife and it's driving me *crazy*."

Another woman, perched on the arm of the couch, plucked the ball of energy out of the air.

"He's probably adopted," she said.

"Why wouldn't he mention that?"

"Maybe he didn't know."

"I think you would know, wouldn't you?"

Soon other people were throwing out ideas: Simon was trans, Simon was gay, Simon had a child with another woman. Mona wondered how she would deal with Phil's love child, were he to present himself at their front door. Graciously, she hoped. She would send Phil's bastard an Amazon gift card at Christmas.

Mona saw the ball of energy floating in the air. She reached out and grabbed it.

She said, "Or Simon was in prison."

"Oh, that's clever!" said the deranged little woman who followed strangers on the street.

Mona was thinking how pretty the ball of energy was, how brightly it glowed, and how many colors there were when you stared right into it, when she saw Will Powers looking at her hair. She dropped the ball of energy on the floor and walked away. The ball bounced a few times and lay there.

———

BARNEY SLINKED THROUGH THE LIVING ROOM, exploring with his nose. There were feet everywhere, a hint of feces on some shoes, the smell of other dogs on pants legs. He sniffed. Cat urine. Hands reached for his head and rubbed him. The refrigerator door opened and he could smell the onion that was thrown out a week before. He could smell ants and ant poison. He could smell the good, rich, moldy smell of cheese. From the bedroom he could smell old sheets, dark closets. Barney knew everyone's secrets: he could smell who was afraid and who was aroused, who dribbled and who spilled. He could smell the sickly-sweet stench of a tumor, long before the tumor's owner knew of her own disease. He could smell bacteria breeding in molars. He could smell cockroach poison behind the refrigerator. He could smell women bleeding and men's underwear crunchy with crusted semen. He could smell the other dogs the people in this room had known. He knew from their smells all their secret, dirty, doggish histories.

———————

"WILL?"

"Mona? Oh wow—"

He seemed so surprised to see Mona, and stared at her so intensely, that she wondered for a moment if he had thought *she* was dead.

"I'm so sorry, Will. I should've gone to your funeral but I was on tour and then I wanted to write a note to your parents to tell them how much you meant to me but I couldn't find the words and I should've and I'm so glad you're not dead."

"Dead," he said.

"That's what I thought."

Mona explained about Kayla Kosterman and how the bar was so noisy.

"I was just heartbroken," she said.

"So how did I go?" he said, smiling.

"I didn't ask."

His smile disappeared.

"You never even asked?"

"Not really."

"I see."

"What difference does it make?" Mona said.

"'What *difference* does it make?' Seriously?"

Mona said, "You're not dead, so what difference does it make?"

Will Powers leaned forward. She backed up. She wondered if she had been mistaken about the hair, if Will was fixated on that little hint of gray, not the amazing wave.

He said, "I saw you walk into this party, Mona, and I thought about leaving. Because I didn't know if I could do it, you know? It was just like, boom, here she is, this is really happening. For twenty years, you and me, the thing we had, the time we spent together, that was a beautiful little thing right up there on my short little shelf of beautiful memories. I polished it from time to time. And I cherished it. And I was fine with never talking to you again. Not happy but fine. Because I thought that you thought it was something special too. And you were married and then I was married and it was probably best, you know, if we just kept our distance."

"I didn't know you felt that way," Mona said.

"You should've known."

"You were always just—"

"I came to your shows sometimes, just to sit in the back row and watch you. Just to be in a room with you. Just to see you again. You didn't even ask how I *died*?"

"But you weren't actually dead!"

"I was dead. For you. For you it was like I was really dead."

"I did care, Will. I did. I cried. I had real tears."

Mona told him about the incident at the dentist's office. This was a few months or so after he died. She had been getting a cavity filled, inhaling nitrous, when that Elton John song, the one about Daniel and his brother and traveling to Spain, came on the radio. Will used to play it on his guitar. Her lips had been paralyzed by the anesthetic, making it hard to blubber without drooling. They stopped the procedure and let her cry. The dentist's assistant rubbed her shoulder comfortingly.

Will said, "But you weren't so upset you went to my funeral."

"There *was* no funeral."

"How much work would it have been to google my name and find out what killed me?"

Mona said, "Do you know how many Will Powers there are? A lot of them die every day. I couldn't concentrate on something like google. I was in mourning."

"Did you wear black?"

"No."

"Cover your mirrors? Rend your garments?"

"No."

"So how did you actually mourn me?"

"I just felt . . . sad."

"I swear, Mona, you are still after all this time the single most self-absorbed person I have ever met in my life."

"Oh Christ, I wish to fuck you were dead," Mona said.

She was startled by his laugh.

"Oh shit, it is so great to see you," he said. "This is the *last* place I expected to find you."

"Screw you, I thought you were serious."

"I was serious but now I don't care. Give me a hug."

Mona stepped in and folded herself into Will. He wrapped his long arms around her. She burrowed her nose into his sweater and stayed there a long time.

"You choked on a piece of lamb," she said.

"Vegetarian."

"You foiled a bank robbery and got shot."

"Me?"

"Autoerotic asphyxiation gone wrong."

"All too plausible."

Mona disentangled herself from his arms. She took a step backward, and he took a step forward, and then they sat side by side on the couch. Mona crossed her legs and angled her body in his direction, so he could really see her hair.

"So, who are you now?" she said.

"They call me Mr. Powers. I teach high school English in Hoboken. And I coach drama."

"I bet the kids adore you."

"We have fun," he said. "You'd love them. They are so bright and so creative—"

"So, Mr. Powers, do you still sell dope?"

That's how Mona met Will. There had been a time when his name had been in certain circles like a trademark, as in the phrase "I need some WillPower." There wasn't an actor in New York City in those days who didn't buy their WillPower from Will Powers, who was himself an aspiring actor, or didn't sample a bowl of the dank WillPower thereafter in his East Village apartment, or didn't spend the afternoon subsequently paralyzed on WillPower and flopped on his couch watching something picked out of Will Powers' massive collection of videotapes despite *really* having to get some shit done, or who hadn't eaten Will Powers' famous spaghetti in his tiny little kitchen, or didn't wake up on his couch, or in his bed, or who hadn't taken a shower in his nasty shower the next morning and sprinted to an audition, only to find herself back in Will Powers' apartment later that day because it would take too long to get back to Brooklyn, and you have a callback at five.

"I've been sober for a decade," he said.

Mona said, "Me too."

He looked at the glass of wine in her hand.

"Ish," she added. "Sober-ish. Not now. Obviously. But generally speaking."

Will laughed again. Phil didn't laugh at things Mona said. Instead he said, "That's really funny," in the places where the laughs were supposed to go. Mona asked him once, "Then why don't you laugh?" "I do laugh." "No, you just say, 'That's really funny.' You aren't *actually* laughing." "Are you seriously fighting with me about this?" "I'm not fighting, I'm interrogating. I'm trying to understand." "I'm supposed to fake my orgasms *and* my laughter?" "That's really funny," Mona said. The thing of it was, Phil *did* laugh with other people. He laughed at the television, he laughed with Aaron, he laughed at all sorts of things. He even told Dr. Billy that he prized Mona's sense of humor. Mona wondered if he laughed with Melanie McDowell, out in the woods.

"Do you remember what a crush I had on you back then?" Will asked.

"How could I forget? It was quite flattering and a little weird."

"You didn't even want to go to my funeral."

"I'll go next time."

"So why did you always say no?"

"I did say yes a bunch of times."

"You know what I mean."

Mona looked at him. "How could I say yes? I didn't want to be a drug dealer's serious live-in girlfriend. The next step after that was drug dealer's wife. How was I to know that you'd get sober and teach high school English? I thought for sure you'd end up in prison and I'd have to get up at four in the morning to ride the bus upstate so I could visit you. With Ziploc bags of dope up my you-know-what. And I hate getting up early."

"Married? Kids?" he said.

"Husband and son. One of each."

"But you're here today."

"So are you."

"My kids are with my ex," he said.

Mona began to cry.

"Are you okay?" he asked.

"I don't know," Mona said, as surprised by the tears as he was. "I don't know what's happening to me today."

Will took Mona's hand. Mona was so *bored* with pushing back the tears, and Will seemed to respond so positively to them. He stroked her hand with his thumb and looked at her—really looked at her—for the first time. He was getting it now about her hair, that today was something special. She fed the tears a little by thinking how sad that someone as fundamentally nice as Will Powers was alone on Thanksgiving, some other man breaking the wishbone with his kids. Milton would have her wipe away the tear here. "Underplay it," he would say. "Bring the words to the front, not you, let Shakespeare talk. *You* act so the audience can feel." But what would it be like to let herself go? Why did she always have to do it Milton's way? Mona looked at Will and saw in his tea-brown eyes a great depth of understanding; she felt for a moment that she could tell him anything, anything at all, and he would understand, without the laborious process of negotiation and interpretation that was necessary to explain things to her own husband. There was no subject of importance to Mona that she could discuss with Phil that the years of cohabitation and continual friction had not rendered either so sensitive through abrasion that it could not broached without provoking a spat of bickering, or else so thick and calloused over with repetition that both of them would be bored. She saw that Will looked at her now with bright, eager fascination. She wanted to say, "It's so nice to see you again," but she found herself crying harder now, past the point where she could bring the tears under easy control.

"It's okay," Will said. "It's all okay."

He wrapped his arm around Mona. He stroked her head. Mona remembered that Will would wrap his arm around a boa constrictor if the snake looked a little sad. Then she remembered that he used to walk over to Washington Square in the afternoon and juggle for tips. Man, there was a guy who could juggle his brains out. She wanted to ask him if he still juggled but she couldn't stop crying. He was trying to be an actor back then, like all of them, he even had talent, but shit, the callback was today? Really? It made no difference talking to Will now that they had not seen each other in decades and that he had died in the interim. The only part of talking to Will now that felt strange was that this Will Powers had the wrong hair. So much of him had been about his long hair, which he wore in a ponytail. Now it was more like this sleazy hipster man-bun thing, even though he was well into his forties. Mona suspected that Will, with a little prompting and an assurance that his audience was sympathetic, could name the hottest girl in his eleventh-grade American Lit class.

"I don't want to get your shirt all dirty," Mona said.

"That's what it's for."

"Thank you for being so nice to me."

Only when she kissed Will did Mona stop crying. She didn't mean to kiss him: she had just turned her face and found his face, rough with stubble, in the vicinity. But as soon as she kissed him the tears shut down and all her energy went into kissing him. She wasn't kissing him for the first time. Will Powers kissed her back. Then he was kissing her for real, his mouth warm against hers. Mona remembered days almost entirely forgotten in which she had done nearly nothing but kiss Will Powers, and the intervening years that formed the bulk of Mona's adult life became insubstantial.

"I'm so glad you're not dead," she said.

"Me too."

"Did you really go to my shows?"

"Like you went to my funeral."

Mona crawled very slowly with the tip of her tongue along the outer edges of Will Powers' lips, feeling the place where his beard and mustache were growing in.

They kissed for a minute or two, tenderly and silently. Mona was filled with regret for the intervening years. She felt like things were right that had been wrong for a long time. She began to think of the life she and Will Powers were, just now, beginning together: the furtive bus rides out to New Jersey, the anticipation almost as sweet as the arrival; the horrible afternoon in Dr. Billy's office when Mona would one day confess everything; the little apartment she and Will might eventually share where the two of them would sit on the couch and kiss and talk all evening long. By the time Mona sat back and Will took a sip from his sparkling water, she had built an entire life with him, concluding with his actual death.

Will broke off the kiss. He had a look on his face as if he had eaten a large meal too quickly and needed to burp.

"Well," Mona said.

"I know what you mean."

The two of them laughed. Both of them were embarrassed for a moment. Then Will asked if she remembered Ecky Riesling.

"Ecky Riesling," Mona said. "The name rings a bell. Why do I know that name?"

"The house in Vermont? Where we shroomed?"

"Oh! Ecky! Of course!"

"I just saw him two weeks ago," Will said.

"No way! How is he? And he had that pretty girlfriend? What was her name? Teresa Something?"

"He left her a few years ago. He just got married again. His new wife is like twenty-three. That's why I went to see him."

"But Teresa was beautiful," Mona said, remembering now for the first time in decades a late-summer afternoon in a grassy field gathering wildflowers with Teresa Something. How had Teresa Something, who wore daisies in her hair, now grown so old that a man would leave her for a younger woman? Who could be younger or prettier than Teresa Something? "And they were so in love," she added.

Will shrugged.

Now Mona knew that he had no more understood, really understood, the wave in her hair than she had understood, really understood, his sleazy man bun.

From across the room, the woman in red leggings let out a shriek of laughter. "So true!" she shouted. The doorbell rang. Mona and Will sat together for a few more minutes mentioning the names of various young people they once knew who had grown up. Mona wondered what this *thing* was that lay between then and now: you couldn't touch it or taste it or see it, but it was *there*, and somehow, all things weighed, it mattered more than anything else.

Finally Will said, "What about your sister? What's she up to?"

"You knew Zahra?"

"Don't you remember when we went to the Met together and saw *Tosca?*"

"We did?"

"One of the tenors was a customer of mine—you really don't remember this?"

"Are you sure it was me?" Mona asked.

"It was you and your sister, both of you in red dresses, your sister was like twenty minutes late, and I felt like the king of the world, walking around with the two of you."

"I wish I could remember."

"Is she still in town?"

Mona took a long sip of her wine. She chewed it a little in the back of her mouth. She liked the cool acid oily mineral taste of it, the way it cleared her sinuses and made her think clearly.

She said, "Zahra's Zahra. You know Zahra."

"It was nice, the way we were friends back then."

Mona didn't say anything for a long time.

"I guess we'll all need to get together soon."

———————

BARNEY TROTTED THROUGH THE LIVING ROOM, carrying an oddly shaped purple bone in his mouth. No one saw him, or if someone did see him, they did not squeal or comment. He had found the thing exploring in the bedroom, under the bed: a largish bone, the texture just yielding and pleasant to gnaw on, the smell familiar and rich. He would have stayed to gnaw his find in the bedroom, where it was quiet and the coats were piled high on the bed, each with their own interesting aromas, but there was a cat. She was hiding in the closet. She hissed at Barney, frightening him. Barney was looking for a place where he could explore his find in peace.

"Is that *me?*" Mona said.

She stood up from the couch so suddenly that Will Powers knew that Mona's mood had shifted, which was to Will Powers not a surprise at all, because, if he now remembered one salient fact from his time with Mona, it was that Mona's mood was *always* shifting, had always been shifting, and would likely continue shifting long after she died.

"I'll be right back," she lied.

Mona drifted toward the wall of the apartment where Vanessa had assembled a lattice of photographs, each in an identical IKEA black-matted Fiskbö frame, each photo documenting a distinct phase of Vanessa's existence, from chubby babyhood to winsome girlhood to ravishing adolescence to her brief but intense spell down at 107 Avenue C to the years beyond. The photo that interested Mona, though, was not the picture of girlish Vanessa graduating from elementary school or tweenish Vanessa riding a pony in Vermont or post-Rabble Vanessa hiking in the Negev or ageless Vanessa and her cousins rowing a boat on a lake somewhere. No, the photo that interested Mona was the photo of Vanessa at the White House, standing side by side with Mona, Milton, and Bill Clinton, all of them in evening clothes with slightly drunken, happy late-night faces.

They were at the White House because Bill Clinton was a Shakespeare buff, and he wanted a night of American Shakespeare at the White House. Vikram's Richard III, a follow-up to his Hamlet, had been their other big hit of the season in addition to *Measure*, so Mona, Vikram, Milton, Vanessa, and a few other luminaries of American classical theater were all invited down one snowy weekend in February to Washington. James Earl Jones was going to trot out some monologues from *Othello* and Al Pacino would do his Shylock, and Mona (Mona!) was right in there with them, playing Lady Anne's seduction for an audience that included the president, his wife, and some Supreme Court justices, as well as an assortment of governors, senators, congressmen, and businessmen.

The first part of the evening had been the playing, up on the makeshift stage White House staff had built out for the evening. Then there had been a reception at which the guests enjoyed what the invitation called a "Post-Theater Supper." There had been eight of them at the table with polite conversation to the left and to the right, the actors from the Rabble having clearly been relegated to faraway regions of the room where invitees of low political importance were left to chat politely with other invitees of low importance. But around midnight the tenor of the evening changed, as guests began to mingle with their digestifs and glasses of whiskey and the celebrities and diplomats and politicians all loosened up. The room got a little louder and the lights a little dimmer. That was when it seemed to Mona all the old alpha males moved in on her simultaneously, as if she were the prettiest little fox in a room full of baying hounds. Far and away the most persistent of her suitors was the chief justice of the Supreme Court, William Rehnquist, who had a theory of *Hamlet* that he was very eager to expound. There was nothing so insistent as a man who thinks he has *Hamlet* all figured out. He was leaning in very close to Mona with stinky breath and explaining the play to her when Vikram tapped Mona on the shoulder and whispered in her ear that it was time to rehearse their lines.

"Mr. Chief Justice, would you be so kind as to excuse me?" Mona said. "Mr. Gupta has just reminded me that I promised my mother that I would telephone her from the White House. It means the world to her."

Then she flashed her cutest smile at the chief justice, who took her hand and with old-world courtliness kissed it. She made a half curtsy in his direction and followed Vikram. The White House staff had made available a little changing room for the actors, so they could perform in costume and then put on their evening wear for the party afterwards. Mona, Vikram, and Vanessa crowded in there, the three of them almost giggling at the audacity of it all as they sniffed fat lines off a hand mirror.

After that the party was a lot of fun. There was dancing and glasses of champagne, and the old men who wanted to flirt with Mona seemed a little more charming, all of them bringing their vintage A-game as they asked her how she memorized her lines or telling her that they had once acted a little too. A congressman from Ohio even got so far as telling her that he was in New York all the time, and it would be his pleasure to take her out for a drink or a meal.

The best part of the party was the president himself. Was there ever a president who exuded good humor like this one? It took Mona an hour or so to realize that the big man who looked like Bill Clinton from the television was in fact the big man at the center of the room radiating laughter and attention, and that her desire to get near him and soak up some of his good energy was the famous charisma at work. Later the president was sitting at a table with Milton, Vikram, and Mona.

"Mr. President, I'd like to introduce you to one of our new stars, Mona Zahid."

"Hello, Mona," the president said, taking her hand, holding it. "I have to tell you, I was stunned."

"Thank you, Mr. President," she said. "I like your work too."

The president laughed a big happy laugh. He said, "Can I ask you a personal question, Mona?"

"I don't know, Mr. President. It depends how personal."

"She says what's on her mind, Mr. President," said Milton. "We brought her in two years ago and she's been tearing the place apart."

"I can see that," the president said. "I want to know why that Anne falls for a snake like Richard. I just never understood that. Tonight was the first time I ever saw that scene and I thought it worked, but I still don't understand it."

"Because he's sexy, Mr. President. And because she doesn't live in a world where girls can say no to a powerful man."

"Powerful men sometimes can't say no to a pretty girl either," he said.

His bow tie was loosened and his collar opened, and his huge face was flushed. But he had a spotlight of attention that was bright and sober. *This* was the real perquisite of being president, he seemed to say: sitting at a table with interesting people like them. Mona couldn't say exactly how he did it, but he was one of them, a downtown actor, an honorary member of the Rabble. If she'd been introduced to him at the Meet'n'Greet as "Bill" from way back in the day when the company used to rehearse in Milton's living room, she'd have believed it. That impression was reinforced by the story he was telling, of playing the Scottish Lord in an eleventh-grade production back in Arkansas, Bill talking about the banquet scene just the way actors talked about the banquet scene, in terms of beats and

squeezing the laughs out of the horror and hunting down the audience where it was hiding. It was hard to believe that in the morning
they'd be back in New York running lines but Bill Clinton would be
on the phone talking to Boris Yeltsin about nuclear weapons. Then
an aide came around and he said, "Will you excuse me, Mona? I
hope you'll stick around and we'll have a chance to talk later." The
way Bill Clinton looked at Mona, she understood that he would
have been happy talking to her about playing Shakespeare all night,
only you never got quite enough of what you wanted, not even if
you were the president. Mona loved it that he pretty much ignored
Vanessa all night long.

Before he was dragged off, the White House photographer took
a picture of them all together, Milton on the left, then Mona, then
Bill, then Vikram and Vanessa. Mona was in the middle, with
those two big men's arms around her back. Milton looked a little
awkward in black tie, but otherwise was absolutely at his ease,
in no way intimidated by the proximity of power. Mona couldn't
look at that picture now without thinking how young they all
looked then. Milton had been a good-looking man, tall and broad-
shouldered, his black beard ahead of the fashion that fifteen years
later would become universal downtown. Not long after he had
his first heart attack and just like that, his beard turned gray and
he was frail. That's when the vultures started circling, when he
was weak.

Vanessa had been so pretty—no wonder she kept the photo on
the wall dead center. Could you tell from the photo that she was
Milton's mistress? Her glance was slightly off-center in the photograph, as if she was looking for him out of the corner of her eye. Her
face was flushed with excitement.

Then Mona looked at herself. She noted the smoothness of her skin, the plumpness of her cheeks, how dark and shiny her hair was. Her sister had helped her pick out that dress too.

Mona actually met Bill Clinton one more time, fifteen years later.

He was in the audience for her Lady M. He found her at her dressing table after the show.

He said, "I don't know if you remember, Mona, but we had the pleasure of meeting a number of years ago. I have never forgotten your performance. You gave me chills tonight."

"I'm so sorry, where did we meet again?" Mona said. "I'm so terrible with faces."

He laughed, and Mona liked him all over again. But he was changed also. The vitality was diminished. He was thin and his voice was reedy. Mona thought he might ask for her number, and wondered what she would say. But he just shook her hand one more time, told her all over again that her performance had been unforgettable, and left. Mona went home melancholy, and despite her nightly melatonin, found it difficult to sleep.

———————

MONA'S EYES DRIFTED across the wall of Fiskbö frames. She knew more of the faces and their stories than she expected: there had been a night, the two of them sitting cross-legged on the couch and working their way through a post-rehearsal bottle of wine, when Vanessa pulled out her family album and showed Mona these very photos, telling her stories about her childhood and adolescence.

Being a Levin was almost as screwy a business, it turned out, as being a Zahid, albeit with a whole lot more money. She had largely been raised by her grandfather: her mother had been injured in a horrific car accident when Vanessa was just a toddler, the long-term result of which was a profound addiction to painkillers that left her most of the day barely responsive; her father was addicted as well, not in his case to drugs, but to the adrenaline and ego gratification of running for political office, burning through the trust fund established for him as he ran three campaigns in eight years, the first successful (lieutenant governor of Connecticut), then two unsuccessful tries for the House. These were all-consuming endeavors, during which Vanessa did not see her father for weeks on end, except to be trotted out for campaign events or photographed for campaign publicity.

When Vanessa was twelve, her mother started a fire lighting a cigarette from a gas burner. Vanessa managed to drag her out, but the entire house burned to the ground. Sometime thereafter, Vanessa went to live with her paternal grandfather. It was Bob Levin who drove Vanessa to school every morning through high school and sat up late at night waiting for her when she went on her first tentative dates; he wrote the checks that accompanied her college applications, and when she decided to go to Bard, once a month drove to Annandale-on-Hudson and stayed in an old B&B off campus, the two of them going for long walks in the woods or talking about the plays in which Vanessa was involved as a burgeoning theater geek. When Vanessa found a place in the Rabble, Bob Levin bought her the apartment on the Upper East Side in a serious building with a doorman, so that she would be safe.

Now Vanessa and Bob Levin were together in the third row, second file of Fiskbö frames, the pair of them standing in front of this very building. Bob Levin was diminutive and sprightly, hardly taller than his granddaughter. He had his arm wrapped around her shoulder, and his gaze was in her direction, a sweetly loving expression on his face.

Mona met Bob Levin once, when he came into the city for a day of medical tests. *Measure* was in the fourth week of rehearsals. It was their off day and Vanessa invited Mona and a few other castmates to a late-night dinner with him at some red-sauce palace in the East Fifties where he'd been going since the forties. Vanessa also invited Milton, who had known Bob Levin since the days when he'd earned a place for himself on the plaque in the lobby of 107 Avenue C as one of the early donors to the Rabble.

It was a tense evening—or maybe it was just Mona. The show was not thriving, and the weak link, Mona thought, was certainly Vanessa. Whatever Milton said on the subject, Mona figured that Vanessa could have used a few years with the cookie-cutter, son-of-a-bitch hacks in drama school. Mona considered Vanessa with the unsentimental eye of a professional and saw a young actress with a good instrument when she could find it, a pleasant mezzo-soprano, but who regularly wandered off her voice, so that even in the snug confines of Burbage it could be hard to hear her. Even after all these years, Mona could hear Moni Yakim, her movement and mime teacher at Juilliard: "The most difficult thing an actor must learn is to stand still." If you think that's easy, try it: Stand up and don't move for the next fifteen minutes, not so much as a muscle. Do it without any sign of visible strain. Now add four hundred and ninety-five spectators. But Vanessa had a distracting fidget, throwing her energy extravagantly all over the place, or stealing other actors' energy like a pickpocket on the subway. In drama school, you learned, really learned, about vowels and consonants—and again, Vanessa needed that. She had lazy diction. You might be able to get away with that if you were doing modern theater or screen work, but this was Shakespeare, where you needed all the help you could damn well get. In drama school, you learned how to play a five-beat line, so that the rhythm informed the sense. Above all, the cookie-cutter, son-of-a-bitch hacks at drama school would have taught Vanessa to act the way a professional does, day in, day out, whether you're feeling the creative groove or not.

Mona by then wasn't the only one in the company wondering why Milton had offered the part to Vanessa. Anne Carman said to Mona, "Well, she certainly must be good at *something.*" But Mona knew that they weren't sleeping together. Vanessa had told her the story of his advances, even asked for Mona's advice.

"You can say no," Mona said.

"I don't know," Vanessa said. She told Mona about the late-night phone calls, and the long lingering pauses in the dark.

"So what's holding you back?"

"It doesn't feel *right.* He's married. He's old enough to be my father."

"So tell him no."

"I don't *know,*" Vanessa said all over again.

Mona had little sympathy for Vanessa's tormented indecision. Mona had gone to bed with some men who asked her, said no to others, but she had never tortured herself about the decision. Mona wondered whether the do-I-or-don't-I drama of it all was what Vanessa liked best, whether *this* was her secret itch that needed scratching. "I am at war 'twixt will and will not," said Isabella, and the only time Vanessa couldn't seem to express that sentiment sincerely was when she was standing opposite her Angelo in Burbage.

Mona looked at Milton across the dinner table as he chatted with

Bob Levin or cast surreptitious glances at Vanessa. His lips were greasy with lamb fat. The notion that Milton had replaced Mona with a better actress—*that* she could, with great difficulty, accept. *That* was a sacrifice for the sake of Art—she capitalized the word in her mind in all sincerity. But the idea that he had replaced her with an inferior actress whom he hoped to seduce . . . soon she was back to the three-in-the-morning wake-ups, staring at the ceiling and reliving the day's rehearsal, remembering the places where Vanessa had stumbled over the meter or failed to find some nuance in a line or phrase. Then she would think about Milton. From the first day in the audition room it had been lies.

When Mona first moved to New York, she had taken a room in an apartment in Hell's Kitchen. She had been there three weeks when she walked into the kitchen late one night and found it crawling with cockroaches, hundreds, thousands of them, every surface covered. They must have been living in the apartment the whole time. She never slept there again. That's how she felt now: that corruption was enveloping her, destroying the thing she loved best.

As for Vanessa—Mona had only disdain. If she wanted to sleep with Milton or just tease him endlessly, that was her business. But Isabella was such a beautiful thing. It was as if Vanessa and her family, basking in their wealth, their Greenwich estates and Upper East Side apartments, had purchased on a whim some glorious painting, then left it in some sooty, smoke-filled room, there to be effaced by ash and grime until some future generation did the hard work of restoring it, if it could be saved at all. There was a *responsibility* in these roles, Mona thought. They were simply too magnificent to treat with casual contempt. Mona looked at Vanessa across the table. She was laughing at a joke someone had made. This infuriated Mona also: every line Mona spoke onstage was the product of endless considered choices—where to breathe, how to arrange her hands and face, where to pause and where to allow the line to sing. Mona would never, had she been Isabella, gone out to dinner and giggled the evening away. She would have been in the studio, at least trying to solve the problem.

Mona looked up from her plate. Vanessa looked at Milton, then looked at Mona looking at her. She began to blush.

Mona might have long quit the production altogether, as Zahra advised her to do, but for that blush; Mona in her most generous moments suspected it was for that blush that Milton had brought Vanessa into the company. There had been a handful of moments in the rehearsal room, perhaps three or four, no more, out of hundreds of hours they had spent together in Burbage, when the tedium of unproductive work was broken by that blush and Vanessa's Isabella hinted at life. Mona was entranced by the blush. It was not just a spot of red in her cheeks: it was a complete dismissal of her psychic defenses. It suggested a remarkable complexity of emotions: of desire and its opposite, of anger and *its* opposite, of surrender and resistance. Vanessa's eyes glittered, her breath seemed to quicken, and for a moment she glowed. Then her face returned to its normal color.

———

THREE FISKBÖ FRAMES to the right of Grandpa Levin: the cast photo from *Measure*, all of them in street clothes, onstage, arranged on risers, Mona to the far left of the lower riser, Vanessa at the center. Mona couldn't remember them taking the picture. They took one like it before every show. It was a press-night ritual. She was surprised that Vanessa put the photo on the wall. It wasn't associated with a happy moment.

Two hours after the photo was taken and just an hour before first call, Vanessa hung up the dressing room pay phone, sobbing.

"What's the matter, sweetie?" Mona said.

It took Vanessa a minute to talk. "It's my dad. My grandfather's had a heart attack."

"Will he be okay?" Mona asked.

Vanessa shook her head.

Mona hugged her. "Oh no," she said. "I'm so sorry."

Vanessa cried on Mona's shoulder for a moment, then said, "Should I go home?"

The question surprised Mona. She had never missed a show and never would; not under any condition whatsoever. Later in her career she would leave a hospital bed with a 103-degree fever, play a show, and return later that night to Mount Sinai. To be off on opening night—as a lead!—was unthinkable. Mona didn't say this, however. She was genuinely unsure if Vanessa would be able to pull herself together sufficiently to get onstage.

"It's up to you," she said. "But you have to decide fast."

"I don't know," Vanessa whispered. "Maybe I should go home."

Mona sent one of the interns to hunt Milton down. The intern dashed up to Milton's office, which was empty, and the rehearsal rooms, where Milton sometimes sat alone and read, were locked. In a moment of internish inspiration, he ran to the Leprechaun, where he found Milton calming his pre-show nerves over a Jameson and cream, as was his ritual.

"I'm sorry about your grandfather," Milton said as he strode into the dressing room. His voice was oddly cold.

Vanessa ran up to him and threw herself at his chest.

"He was doing so well," Vanessa cried. "The doctor said he was just fine when I saw him last time."

"Guess they got that one wrong," he said.

"I'm not going on," Vanessa said. She had decided. Mona was sitting in the old green easy chair that had lived in the corner of that dressing room for almost thirty years. She used all her art and skill to sit as quietly as she possibly could, hardly even breathing. A series of varied forms of happiness unfolded before her: the happiness of triumph, the happiness of revenge, the happiness of vindication, the happiness of opportunity. Now Milton would surely see what everyone else could see: that Vanessa was not one of *them*. Mona was off-book as Isabella. There was a full house out front, waiting impatiently. Vanessa continued to weep on Milton's chest. She could not possibly go on like this. It would be cruel to push her like this in front of a full house.

Milton let her cry another moment and then kissed her. "Forcefully," Mona would later admit, was the correct adverb to describe the kiss. He pushed her hard against a makeup mirror, Vanessa grunting slightly when she made contact. For a moment she resisted the kiss. Then she kissed Milton back, her kiss equally forceful.

Vanessa was on that night and every subsequent night of the run, but Mona never saw a better performance out of her—a better performance of Isabella, period—than she gave that first night. Mona knew the real thing when she saw it. It was all a question of what you wanted out of life. She would have given anything to have been kissed like that, if such a kiss could produce such effects.

———

THEN, IN THE FOURTH ROW, third rank of Fiskbö frames, there was the black-and-white photo of *Measure* that had accompanied the review in the *Times.* The photo was from one of Isabella's scenes with Angelo, Vanessa dressed in a nun's habit, her face upturned toward the lighting, arms outstretched, her cheek so dark with blood that it looked almost like a bruise.

Vanessa's Isabella produced one of those brief, intense squalls of excitement that from time to time sweep New York theater. After the review, Mona found herself fielding calls from long-lost elementary school friends asking if she could help them find a ticket: everyone wanted to see the show before it transferred, as it inevitably would, to Broadway. There the delicacy of Vanessa's fragile creation would be lost in a big, echoing house filled with tourists. Only in the Rabble's intimate theater where half the audience was within arm's length of the thrust could you see the blush on Vanessa's cheek.

Peggy Trimble, the stage manager, had a strict rule that actors were to remain in the dressing rooms while offstage. Nevertheless, Mona would drift around back of the hall, still in costume, to watch from the vomitorium-left as Vanessa made her entrance: "And have you nuns no farther privileges?" Isabella said, *blushing*— and the play opened up like a tropical flower, glorious and rotten. "Are not these large enough?" "Yes, truly. I speak not as desiring more." Every night there was a different sense to the lines, a slightly different shifting pattern of emphasis and blush and fear and desire that produced a new Isabella that Mona had never seen before. Now she blushed on "privileges," then on "truly," now on "desiring." Some nights she was alive with religious passion, other nights she burned with barely concealed sexual frustration; watching the performance night after night, Mona came to see that they were somehow the same. Some nights she all but yielded to Angelo, and other nights she exploded with martyred outrage as he confessed his monstrous desires. The only constant was that air of haunted fragility.

Mona could sense the intensity of Vanessa's affair with Milton. Before shows Vanessa would sit backstage, paralyzed by stage fright. Only Milton could calm her down. More than once Mona saw her burst into tears, burying her head in Milton's hairy neck as if he were Aslan. Once he was caught up in traffic, an accident on the Brooklyn Bridge. Peggy Trimble called, "Beginners!" and Vanessa, in such a stunning lapse of theatrical convention that it might have ended another actress's career, simply refused to budge. Milton arrived twenty minutes after curtain and Vanessa kissed his face, over and over again.

As the run of the show continued, Mona had the sense, almost frightening, that the part had begun to play Vanessa. Her skin, always pale, now seemed bloodless, and Mona saw her fingering her bracelets before the show like prayer beads. Mona no longer stayed in her apartment after shows, even when she was invited. She preferred to sit on the subway for an hour after midnight and stare at the homeless and the deranged, as they confronted their imaginary enemies or confided to their invisible friends.

DEEP IN THE RUN THERE WAS AN INCIDENT. There was no Fiskbö frame on the wall to commemorate the event, but Mona recalled the moment with precise clarity nevertheless. They were in the rehearsal room. Milton had rethought his Act Four, and decided the cast needed a few days' work: to the frustration of his actors, he was forever tinkering with his shows, reblocking a scene or simply rehearsing it if he felt something was missing.

He had his hand gently on Mona's shoulder, Mona not remembering why, something about dipping her head on the upbeat, when the door of Burbage swung open and his wife Susan was standing there with the fire extinguisher in her hand. Mona hadn't met her, but she knew her face from the framed photograph on the credenza in Milton's office.

"You whore," Susan said.

Mona stood there paralyzed. She started to say, "Not me! She's the—" Then she stopped herself.

Susan lifted the nozzle of the fire extinguisher in Mona's direction.

Mona had never seen Milton look frightened before.

"Go home, Susan. Just go home. This is Burbage," Milton said, groping for a note of authority.

Mona looked at Vanessa in the mirror. She had on one of her ankle-length peasant skirts and a thin cotton T-shirt and all those bracelets. She was shamefully beautiful. It would have been so much better at that moment if she were just a little more plain.

"Why should I go home? What's at home?"

"This is a rehearsal," Milton said pitifully. "We're working."

"You sick bastard. How old is she anyway, Milton, twenty-two?"

Susan was still staring at Mona, Susan *still* not understanding, Mona thinking, *Twenty-two? Really?* Mona thinking that Susan was a pretty woman, far prettier than she imagined, well turned out for a morning of madness in tailored beige slacks and an open-necked shirt, silk scarf tied expertly around her neck. Her hair had the groomed look that only comes from good product and good judgment and a half hour at least with a blow dryer. She had met Milton as a member of the board; Mona had heard that she was a big shot at McKinsey. Her makeup was expertly done. Mona thought to herself, Why isn't she good enough? What's wrong with her?

What more could a man want? If you want passion—just look at this woman, waving a fire extinguisher like an Uzi.

The whole room was silent, as if they had dried on their lines and were waiting for Peggy Trimble to prompt them.

Then Vanessa said, "I'm so sorry," her face a brighter blush than Mona had ever seen on her before.

"And who are you?" Susan said, still not figuring it out.

"I'm Vanessa Levin. And I love him. I'm sorry but I do."

Mona thought this might have been the bravest thing she'd ever seen.

The nozzle of the fire extinguisher swiveled away from Mona.

"He doesn't give a shit about you. Tell her, Milton. Tell her."

Mona would later spend considerable time trying to interpret the silence that followed. She saw Vanessa staring at Milton, smiling almost, as if expecting absolutely that he would tell their special truth. The silence extended itself uncomfortably, the kind of thrilling silence that is almost impossible to produce on a theatrical stage. Nobody in the audience of actors and techs coughed or rustled or even breathed.

Then Mona could see Susan squeezing the handle of the fire extinguisher. "God damn it, how does this thing work?"

"There's a little pin," Anne Carman said. "You have to pull the pin."

"What pin?"

"There," Anne said. "It won't work unless you pull the pin."

Susan stood there a moment. She stared at the fire extinguisher. "Fuck all of you," she said. She threw the fire extinguisher to the ground. It landed with a thud. "Don't come home," she shouted at Milton. "And Vanessa, sweetie, let me tell you a secret. He has probably fucked every woman in this room. And he'll lose interest in you just as soon as some new thing comes along."

Susan slammed the door of Burbage behind her. Vanessa stood in the center of the room, tears silently streaking down her lily-white cheek, achieving now the most perfect incarnation of humiliated, humbled Isabella that Mona would ever see. Not even Milton knew what to do. His jaw hung slightly open.

After a minute that felt like an hour, Anne Carman said, "He hasn't fucked me. I want that to be known."

"Not me either," said Peggy Trimble.

"I *wish* he'd fuck me," said Party Tom.

It was strange to Mona, thinking back on it at a remove of decades, the wave of laughter they produced. It was uncontrollable, hysterical. "Let's get back to work," Milton eventually said, and amazingly, still laughing, glad to have been witness to the day's spectacle, get back to work was just what they did, because gentle, generous, giving people the members of this Rabble certainly were not, nor ever claimed to be.

3

She couldn't have been older than twenty, the girl who was interrupting Mona's thoughts. Mona noticed her looking at her, step forward in her direction, step back, then look at her again. Finally Mona turned toward her and smiled. Only then did the girl move forward and say, "You're Mona Zahid, aren't you? I just adore your work. You're the reason I want to be an actress."

"I love you," Mona said.

"I made my parents buy me a season ticket and I've seen everything twice."

"What's your name?" Mona asked.

"Coral."

Mona was enchanted by the old-fashioned name, so appropriate for this girl who did indeed look like she belonged in a nineteenth-century daguerreotype, staring gravely into a camera lens.

"Would you like a glass of wine, Coral?" Mona asked.

Coral was still so young that the question made her smile shyly. Mona wondered if she was old enough to drink.

Mona said, "Why don't you go find us a nice bottle of white wine hiding in the fridge someplace and then you can tell me your story."

"I'll be right back," Coral said, and headed toward the kitchen.

There were too few chairs for all the guests, so Mona settled herself in a cozy nook on the floor beside the window. Here she was protected from the room on one side by the couch; there was a wall behind her and a wall to her right. She shared her grotto with a palm, leaves and branches high above her. She couldn't believe that no one else at the party wanted to hide in this excellent little cave.

There had been a time when one of the men would have rushed to offer her a seat; she wouldn't have been able to sit alone on the floor for a minute. But she was growing invisible now, she thought. A woman makes her own light: Old Tom always understood. The light Mona required to be seen used to blaze forth spontaneously from her. She hadn't thought about it much in her twenties, when she at once accepted and begrudged the fact that no one in any room would ignore her, that wherever she went she would be seen. Hypervisibility had been Mona's superpower. In her thirties, she had begun to notice the light ebbing from time to time. Now in her forties, the fire required constant stoking. She knew how to play a beautiful woman: with an effort of will and the application of skill, she could blaze, but it required ever-increasing energy.

Mona thought it might be time to leave the party but was overwhelmed by the prospect of finding Vanessa, thanking her for her hospitality, and promising to find her some other time. She was overwhelmed by the notion of doing anything. Just the thought of saying all those lies made her feel empty and tired. Perhaps it was best to postpone her visit to Milton.

What enthused Mona was the prospect of boring that young girl half to death. She had always wanted a protégée. Mentor was a role she could get into, at least for the duration of the afternoon. She could assign her little errands. *Coral, would you be a darling, my phone is dead, would you find a charger? Coral, I'd be so grateful, do you think you could find me a little sparkling water with lime?* The girl would consider this an afternoon to treasure for a lifetime, an anecdote for her grandchildren.

Mona crawled out from the grotto. Somebody had left a very

nearly full glass of rosé unattended on the coffee table. Still moving forward on all fours, animal-alert, eyes windshield-wipering from side to side, she swiped it and retreated back to safety.

Vanessa's Isabella never really recovered from that scene in Burbage. Mona didn't know why. Something in her confidence was lost, the way an athlete, after a painful defeat, might lose her most sensitive touch thereafter at the most critical moment. The performance degenerated ever so subtly, performance by performance, over the rest of the run into something that by the end was a sad shadow of something that had been beautiful. Audiences walked away privately confused by the commotion the show had produced. Then, as they strolled toward the subway talking the play over, they convinced one another, because the tickets were expensive and they didn't want to see themselves as chumps, that they had been in the presence of greatness after all. Mona wanted to run after them and shout, *No, this show was special once, it really was, you have to understand. I never saw anything like it.*

When the run limped to an end, Milton offered Vanessa a slate of minor parts for the next season. Vanessa quit the company rather than accept the offer, although there was still a year remaining on her contract. Even now, even after all these years, from a strictly professional and artistic point of view, Mona didn't think that Milton had wronged Vanessa when he demoted her from company nobility, no matter what the *Times* would later say:

> When Ms. Levin ended the affair, she said, Mr. Katz demoted her within the company ranks. She was no longer offered the lead roles which Mr. Katz had promised her when he hired her, and no longer cast her in productions he directed, depriving her of opportunities for vital mentorship and coaching.

The greater and unforgivable offense, by Mona's lights, had not been to demote her, but to promote her prematurely; having seen her extraordinary talent, he had wildly overestimated his capacity to shape it; and having failed to shape it, he lost interest.

Mona sat on the floor preparing a monologue on the nature of artistic success. She wished that she could pluck her own mentors, Anne Carman and Old Tom, out of her memory and hand them over to this girl entire. Those were Mona's people, her tribe. "There," she would say. "Listen to *them*. That's what's required if you really want a career as an actor. But it won't be as fun or easy as you think. It's a hard job if you take it seriously."

Anne Carman had been in her sixties when Mona joined the company. Now *there* was an actress. Half of what Mona did nowadays was just imitating Anne, which, Mona supposed, was the way the business worked, an uninterrupted chain of influence reaching all the way back to the Globe itself. Actors watched one another and borrowed what they needed. Mona had never known an actress who could convey more emotion with her hands alone, either wiping away the ghost of a tear, or pointing, or touching the other actors on the stage. She taught Mona that the listening was every bit as essential as the talking, and you listened with your whole body. When Anne Carman listened, so keen was her attention and intensity, the audience listened too. She made everyone onstage with her a better actor. Mona could remember vividly decades later the moment in *Hamlet* when Anne's long tapered hands stole the show. Hamlet has just stabbed Polonius, and in Milton's staging, it was a bloody brutal business, Polonius not dying easy, but staggering downstage to collapse in a pool of slow-puddling blood. The emotional heart of *Hamlet* was a tragic death and it wasn't either of the Hamlets, old *or* young. Milton had Vikram, his Hamlet at the time, practice for the murder by stabbing a side of beef to get a feel for things, then he explained (no one was quite sure how Milton knew these things) that the real problem was getting the knife out of Polonius's side, not in. Milton felt it very important that the audience see a man die here. Polonius lay onstage bleeding, gurgling, and dying for two excruciatingly long stage minutes, his blood settling into a thick pool center-stage, eventually coating the hands and clothes of each and every character as they tracked it from one corner of the house to the other. Mona in later years could imitate but not entirely capture the effect of Anne Carman's hands as they writhed over the body. The audience knew from their motions alone, twisting into spasmodic little knots, the viciousness of the murder and the gravity of the crime. They were the hands of a mother, unable to speak, who has just seen her beloved son commit an unspeakable act. The tension created by the hands built, and built, until finally Vikram snapped at his mother, "Leave wringing of your hands!"

It was ten years now since Anne Carman was found dead on the sidewalk in front of her building in Queens. Milton had kept her on payroll for the health insurance, which allowed her the home health aide so she could stay in her own apartment. The home health aide had gone to buy groceries when Anne Carman crossed the living room, opened the window, and climbed out.

Mona looked around for—what was her name? She could see her in the kitchen, standing near the refrigerator, flirting with a boy her age. All thoughts of Mona, of the stage, forgotten. She was flicking her golden hair back and forth, the boy enchanted by her rays of light.

Mona was surprised how many actors she knew had committed suicide. That was something Old Tom had pointed out to her. "This profession makes terrible preparation for life," he said to her. No other profession was as associated with an activity of childhood, and when the childhood ended—what else was there to do? Old Tom was a proponent of the thesis that Shakespeare himself died by his own hand. He proposed his thesis with no argument or evidence because Tom wished to convince no one; he only felt, he said, that he had come to know the man very well after all these years, had lived side by side with Shakespeare and his lifelong struggle with depression, the evidence for which was found in every play, and he was sure that Shakespeare, seeing his powers diminish and finding himself facing old age in miserable Stratford, must have been very tempted to bow out on the same terms he offered so many of his most beloved heroes.

Anne Carman's memorial service was one of the last times that Mona's generation of the Rabble was united. There was Old Tom, now ever so frail—Mona couldn't escape the suspicion that Tom at the end was playing one of his famous old men, hamming it up just a bit for effect: the trembling hands, the piccolo voice. There was Milton, grave and stately. A dozen others. Vikram didn't show up. He had sent a large bouquet of flowers, which was supposed to mean what to whom, exactly? The funeral was held at the Episcopalian church in Queens where Anne Carman had been an improbable but regular attendee, the actors arrayed about the empty pews together with Anne's health aide and two or three others who had known her over the years, but the real memorial had been the after-gathering at the Leprechaun, where the old gang told their best Anne Carman stories and recited lines in her honor. When it was Mona's turn to speak, she recited Gertrude's description of the death of Ophelia. But it was Old Tom, stately Tom, wise Tom, who produced that evening's moment of transcendent grace. He lit a cigarette, took a drag, and placed it in the ashtray in front of him. "Anne asked me to read this," he said, and spoke that most heartbreaking of the sonnets, the one that begins, "No longer mourn for me when I am dead." At a certain moment Mona ceased to hear Tom's voice and heard Anne's: "For I love you so, / That I in your sweet thoughts would be forgot, / If thinking on me then should make you woe."

If Coral ever came back with that bottle of wine, Mona would tell her about Old Tom and how he came to every rehearsal in suit, tie, and polished leather shoes, attire that in and of itself was an education in seriousness and intention. At the start of rehearsals, he took off the jacket and hung it up neatly.

Milton had known Tom back in the sixties, when the two of them used to put on guerrilla theater. That was when he was known as English Tom. Then Milton brought him back into the company three decades later to play his old men. He had been a middling, jobbing actor all his career, a packhorse in other men's great affairs, until he discovered a brilliant capacity for the Poloniuses, the Prosperos, the Master Shallows of this world. These performances had not gone unnoticed by critics or the public, and he had become toward the end of his career an unlikely star. The trick to playing old, Very Old Tom once told Mona, was that every old man stares in the mirror and sees the young man he was. You play the young man and let the audience see the old man. "And who did you used to be, Tom?" Mona asked him. "I once vomited in John Gielgud's loafer," he said. "And he called me a beautiful, silly boy."

What people didn't understand was how hard you had to work to get those kinds of performances. It had been an education to learn what Tom did to prepare for each role. He used to haunt an old-age home, sitting in the corner with his big sketch pad. He'd sketch the inmates for hours, concentrating on details: the palsied hand, the off-center glance, the look of fear in a forgotten phrase. Then it was hundreds of hours in a studio, in front of a mirror, getting the gestures right, learning to make the tremor his own, so it was built into muscle memory and could be reproduced on demand, night after night. Every one of his old men was different, an artisanal creation. Polonius didn't just have a tremor: he fought the tremor, was frustrated by the tremor, was horrified by it.

Tom was afflicted by the worst stage fright Mona ever saw. Mona used to hold his hand before he went onstage. "This never used to bother me," he said. Sometimes he'd turn to Mona right before curtain-up and say, "Lord save me, I can't remember my lines." But he never failed to step onto the stage, never missed a show.

Mona looked around for the girl. She might have left the apartment altogether, hand in hand with her newfound friend. Mona got up and went to find her own bottle of wine. No one noticed her. How strange it was to be invisible! Did she even appear in the mirror? There wasn't a single mirror in the living room—why not? Didn't Vanessa understand the importance of mirrors to open up the space? Also—they were nice for making love. Did Vanessa have lovers? Surely there would be men attracted to that bosom and curves. Mona would have put a mirror right there on the wall, reflecting the windows and the couch. *Sweet little Coral!* she thought. *I had so much to teach you about interior decorating, about making love, about acting. Come back and ask me how I found my way. That was me, right there, on the wall, that was Vanessa, that was us.*

In the kitchen, Mona opened the refrigerator and took out a bottle of white from the side rack. No one stopped her. She might have started slipping wallets out of purses, rings off fingers. She was sprightly like Ariel, crafty as Puck. Only Barney, chewing steadily on his purple bone under the kitchen table, saw her. Mona took the bottle and waved it in Barney's direction. *Would you care for a glass?* she thought. *No, thank you,* he replied. *I am intoxicated enough.* Mona took the wine back to her little grotto. She could live here, she thought. Make her cave cozy. Throw pillows on the floor. A wine rack. No Bruce, no Sheila, no Rachel, no Phil. Certainly no Milton. She poured herself a glass and sipped it. Delightful hints, she thought, of elderberries and toe sweat. Fruit forward. One of the other guests, not noticing Mona on the floor, looked out the window onto 71st Street. Mona, crouched at his heels, began to growl softly.

———————

THERE WAS A LITTLE ACTOR IN THE PARTY.

He couldn't have been older than six, in a rumpled Dora the Explorer T-shirt. He had a thick head of dirty dark hair and simply the biggest pair of sticky-out ears Mona had ever seen in her life. Mona wondered if he would ever grow into those donkey things. He was sitting cross-legged across the room, staring at Mona staring at him. Mona didn't know how she had missed him this whole time. She tilted her head and he tilted his, then she slowly inserted her finger up her nose. By angling her head slightly, she made it appear that the finger was traveling digit by digit up into her skull. Then she sneezed the whole hand out. The boy smiled at her. She waved him over and he crossed the room and sat down next to her.

"I don't like to brush my teeth," he said.

"Who does?" Mona said. "I haven't brushed my teeth in a week."

"You're kind of stinky," he said, and collapsed in giggles.

"Thank you."

Mona couldn't have asked for a more exciting conversational partner. The last time she had felt this intrigued was God-knows-when.

"What's your name?" she asked.

"Elias."

"Elias, would you like to be my boyfriend?" she said.

"No," he said.

"Please?"

"Okay."

"Only I'm married," she added. "You should know that."

"Me too."

"Who are you married to?"

"I don't know."

"That's the way I feel sometimes too."

Just as soon as Mona said that, she knew that she had made a mistake.

"That's not *true*," he said.

Elias looked at her severely. Mona understood: he didn't like that kind of cynicism. He valued sincerity.

By way of apology, Mona flopped on the floor, shot dead.

"They got me," her corpse whispered.

The boy threw himself flat on the floor beside her. He took out his pistol and fired a few desultory rounds in the direction of their assailants, then looked around to see if he was in trouble.

"I'm not supposed to shoot people anymore because I bited Yasmine."

"Do you like to shoot people?"

"Yes, but I'm not allowed to shoot anyone."

"Because you bit Yasmine."

"Yes."

"Why did you bite Yasmine?"

The boy looked at the space between them. Things were going too fast. He wasn't ready to talk about these things.

"I bet she was delicious," Mona said.

"Yasmine's a *person*," he explained.

They sat in silence a moment.

"I bited Yasmine because I wanted to," he finally confessed.

For the first time in her life, Mona thought she understood a man. This was what relationships were based on: total, complete honesty. If only she could get the others to achieve this same level of transparent, courageous self-knowledge. Bruce would say, *I bited that fraud William Shakespeare because I wanted to.* Phil would say, *I'm in the woods biting Melanie McDowell because I want to go in the woods and bite Melanie McDowell.* Milton would say, *I bited the girls because I wanted to.* The *Times* would say, *We bited Milton because we wanted to.* Angelo would say, *I bited Isabella because I wanted to.* The world was going around biting the world because the world wanted to.

"Did Yasmine cry?"

"She was fake crying, like boo-hoo-hoo."

Mona leaned over and bit the boy's big, sticky-out ear. Not hard enough to draw blood, but hard enough to hurt, to feel the tender skin under her sharp teeth, and she hung onto it for a long moment even as he squirmed away.

"We're not allowed to bite or kick," he said. "No biting."

"But I wanted to. I really did."

"Why?"

"You looked delicious."

"I'm a *person*. And—"

It was then that Barney found the two of them in their little cave. He was still carrying the large purple bone, which he deposited proudly in Mona's lap. The thing was covered in dog slobber. Barney sat directly in front of Mona panting, eager for her to play.

What followed Mona would later consider a miscalculation. The miscalculation, essentially, was this: that it was possible to throw this obscene object across a crowded room of Thanksgiving party-goers, the thing followed by a bounding beagle and a madly shriek-ing six-year-old boy—and not thereafter be the object of every eye in the room. The degree of ensuing destruction surprised Mona. There were overturned wineglasses and plates, and one of the plants—did Vanessa really need so goddamn many? what the fuck was this, a terrarium?—lay on its side, hemorrhaging thick black dirt into the carpet, and somehow in the frenzy one of Vanessa's Fiskbö-framed portraits on the wall had taken a full-on blow from the device, now vibrating loudly, and smashed on the floor.

Mona, now no longer invisible in any way whatsoever, sat on the floor and looked up at the crowd of Thanksgiving partygoers and said, "I don't know what got into him, he's usually such a good dog."

4

Mona woke up in a strange bed in an unfamiliar room. It took her a moment to slot the memories into chronological order, an activity that felt not unlike putting together the big thousand-piece jigsaw puzzle that she and her sister used to haul out of the closet on snow days. The reason that puzzle never got built was that two or three puzzles at least had been thrown in the same box over the years, each puzzle incomplete: the Taj Mahal was on the box cover, but there were bits and pieces of sleeping puppies in a heap and a sailboat on a lake intermingled therein.

Now the picture on the box was Mona's Big Day Out, but Mona was having trouble finding the corners and edges. There had been Bruce, there had been Sheila—that felt very long ago, pieces from another box. Rachel was in town, Mona knew that. Too many hours had passed from morning until now to account for Mona's confusion. Mona had gone out to get parsley? Then there had been the walk across Central Park? She had visited a Starbucks?

Then she found a corner piece: she was in Vanessa Levin's bed in Vanessa Levin's apartment.

But the pieces she discovered thereafter simply wouldn't adhere. There had been several bottles of white wine, both before and after the Incident. Barney was in disgrace. Mona was in disgrace.

At a certain moment Vanessa was saying, "We have a tradition that every year, we all have to say something we're grateful for. And I'd like to say, I'm grateful we can celebrate this day together."

They had gone around the room. Mona said, "It's been far too long since I've seen Vanessa, and I'm happy to be celebrating Thanksgiving with my old friend. And I'm so happy to be here with all of you. I love you all so much."

That cluster of memory was adjacent on the card table of Mona's consciousness to another. It was either earlier in the evening or later, or, Mona conceded, the event in question might well have occurred on some other evening altogether. Mona had received who-knows-how-many warnings in her day on the deleterious effect on memory of mixing alcohol and the opioids—and they had all been right, she conceded. Mona had been asked to recite and she had said demurely, "I hope I don't dry." Then she had recited one of Titania's speeches from the *Dream*, which Mona well knew she could recite in a coma without drying, so firmly imprinted was it in her synapses and cerebral cortex. "That was so beautiful," a girl had said. Coral. So it was this evening.

At some point in the evening she had called Phil.

At some point in the evening Will Powers had asked her not to contact him again, because she would be dangerous to his sobriety.

At some point in the evening Barney peed on the kitchen floor because she forgot to walk him, which was bad, bad, bad.

At some point in the evening she had told Vanessa to go sleep in her own fucking bed. Apparently Mona had been in Vanessa's bed at the time.

Mona slipped her feet over the edge of the bed. An alarm clock on the bedside table insisted that it was 12:24 a.m., which was either far too early or far too late. She felt wide awake and refreshed. She wondered if she might not have missed a day somewhere. Her dog was asleep on the floor beside the bed, a look on his face of beatific contentment. Mona dropped down on the floor and wrapped an arm around him. He rolled over in his sleep and lazily licked her face. Mona hoped Barney would live forever. There was that line from *Measure*—"this sensible warm motion to become a kneaded clod." That was dying. Mona thought about that line all the time. Barney was all sensible warm motion. He sensed things, he had good sense. She liked his dank musty smell, the way he squirmed a little to accommodate the weight of her head on his thorax. Mona petted him gently. She massaged his long floppy ears, caressed his temples, and rubbed his whiskers back against his snout. Mona sometimes thought that Barney was the only creature in this world who took her seriously, who worried that she made good choices, and didn't judge her when she failed to. Mona was at a point of still and quiet apogee: she had far too much junk in her system to feel the hangover she knew was brewing. Minute by minute, the pills she had taken would catabolize away and the hangover, the lack of sleep, and the emotional disorder of the day would solidify into a crushing headache. For the moment, though, she felt surprisingly clearheaded and good.

Mona lay on the floor and thought about her father. She hadn't thought about him in a long time. He was found in his RV in the parking lot of a Walmart in Wisconsin. A local sheriff's deputy called Zahra. Hafez had been in the vehicle for two days apparently, before Walmart security noticed him. There was a rabbit in a cage on the passenger seat beside him, the sheriff said.

"A rabbit?" Zahra said.

"Yes, ma'am. A gray and white lop."

In any case, the sheriff said, he was very sorry for her loss—but did Zahra think she'd want the rabbit? Because, the sheriff's deputy continued, he'd been keeping that rabbit in his house until he heard from her (that's the kind of place Fuckbum, Wisconsin, is, his voice intimated, unlike whatever coastal urban hellhole *you* live in) and his daughters had grown fond of it.

"Are you serious?" Zahra said.

"Yes, ma'am."

"My father is dead two days and your daughters want his pet rabbit?"

"Yes, ma'am."

"I want the fucking rabbit," Zahra said. "Screw your daughters."

When Zahra and Mona flew out to Wisconsin in the dead of winter to incinerate their father and get his rabbit, the deputy sheriff told them the rabbit had crawled out of his cage and gotten lost in his backyard. Zahra knew he was lying—but what were you going to do? The pair of them spent four days in Suckass, Wisconsin, arranging the details of Hafez's cremation, getting drunk every night in the crappy motel room, when on their last afternoon before they drove back to Milwaukee, Zahra shouted "Stop!" just as Mona was pulling out of the motel.

Mona said, "Don't scare me like that."

"It's Dad's rabbit."

There was a white rabbit standing on the snow-covered median of the two-lane highway, black eyes staring at them intently. Mona said, "You get down." As soon as Zahra was down, though, the rabbit started sprinting across the highway and then through a large open field. Mona was out of the car too and both sisters were sprinting across the hard, icy ground, slipping and sliding, trying to catch the rabbit, but it was out of sight and gone. Zahra and Mona never figured out what her father wanted with that rabbit. It drove them crazy. Hafez wasn't the kind of guy who adopted pet rabbits—but there he was, found dead with a rabbit. Zahra promised Mona this would be the first thing she was going to ask him when she met him on the other side.

Mona thought about this and a lot of other things lying on the floor of Vanessa's bedroom with her arm wrapped around her beagle. The rabbit must be at least seven, eight years old now. How long did a rabbit live?

———

VANESSA WAS SITTING ON THE COUCH. She had a blanket over her shoulders and headphones on. She was staring at her iPad. Mona wondered whether she could just sneak out the door. She knew that she was in trouble. But Vanessa saw her and smiled. She took off her headphones and said, "You're awake!"

"I'm so sorry," Mona said. "I made such a mess of your party. Everyone was so nice and I was so terrible."

"It was quite a performance."

"I don't know what got into me. I don't usually go to parties."

"I can't imagine why not."

"I think Barney and I should go now."

"It's the middle of the night."

"We'll just jump in an Uber," Mona said. Her phone had somehow charged overnight; she had been readmitted to civil society.

"Would you like a cup of tea?"

"Maybe some tea," Mona said, wondering what she was supposed to do with her night, where she was supposed to go. She would head home to Phil, she supposed. She began to remember the details of their conversation. She had called him late in the evening. She asked him why he never laughed at her jokes. "Of course I do," he said. "Like what?" she said. "Why don't you come home and we'll talk about it?" "I am so hot for you. Want me to take the phone in the bathroom?" "Where are you?" "I am so in love with your penis." "Mona, I think—" "Do you want to talk to Barney?" Mona put the phone up to Barney's ear. She heard Phil say, "Mona? Mona, are you there?" She took the phone back. She said, "It's just that I hate being boring and I bore you." "You don't bore me, Mona. We're married, that's all," Phil said, unable to disguise the boredom in his voice. "It's *boring* to be married." "Of course it is. That's the point of it." "I don't see the point of it." Phil said, "I got the pies from Dora's, the one you like." "What flavors?" "Boysenberry and apple." "Did you leave me some?" "Of course." "Did everyone have a good time?" "My mom wanted to call the police because you never came home." "Why didn't you?" "I figured you'd call eventually. But I'm worried." "We have to make some changes," Mona said. Phil said, "Like what?" But Mona couldn't think of one thing to say.

Mona followed Vanessa into the kitchen. She saw her filling the kettle and set up cups. Vanessa said, "Herbal or real tea?"

"Real tea?"

"Earl Grey or the other kind?"

"It's all the same to me."

"I do herbal."

"Whatever you do I like too. You know, I think I'm just going to go."

"Stay for a cup of tea."

Mona started to say something about Elias and how much she liked him, or ask a question about the party. Instead she said, "Milton's dying. I thought you should know. That's why I came."

Vanessa had been rummaging in a drawer for teaspoons. She stopped and looked up. Mona had the postcard in the pocket of her vest. She fished it out and showed it to Vanessa, who read it carefully, then flipped it over and looked at the photograph of Mona on the cover.

"You were always his favorite," Vanessa said.

"Me?" Mona said. "That's not how I remember it."

"The two of you were always whispering in the rehearsal room. The little jokes. I heard him say that he hoped you would take over when he left."

"He said that? Really?"

"More than once."

"I didn't know that."

"I guess there was a lot about Milton you didn't know."

Mona looked around for Barney. He had followed her into the kitchen. He was lying on the floor, panting gently.

"I think he really loved you," Mona said. "He went to pieces after it ended."

Vanessa poured hot water in both cups. Then she added tea bags. She said, "Mona, why on earth did you come to my house after all these years to tell me this?"

"I thought you might want to visit him."

"Why would I want to visit Milton?"

"I don't know—I just thought you might want to clear the air."

"Clear the air like there was some misunderstanding? Mona, I had an affair with him when I was twenty-two and he was fifty-whatever. When I stopped sleeping with him, he fired me. The man left me a nervous wreck."

"When you left him he had a breakdown. He had a heart attack," Mona said.

"Mona, why on earth are you defending Milton?" Vanessa's voice turned husky and accusatory. "That's the way it always felt even then, like you were trying to sell Milton to me or something.

I remember us, the two of us, right here, and I asked you what I should do about Milton and you kept telling me to go for it. Why on earth did you say a thing like that?"

Who could know anything for sure after all these years? How could she have known then that she'd be accountable for her words now? Vanessa rummaged in a cupboard. She found a little bear of honey. She squeezed it into her tea, then squeezed more, then kept squeezing.

Vanessa said, "I had no business being in that company. I was in no way ready for that kind of pressure. And I had no business at all being Milton's mistress. And the fact that they were mixed up like that bruised me in ways you can't even begin to imagine. He should have protected me and nurtured me. That's what you do with young people! That's what you do with young actresses! And instead—look at me!" Vanessa gestured at the little apartment. "I'm still sleeping in the same bed I slept in when I was with Milton. You know what my therapist said? He said Milton nailed me into that moment in time and I never moved forward."

Vanessa put down the bear of honey and walked away. Mona heard water running in the bathroom. Then Vanessa closed the door.

Vanessa came back to the kitchen and said, "Thanksgiving's always such an emotional day for me. I always end up crying."

"Do you still act?" Mona asked.

"The day I walked out of 107 Avenue C, I thought to myself, *Thank God I don't have to do that anymore.* And I've never once changed my mind."

"Why did you hate it so much?"

"Are you asking sincerely or are we debating?"

"Sincerely," Mona decided.

Vanessa chewed her lip.

"I guess I was never meant to be an actress," she finally said. "I didn't want all those people looking at me like that, when I was so naked. Milton got me to do things that I never wanted to do."

"Then why did you walk into the rehearsal room in the first place?"

"I was too young to know that I could say no."

"You know, you could just say 'Fuck off' to Milton. He responded very well to that."

"Mona, that's the thing. I didn't know that. That's what I'm telling you. I didn't know that you could say that. Before I met Milton, I had one boyfriend in my life. I had stuffed animals on my bed. Milton came to see me in my *school play*. He offered me a place in his company that very night backstage with my parents standing not five feet away. My mother took me aside and told me this was an opportunity of a lifetime. Shit, *my mother* would have gone to bed with Milton in a heartbeat. How could I have understood what he really wanted from me?"

Barney's rear paw flicked forward to scratch a spot behind his ear. Vanessa sipped her tea.

"The cat is still in the closet," she said. "Poor thing probably won't come out for a week."

"I would have found it exhilarating," Mona said softly.

"Exhilarating? Are you *serious*? I was scared to death the whole time. What's exhilarating about that?"

Mona didn't have an answer. Frankly, it all sounded exhilarating to her: to be Isabella, to be Vanessa, just to be young. She wondered when exactly all emotions but grief, anger, and gratitude had become playacting. Those were the three emotions you were allowed after a certain age. Exhilarated was off the table.

Vanessa said, "I just wish that somebody had told me back then that there was another way to play the role."

"Like how?"

Vanessa got up off her stool and began fussing in the kitchen, sponging down an already clean counter and unloading the dishwasher. While she worked, she told Mona about a touring production of *Measure* that she put on with the Public a few years ago. "It was the first time I saw the play since I did it with Milton. The Public took a touring show to Queensboro Correctional Facility. It's a women's prison. And you should've seen it, Mona. These women, they *understood*. They were shouting and screaming, they booed and hissed and cursed Angelo. It was intense. And I got it. For the first time, I understood. Isabella was a *victim*. She was being asked to do things she didn't want to do, and she was angry. I was so proud of her, the way she just said no. I wished that I had had the courage to say the same thing. And something just went nuts inside me. I started to shout also. Afterwards my supervisor came over and was like, 'Vanessa, please control yourself.' And I was like, 'Fuck you. *I'm* the one who's supposed to control myself?' And that's how I wish I had played the role. I just don't get it how everyone came to my show all those years ago and didn't see what these women in prison could see."

Mona didn't know if she should say what she was thinking. She had seen the same show, when it played in the park. It had been mediocre. There was a line from *Antony and Cleopatra*: "She shows a body rather than a life." That was the difference between *that* Isabella and Vanessa's.

Mona said, "Your Isabella was the single most extraordinary performance I've seen on a stage in almost thirty years of professional acting."

Vanessa looked Mona in the eye, her shoulders tensed.

"And I owe it all to Milton. That's what you want to say. Milton fucked the role into me and—"

"No. That's just the opposite of what I'm saying. Milton was never onstage. You were."

Vanessa started to say something, stopped, started again, and stopped again. A hint of red appeared on her cheek.

Mona asked, "Can you do it on command?"

"Do what?"

"That blush. I've wanted to ask you that since the first day I met you."

The blush deepened. The blush was like some communication with the deeper, inner Vanessa; it transcended her words and thoughts.

"It used to bother me so much as a kid."

"I can imagine."

"It's just a part of me, I guess."

Mona said, "I would have given anything to have the kind of talent you had. It drove me nuts that I couldn't do what you did."

Vanessa turned away from Mona and put away the last of the silverware. When she turned back a minute later, the blush was gone. Her face was pale and clear. Only later did Mona realize that she hadn't answered her question.

Mona said, "I have to play Cleopatra soon and I'm scared to death. Most of the time I just don't think I could possibly care enough about anything, much less Antony, to play the role right."

"But you were so wonderful last night!"

"I was?"

"You were *amazing*."

"I've been doing that old Titania bit since high school."

"The Titania was good but the Cleopatra was *awesome.*"

A hint of memory, like something from a dream. She had played the death scene. "Give me my robe, put on my crown; I have / Immortal longings in me." There had been some nice little business on the robe and crown, the woman in red leggings and her friend springing up to cloak her in the blanket from the couch, covering her head in a scarf. Mona-but-not-Mona leaning over Will Powers, exaggerating-but-not-exaggerating her drunkenness, saying, "Now no more the juice of Egypt's grape shall moist this lip." It was all so tantalizingly close to memory: not the gestures, not the words, but a certain way of feeling... had it been excitement? She would see Antony again.

If Vanessa saw anything odd about Mona being unable to remember the events of just the night before, she didn't let on. She said, "I wish I had recorded it for you. You were so good."

"And you say I didn't embarrass myself?"

"We stayed up late just to listen to you."

Mona wanted to ask more questions, but she had been an actress long enough to know better, to know that whatever she did last night could not be reproduced, would have to be found again the next time she said those lines.

Mona said, "I am so hungry. I can't remember the last time I ate anything."

"We have so much food in the fridge."

Vanessa opened the refrigerator door. Mona saw rows and rows of neatly packed Tupperware. She said, "We've got the chili and the roasted butternut squash and some hummus and these seitan meatballs things? They were good? And I think there's also some stuffing thing someone brought. It's all good. Do you want me to make you a plate?"

"Please," Mona said. "And thank you. Thank you for being so nice to me."

"I always liked you, Mona. That first day in the rehearsal room, I was scared and you were so kind. And you didn't have to be."

Vanessa opened a cupboard and pulled out a plate that she loaded with a variety of orange and brown food. She added some green accents. Then she put it into the microwave. She tapped the button rhythmically, and the plate began to rotate like a fairground carousel. Then she prepared another one.

"Mona, whatever you think, I don't hate Milton. But it's a fact that after what Milton did to me, I started eating and never stopped."

"And that was Milton's fault?" Mona said.

"Please, Mona, don't fight with me."

"I'm not fighting, I just think it's kind of ridiculous to blame—"

"I was pregnant," Vanessa said.

"When?"

"In Burbage. When his wife burst in. With the fire extinguisher."

"I didn't know that."

"No one did. Just Milton."

Mona watched the plate of food turning around in the microwave.

"I was so scared," Vanessa said. "It was funny to all of you but I thought she was going to kill me. I didn't know what that thing was in her hands, I thought it was a gun, I really did. And all of you were laughing. That's when I knew Milton wasn't going to take care of me ever, when I stood up in front of his wife and God and the whole wide world and said I loved him and he just stood there, and he didn't do *anything*, just stood there."

"I'm sorry," Mona finally said. "If that means anything."

"You didn't know."

Vanessa opened the microwave door and casually tapped the food with a finger to see if it was hot. "Another minute," she said, and licked the brown sauce off her finger.

"That's when I decided not to have the baby," she said, her voice now matter-of-fact. "I told Milton it was a miscarriage, and you know what he said? He gave me some flowers and asked if I was going to be off. That's what he said. I said, 'You damn well better believe I'll be off.' But I did the show anyway."

The microwave beeped. Vanessa went to pick up the plate. It was hotter than she expected. She juggled it with her fingertips and set it down on the edge of the counter, where it balanced for a second, and toppled onto the floor and smashed. Butternut squash tumbled across the floor, seitan meatballs rolled into corners, stuffing splattered across the hardwood floor.

"Oh fuck!" Vanessa said. "Can't I do anything fucking right?"

The noise of the accident and the smell of food woke Barney up. He looked at Mona. Before she could say anything he scooted across the kitchen, sniffed dubiously at a vegetarian meatball, then retreated in disappointment out of the room.

"It's okay," Mona said. "I break things all the time. I really do."

"I'm such a fucking klutz," Vanessa said.

Mona came around to the other side of the counter. She looked under the sink and found a garbage can, then began to pick up pieces of broken ceramic and throw them away. It was an old thin china plate with an elegant teal pattern. The shards were still hot in her fingers. Then she began to scoop up the old food and throw it in the garbage can too.

"Here," Vanessa said, handing her a paper towel. "You don't have to do that. I'll do it."

"We can do it together," Mona said. "It smells good."

"Watch your feet, there's broken plate everywhere."

"Where's your broom?"

Vanessa found a broom and dustpan in the hall closet. She handed them to Mona.

"My one job in life is to preserve this set of plates for my posterity. My grandmother received them from her parents as a wedding present. In the old country. They were the only thing she and my grandfather brought with them. It's one of those stories, she had to smuggle the plates away from the village in her underwear or something. They get to this country and these plates—they're like *everything* to her. She got old and she died and she gave the plates to my mother. My mother if anything was freakier about Grandma's plates than Grandma. She had them in the special china cabinet and sometimes I'd come in at night and I'd catch her sitting in front of the plates, just looking at them. So she gets sick and she gives them to me. And it's clear my mission in life is to preserve them for Elias's eventual wife, who will pass them along to Elias's eventual daughter. Our entire family exists to sustain the passage of these plates through the generations. And this is the third of eight that I have broken."

When the plate was cleaned up, Mona said, "You sit down. Let's try again."

Vanessa sat on one of the high stools of her open-plan kitchen. Mona put the other plate in the microwave and turned the machine on.

Mona said, "Why do you use these plates if they're so valuable?"

Vanessa chewed on her lip. There was a stray leaf of parsley on the counter that she rolled into a small ball.

"Because I hate the plates. And Elias's got enough problems without the plates hanging over him. I'm hoping that they'll all break and I'll be free of them. So the rules of the game are that they must all break in honest accidents. If I throw them away, Grandma will haunt me. But if they break honestly, then I can get rid of them and Grandma's spirit can go away."

"These are the plates?" Mona said, gesturing at the stack in the still-open kitchen cupboard.

"Yes."

Mona picked the topmost plate off the stack. She raised it chin-high. She felt a giddy manic wave surge over her. Now her hand was just above her head, primed. Her hand was almost open when Vanessa said, "Mona, don't you fucking dare."

MONA WOKE ON THE COUCH, wearing a pair of Vanessa's pajamas. Barney was on the floor beside her. Vanessa had insisted that they sleep over.

"Where are you guys going to go in the middle of the night?" she said. "Let me make you up the couch."

"We've been so much trouble."

"At this point, one more night on my couch is no trouble."

Vanessa went into her bedroom and came out a moment later with a sheet, a pillow, and a comforter. Mona stood up.

"I'll help you," she said.

They stretched out the sheet and tucked it under the cushions. Then she floated a comforter across the sheet.

"There you go, nice and cozy," Vanessa said.

Mona expected that Vanessa would excuse herself to her bedroom for the evening, but she sat down on top of the comforter. She pulled her legs up under her. Mona suppressed a yawn. Vanessa still wanted to talk.

It was maybe eighteen months ago, she said, and she had been walking to work in the morning when, despite her misgivings, she listened to a podcast with Milton. The podcaster was a young man, his voice a fruity, mellow tenor. "We're here with Milton Katz, looking back on blah-blah-blah, fifty years doing blah-blah in his own unique, inimitable way," the interviewer said.

He's in love with Milton, Vanessa thought, the way young men sometimes were; they longed for Milton's simple scheme of life, his all-consuming energy.

She had not expected Milton's voice would stir up, after all these years, so many emotions. She sat on a bench opposite the Public, and even though she was now late for work, kept listening.

Toward the end of the long interview, the interviewer asked Milton to list his favorite productions, the shows he had put on over the years that he looked back on with pride.

"Well, they're all failures," Milton said. "That's just the nature of the work. You never put on a show where you get the play right and put it away in the closet and decide it's done."

The interviewer was persistent, however, and coaxed out of Milton the sought-after listicle.

Milton mentioned four or five shows, some before Vanessa's time, some after. Then he said, "We did a *Measure for Measure*, it must have been twenty years back, with a young actress. From the first time I saw her, I said to myself, 'This girl is made for the role.' I brought her in straight from college. Got a lot of flak for that, but I trust my eye, I trust my gut. Turned out to be the only show she ever did for us, but it was like she was born for the role. And I never thought we did that show better."

"What was her name?"

Vanessa, listening, held her breath, and it took Milton so long to answer that she had to let it go. Not long after that, she said, just a matter of months, the reporter from the *Times*, Angie Steinmetz, called her.

Now, through the open bedroom door, Mona saw Vanessa asleep on her own bed. She could see the clock on the kitchen wall: it was five minutes to six. She tiptoed into Vanessa's bedroom, where she found her own dirty, familiar clothes in the dark. Then she changed in the living room. It occurred to her that she had a show that night: it was Friday morning. That evening, she'd be Maria, dancing around Clara Huskins' stage. "Bring your hand to the buttery bar and let it drink," she'd say with a MILF-ish leer. She'd *sashay in* stage left and prance out stage right.

Mona went into the bathroom to find something for her hangover, which now was beginning to explode. Vanessa had three full boxes of Q-tips. She had makeup remover, and six different face creams, and a single-application treatment for a yeast infection. Mona had just about given up hope of finding her medicine when she realized that there was another cabinet behind the mirror, where she found a row of little yellow bottles. Nestled between a bottle of amoxicillin and a bottle of Zantac, she discovered, almost untouched, a bottle of Percodan. Mona picked the bottle up, twirled it in her fingers. She saw two visions of her life unfold before her: only one involved leaving Vanessa's apartment with that minimum modicum of dignity she had hitherto considered essential to her well-being. When she heard Vanessa grunt in her sleep, she slipped the bottle of pills into her vest pocket.

Then she walked into Elias's bedroom. He was in his bed, hugging a stuffed giraffe. Mona sat and watched him dream. He was moving slightly and twitching his lips. A large elephant sat crumpled on his haunches protecting Elias from the stuffed lions. There was a long soft snake at the end of the bed. Mona moved a friendly-looking polar bear in front of the lions, and she put the snake on the floor, the best she could do under the circumstances.

ACT FOUR

KING HENRY VI

O God! methinks it were a happy life
To be no better than a homely swain;
To sit upon a hill, as I do now,
To carve out dials quaintly, point by point,
Thereby to see the minutes how they run,
How many make the hour full complete;
How many hours bring about the day;
How many days will finish up the year;
How many years a mortal man may live.

1

Mona and Barney were standing on the sidewalk outside Vanessa's building, the pre-dawn air far colder than she expected, when, reaching for her phone to order an Uber, she realized that she had left it, still plugged into the wall, on Vanessa's bedside table. She knew exactly where the phone was, but nevertheless patted the pockets of her vest twice.

Mona sighed. The gesture was more expressive of despair than a scream. It came from the deepest recess of her diaphragm and soul and expressed her innermost conviction that she was the greatest idiot in the world, that she was a loser and a screwup, and that she could do nothing right and did everything wrong and had been this way since birth. Barney looked at her anxiously. "It's okay," she said to the dog, who waved his tail gently a moment. She leaned over and rubbed his head. Barney was unconvinced that everything was okay, convinced in fact of the contrary proposition: that everything was strange and disordered and he had found himself in a scary place at a scary time. He began to pant.

Mona stood under a streetlamp and took a quick inventory of her situation. It was almost six in the morning, she figured, reaching for her phone to check, then remembering all over again that she was a moron. She had her plumping lip gloss, somewhat used, her lips still stinging from its last application; her vape, in which she estimated there were still a good three or four solid puffs; a bottle of stolen narcotics; and a crumpled dollar bill and some change. She had a worried-looking beagle on a leash. She was all alone on a Manhattan street. Her good hair was long gone.

There was no way Mona was going back for the phone. She supposed that she could just walk across the park and go home. That was the reasonable course of action. But there would be gloating on her return, hidden under the ostensible worry and concern. Rachel would tweet Mona's sad homecoming, as no doubt she had been tweeting all through her absence. Sheila would make her tea and insist that Mona tell her every lurid detail.

But the worst part—the part that was simply too horrible to consider—would be the questions from Phil: "And you spent the night where? Doing what? And why didn't you have your phone?" Mona didn't think he would be jealous; he would be concerned, which was so much worse. Almost certainly Phil would use the occasion of her flight to insist that she make an appointment—"just to talk things over"—with Dr. Grossbart, who did not sell his services cheap on Groupon like good, friendly Dr. Billy, but was in fact a serious, very expensive psychiatrist. Mona's relationship with Norm Grossbart and his prescription pad was another of her long-running points of negotiation with Phil. "See Dr. Grossbart" was itself a domestic euphemism for "Go back on an antidepressant." Phil brought the subject of whether Mona should see Dr. Grossbart on a regular basis, so frequently discussed that the *meta*-subject—the subject of whether Phil should discuss the subject of Mona and Dr. Grossbart—was itself discussed more than once in the safe confines of Dr. Billy's home office. Strangely, the meta-subject had come to absorb all of the emotion that both Mona and Phil assiduously avoided while discussing the subject itself, which the two of them discussed in insistently bloodless terms: Phil, for his part, knew there was a difference between insisting your wife play Frisbee with your friends and asking her to take a daily mood-altering medication, and so he displayed a not-entirely-convincing pantomime of modesty (eyes cast down; soft, hesitant voice; one hand holding the other) whenever he brought the subject up. Phil himself had been on Zoloft for years and was unequivocally enthusiastic about the result. Mona for her part knew that she wasn't allowed to demonstrate much by way of strong emotion in these conversations because it would be immediately seized upon by Phil and Dr. Billy as evidence that she needed to be on medication. So whenever the subject of Dr. Grossbart arose she pretended that she was a bomb-sniffing dog who had been trained not to make loud noises near suspicious suitcases. She wagged her tail and nodded seriously, and ended the conversation by kissing Phil on the cheek.

Mona suspected that Phil's love for the medicated Mona was deeper than his love for the unvarnished woman. Mona had tried two or three different spells on the antidepressants over the years. The antidepressants, as predicted, alleviated her heartache and anxiety, made her less troubled and better behaved, had rendered her, as promised, *happier*. Mona appreciated that when she took the antidepressant, unpleasant swaths of her emotional life *did* simply disappear: the dry cleaner incident, for example, probably would not have happened if Mona had been on Zoloft. She was able to walk down almost any block on the Upper West Side when she took the daily pill without fearing that some long-lost acquaintance might jump out of a stairwell wanting to grab coffee. Mona was quite sure that if she had been taking an antidepressant, she would not now be standing on a sidewalk on the corner of 71st and Third well before dawn with two dollars and change in her pocket.

But every time Mona had gone on an antidepressant, be it Zoloft or Effexor or Prozac or Wellbutrin, she had soon enough gone off them again, not just because they made achieving orgasm as frustrating as some rigged carnival game, or caused her to gain a roll of belly fat that even now she had yet to lose, but also because she felt as if she were just very slightly less of an actress under their influence, because she was just very slightly less Mona Zahid. This was something that others in her entourage denied, but Mona was convinced that the limits on her emotional range that the antidepressants produced, both on the top *and* bottom, rendered her playing sterile and listless. She didn't much feel like acting when she was on the antidepressants, and when onstage she felt as if she lost some subtle connection to her audience.

Mona stood on the sidewalk outside Vanessa's building, shivering slightly in the early-morning air. A sharp wind was blowing off the East River.

You should see Milton, she thought. *You shouldn't put it off any longer.*

Mona knew that the voice in her head was telling her the truth. She didn't know what else she could do. *You could go later,* she thought to herself. *The last thing he wants is to see you now, reeking of booze. Go home, get some sleep, call him and see him over the weekend.* But Mona knew that if she didn't go now, she'd probably never go. She'd go home and fight with Phil or Rachel or Bruce. The day would pass and then another, until it was too late.

Mona did a few mental calculations. Milton's townhouse was just across the river. It was a couple of hours' walk, maybe an hour and a half if she walked fast.

———

MONA WALKED DOWN LEXINGTON FEELING BAD. Her head was pounding something miserable now, the hangover swinging from the monkey bars of her soul. She regretted absolutely everything. She regretted stalking out of the house yesterday and ruining everyone's Thanksgiving. She didn't understand now why she had done that. She regretted that while this would not be Aaron's only memory of her, it would forever be *one* of his memories of her, and that Thanksgiving would thereafter be associated with his mother's act of lunacy, to be discussed in years to come when he hosted Thanksgivings of his own. "My mother could be a real piece of work," he would tell his future wife. Mona wondered if she could ever go home again. Perhaps they simply wouldn't take her anymore. She regretted both marrying Phil and treating him so poorly. Mona's regret was not sadness or melancholy or depression or gloominess. It was intense and active. *Something's not right with me*, she thought. This was not the kind of regret that inspired you to reform. This was the kind of regret that made you ache inside in misery and shame and self-directed disgust. She regretted drinking too much: she regretted bottle one and bottle two, the bottles regretted individually—*why on earth did I start?*—and collectively—*why didn't I stop?* She regretted the way her stomach felt. She regretted swiping the bottle of pills from Vanessa's bathroom; she regretted it so much that she didn't even take one of those pills, which would, she knew, wipe out regret at its source. She didn't think she deserved to be regret-free. She looked back at her life, and saw only things to regret: she regretted that when she was thirteen she dropped out of piano lessons, just when she was getting good enough to play the first of the Beethoven piano sonatas. She had begged and pleaded for the lessons, and her father had taken a second job just to pay for them. This was a pattern in her life, in which she committed and abandoned life-improving activities at terrible cost to others. She regretted being who she was. She regretted kissing Will Powers, a clear if minor act of marital infidelity, which left her now with a distinct feeling of ick. She regretted her inability to maintain intimate female friendship, the kind that required careful cultivation over decades and that so many other women seemed to have with their group chats and all-girls' vacations, so that she had arrived at middle age without one real friend she could call on now in a moment of crisis. She regretted that she had not had a second child. She regretted that she hadn't gone to live with Vikram Gupta in LA twenty years ago when he asked her to. She had flown out to California and spent three weeks with him in his little apartment and loved it, for all the usual reasons people love California: the sun, the light, the lazy mornings on Vikram's redwood deck. Then she had flown back to New York and told Vikram that things were over. It had been a choice between the work with Milton and the love with Vikram. A year or so later she met Phil. Mona had bottled up her regret for that decision in her soul's cellar for decades. Now the vintage was ripe and she swilled it down in the space of time it took her to cross from 62nd to 61st Street. How different her life would have been.

But more than anything, she regretted that she didn't pee before leaving Vanessa's apartment. Walking was almost painful. She felt as if her bladder had been inflated to grotesque dimensions, like a beach ball. She began to consider peeing right where she stood, on the corner of 61st and Lexington.

Mona had actually never peed on a New York City street, not just because she considered peeing on the street low-class, but because she associated the act with Zahra at the moment of her greatest humiliation. Mona's mood picked up slightly as she remembered the incident. It must have been just after they moved to New York; this was the very early nineties, when she was just starting at Juilliard. They had been coming home from a party not very far from where Mona was right now, as it happened, when Zahra announced, "I have to pee. Look out for me." Zahra's pleasure in peeing in public went far beyond the relief afforded her bladder: it was like some act of feminist liberation, together with a minor act of exhibitionism. "Please don't," Mona said, already embarrassed. Here was a bright red line that divided the sisters, neither even close to understanding the other on this point. For a woman whose life consisted of the public revelation of her most vulnerable, shameful, intimate emotions, Mona actually was something of a prude when out and about. To be sure, she had once had sex in the lobby of an apartment building in Brooklyn, or come very close at least, so close that there was little reason to debate specifics—had she been caught in the act, her shame would have been quite the same. But that was an exception. Peeing in the street was like showing your boobs at Mardi Gras: you were either the kind of woman who thought it was fun, or the kind of woman who didn't. Between the two camps of conduct, there was only contempt. "Don't be a loser," Zahra said, who had in fact amassed more beads than a modest woman should when she went to Mardi Gras with her college friends. Mona wondered whether Rachel knew these things about her mother, or whether Rachel could imagine her mother squatting agilely on 64th just off Park, pulling up her skirt and tugging down her underwear, and happily emitting a trickling yellow river. Mona was certain that neither Rachel nor any other member of her generation would quite understand the full emotional significance of the name "Jacqueline Kennedy Onassis," particularly to those who grew up in a household where Aristotle Onassis's abandonment of Maria Callas in favor of Jacqueline Kennedy was mourned with an intensity typically associated with the deaths of martyrs, or of the fact that when Zahra looked up, still squatting, Jacqueline Kennedy Onassis was staring down at her, Jaqueline Kennedy Onassis improbably alone on the street and dressed in the most beautifully tailored cream slacks that Mona had ever seen. "Girls, *really*," Jacqueline Kennedy Onassis said. But Mona knew that she could make Rachel understand the look of absolute judgment and disgust on Jacqueline Kennedy Onassis's lovely, coiffed face, because it was imprinted quite permanently on Mona's soul. Now Mona regretted all the times she had not peed beside her sister in the night.

Mona found a little alcove where two garbage cans were chained up; there was space for a third. It was in this spot that she nestled herself. *Look out for me*, she said to the ghost of her sister, who she hoped was hovering invisibly beside her. In one swift gesture she pulled down her leggings and underwear and sank into a crouch. Soon she felt better.

BARNEY WAS NOT WITHOUT OPINIONS on all sorts of things, but he rarely expressed them: he preferred his kibble heated up for half a minute in the microwave before being served, but he did not refuse it straight from the sack; he enjoyed walking into the wind where the smells were richer over walking with the wind, but again, if Mona decided otherwise, he was obliging. Now, however, he made a decision. He was done adventuring. His paws ached, his haunches were sore, and he had skipped the better part of a night's sleep. He had been dragging a few steps behind Mona now for several blocks, Mona correcting him from time to time with a little tug on the leash. Barney sat down on the corner of 34th and Lexington and refused to budge.

Mona looked down and saw her dog looking up at her with obstinate, almost angry eyes, such an unexpected display of independence on his face that she laughed.

Barney did not understand what Mona said next—"Let's just take the subway, buddy"—but he gave her the benefit of the doubt and allowed himself to be led down a nearby flight of stairs.

Barney did not realize it, but Mona's decision to take the subway was an act of courage on her part. She had not taken the subway in over a year, on account of a video that had made the rounds on social media. Everyone had seen it: the blond tourist filming his blonde girlfriend, goofing off and smiling, both of them in bright red sweatshirts, him filming her, then turning the camera on himself, then back on her, both of them exuding the happy glow of a young couple out on vacation in the big city, neither of them noticing the old man falling to the tracks behind them. The video stops with the shriek of the train's brakes. The video was always accompanied by warnings serving as black enticements: "Don't watch this if you're easily upset." "Warning: Serious triggers if you are a human being." "Hard-to-watch content." But also: "Horrible to watch but amazing." "So beautiful." "Changed my life." She watched the video and watched it again. The man, who might have been in his seventies, with a halo of gray hair, his body spectral and long, didn't fall into the tracks: he floated, his back above the tracks, no hesitation at all, arms widespread. He seemed to hang in the air. The train hit him before he even landed and he seemed simply to disappear in midair. The video, magnified still further, revealed that just before impact he bore a radiant smile. Commentators on the internet would later time the duration of his fall and argue over whether it was consistent with the laws of physics.

Eventually the video was taken down, but not before the MTA

had registered a dramatic if temporary drop in ridership. Mona saw the video just after Zahra died and it had affected her powerfully; this stranger's death and her sister's death were psychically fused. She stopped taking the subway too. Phil had considered Mona's refusal to take the subway as a kind of personal affront. "You know the subway is statistically the safest means of transportation, don't you?" he would ask. "Kilometer per kilometer you're in way more danger in a car." Phil would inevitably speak in metric when he wanted to impress upon Mona the awesome weight of science. She would insist that she was not frightened precisely of the subway, it simply upset her, in a way she could not explain but that she wished that Phil would intuitively understand. Only Aaron seemed to get it. "We can take a bus," he said whenever the two of them needed to go downtown.

Now Mona found the courage to go down the subway stairs. The entranceway was lit by a flickering fluorescent strip. She considered how to sneak herself and her dog on the train. Barney was not permitted on the subway, but Mona had acquired a card from an online psychologist labeling him a service animal necessary to her emotional well-being, which usually was sufficient, together with Mona's most imperious glare, to convince even the most recalcitrant subway official that it was best to allow this high-strung woman and her calming beagle to go about their business. That the card was in her purse at home was one of Mona's pressing concerns as she walked into the station; the other was that she did not have a MetroCard or enough money to buy one. It had been decades since she had last jumped the turnstile.

Mona was pleased to see, as she and her dog approached the turnstiles, that they were deserted. Now her mind was fully occupied with the problems at hand. She would jump the turnstile first, holding the leash off to one side, and then she would call Barney, who even at his full height with head erect could pass under the metal bar. Mona placed both hands on the cold steel railings, nonchalantly swung her feet into her chest, shifted her momentum forward, and then, just as she landed, lost her balance: the leash had tangled on the turnstile itself. She tumbled face first onto the concrete platform. One hand was free to break her fall, but only in part, the rest of her momentum absorbed by a largish wad of chewing gum into which she burrowed her forehead and hairline. The pain was considerable and immediate, and not assuaged in any way by the realization that there had in fact been onlookers at the turnstile, all of them staring at her somberly in the fashion of New Yorkers enjoying a fellow citizen's misery. Barney scooted under the turnstile and began to lick her face tenderly, with particular attention to the places where the smell of spearmint was predominant.

Mona's deepest desire was to huddle into a ball and sob, but she forced herself instead to her feet, turned in the direction of the small crowd of indifferent observers, and offered them the same glowing smile she might have given had a crowd at Lincoln Center arisen in spontaneous applause. Then she bowed, held the bow a beat, took Barney by the leash, and waited for her train, which pulled into the station shortly.

2

All around Mona Brooklyn was coming to life: a man in a business suit left a neighboring apartment building, announcing to his phone and Mona alike that it was so typical of Mark to have them come in, when even Fixed Incomes, fer crissakes, was off for the long weekend. Then came a trio of joggers, all in spandex, their eyes glassy and focused on the far horizon. A woman walked her golden retriever, a canine Cleopatra, whose scent, drifting clearly on the wind, entranced Barney, who despite being neutered himself could from time to time be struck by the infinite variety of feminine allure. The dog's owner, also on her phone, said, "Is Mom there? I don't care if she's sleeping. Unless she's dead, she'll wake up for this."

Mona rang the doorbell of Milton's townhouse. She shivered and rocked from foot to foot. Was Milton even home?

Joralemon Street had always struck Mona as an unlikely place for Milton to live, this corner of Brooklyn Heights which seemed to incarnate in brownstone architecture and cobblestones everything the Rabble in art ostensibly disdained. Milton insisted on giving a little spiel about the street to all his guests, taking them out on the front step, pointing first one way and then the other, and saying, "So this street is named after a grumpy old asshole named Teunis Joralemon."

Mona had heard the speech many times over the years.

"Mr. Joralemon was born in 1766, and if memory serves, died about 1840. Wore many hats in his day, did Mr. Joralemon—

saddlemaker, deacon, lawyer, and a judge. Mr. Joralemon emigrated from New Jersey, although we don't hold that against him. Bought up over the years all the land from about there where you can see the River Deli all the way about up to there. Farmed that land, used it to grow vegetables, which he'd take across to market in Manhattan on a rowboat. His big fight in life was against the crosstown streets, which cut up his land. First with Henry Street, then Clinton Street. Lawsuit after lawsuit, fight after fight. Lost 'em all, in the end. In this city, change is inevitable. You can't fight it. The new generation comes in and lays down crosstown streets right through your farm. This right here, where we're standing, is where he had his farmhouse. Burned down in 1842."

The fact that Milton was now himself a resident of Joralemon Street was the product of his marriage to Susan, who, together with her first husband, had purchased the townhouse in the early nineties. They had just completed its restoration when her husband died, choking to death on an overcooked moose steak on a hunting trip to the Boundary Waters, a demise as improbable as it was horrible. Mona did not believe that Milton married the widow Robertson only to become the proprietor of the townhouse, but she supposed that the townhouse and all it represented had been, in addition to Susan's wry sense of humor and obvious sharp intelligence, one of her understood virtues: Milton had arrived at his early fifties, despite the good salary the board paid him, but burdened with a significant alimony and a lifetime of financial improvidence, living in a one-bedroom rental on the Lower East Side, a ten-minute walk from 107 Avenue C. The one-bedroom was before Mona's time in the company, but she heard from Anne Carman and Old Tom that the apartment was more appropriate to the bohemian legend of Milton than the increasingly bourgeois reality. The one-bedroom and all *it* represented had been as seductive to Susan, Mona supposed, as the townhouse had been to him.

Should she ring the doorbell a second time? She stepped back from the stoop and looked up at the house, searching for signs of life. The second-floor windows were dark and curtained, but on the third floor, one of the windows was open.

Mona had always liked Susan, from the first time she saw her wielding the fire extinguisher in Burbage with such exquisite menace. She had always been intimidated by her, frankly. At fundraisers or the little parties she and Milton hosted from time to time, Susan would greet her on this front step, always just slightly more elegant than Mona, her hair more perfectly smoothed, her makeup a little better, resplendent with the easy confidence that comes from success after success in business in Manhattan. Mona had the impression that here on Joralemon Street, Milton accepted Susan's style, taste, domestic values without much demurral; the Milton who ruled with absolute authority at 107 Avenue C, and who made more than one set designer cry with his unyielding opinions on the shape of a doorknob or wall sconce, left the house more or less as he found it. Susan and her first husband had designed the interior of the house in enthusiastic if not slavish imitation of an English country house, the place put together over a few years to look as if it were the product of several centuries: the walls were covered in ornate wallpaper, the furniture, acquired from antique dealers and at auction, was heavy and upholstered in striped chintz. Milton, sensibly realizing that this was a set on which he could act out his most outlandish fantasy, made only one change on moving into the townhouse, ordering the construction of floor-to-ceiling bookshelves in the living room and front hallway, which he filled with his own library.

Mona sat down on the stoop. She would have wagered after the fire extinguisher incident that Milton's marriage did not have long to run, but she would have lost: not only did they stay together, but when Mona saw them thereafter, they seemed to have an easy familiarity that Mona sometimes wished she had with Phil, finishing one another's sentences, Susan casually draping her arm around Milton's waist and calling him "Katz."

Mona decided to ring the doorbell a second time.

The last time Mona was in the townhouse was four years ago, at the wake following Susan's funeral. Mona had never understood the custom of throwing a cocktail party following a death, but Milton believed in these domestic rites—and he knew, moreover, that Susan, who had Irish heritage, believed in them. The house had been packed with Susan's family, who came down from Boston in large numbers, and her colleagues at McKinsey; the whole board of the Rabble was there, and friends of Susan's Mona had never met before, all members of that class of thoroughly adult New Yorkers in whose company Mona never felt particularly comfortable. Mona spent the better part of that evening condoling with Susan's housekeeper, a Polish woman named Karolina, whom Mona had liked on account of her evident, unfeigned distress at Susan's death. She had known Susan for years, from long before Susan was married to Milton; it was to Susan that Karolina, confused by a divorce that involved both Polish and American law, had turned when her separation turned nasty. Susan had helped her to hire an attorney who specialized in such complicated affairs, and had explained more patiently than the attorney herself the details of the complex divorce agreement.

A waiter from Milton's usual caterer circulated through the room with glasses of white wine. Mona took one and then another, and before long, the wine on an empty stomach gave her a headache. "Do you think Susan has—had—any Tylenol?" she asked. "My head is just pounding."

"Come," Karolina said. She led Mona through the house to a small, quiet bedroom on the first floor. Then she put her hands on Mona's cheeks. "Is okay?" Karolina asked. "I am intuitive healer." Mona felt the hand press and squish against her face. Soon her headache began to pass. "Is very difficult time," Karolina said.

"That was amazing," Mona said. "Thank you."

"I do always for Susan too."

Mona took Karolina's business card: "Karolina Symbocyka. Intuitive Healer. Practitioner of Holy Hands." She found the card in her purse a few weeks later, when Phil was complaining about his back, as usual. She asked if he wanted her to make an appointment.

"I don't do quack medicine," he said.

"She really helped me," Mona bristled.

"That's because you're so suggestible."

Mona took this first as a criticism, then as a compliment, then as a criticism again.

Mona soon lost the business card and didn't think of Karolina thereafter. She was surprised, then, when Karolina, wearing a flannel bathrobe, opened Milton's front door, her eyes clouded still with sleep. Mona's first thought was that Karolina must be Milton's lover. Her face went red. She felt all the absurdity of her overnight trek, of her worries for Milton. The well-padded bosom in front of Mona had been Milton's cushion as he tumbled through life. The notion that Milton had taken up with his housekeeper—Mona couldn't say why it shocked her, but it did. Had this been going on for a long time? Had it even been there before Susan's death?

"I'm sorry to wake you up," Mona said. "We met once. At Susan's funeral."

Karolina rubbed the sleep out of her eyes. "I remember you—" she said. "I never remember name of anyone."

"Mona. I work with Milton. Or I used to. I came to visit him."

"Milton is still sleeping."

"Is he . . . okay?" she finally asked.

"He is very tired after last week. Maybe is better you to come later."

Karolina looked at Mona skeptically. She was suddenly aware of the appearance she must be making: she had snatched a few hours' sleep here and there over the past twenty-four hours, but she supposed she must look tired, unwashed, ungroomed. She wore no makeup to hide her exhaustion, or the faint smear of gum on her forehead. She had been wearing the same clothes far too long. Her unhappy dog glared sullenly.

"I think Milton would like to see me," she said, pulling the crumpled postcard from her pocket.

Karolina looked at the postcard carefully, comparing the face on its front to Mona's face now. She turned it over and read what Milton wrote.

"Please to come in," she said.

———

KAROLINA THOUGHT MONA should know about the incident the week before.

Mona was in Milton's kitchen now. She had wanted coffee, but Karolina had offered her instead a strange tea, which tasted of herbs and mud. Barney was lapping from a bowl of water that Karolina, unprompted, had offered him.

Milton, Karolina said, had left the house a week ago, by himself, while she was at the dentist. When she came home in the late afternoon, the house was empty, which was unusual. "How you call, the man who lives in a cave? Milton makes like herman since I am living here. He never goes out." Karolina's concern only mounted as the hours passed and night fell, Milton still missing. Eventually she called both the police and Milton's daughter Ginnie in Arizona.

Well after midnight, the doorbell of the townhouse rang. Milton was on the stoop, with two policemen beside him.

"Do you know this man?" said the smaller of the two policemen.

"That's Mr. Katz," she said.

"Does he live here?"

"This is my house," Milton said, his voice lacking the note of certainty ordinarily associated with such a declaration.

"We found him. Not far from here. He was going door to door, ringing doorbells. He remembered his address but couldn't find it."

The sadness of the moment and its implications registered with Karolina. Milton's light sweater and thin cotton pants, both covered in dirt, were inadequate to the cold fall night.

Karolina told Mona that she wanted to take Milton immediately to the emergency room—he looked tired and confused. "But Milton, he does not want to go. I say, 'Please we must go now.' But he refuses."

The next morning, she succeeded in dragging Milton to the emergency room, where he spent a long day undergoing a battery of tests. The doctor who conducted the tests was small, no larger than a girl, and looked as young, Karolina thought, as a girl also. She came out to the waiting room, where Karolina had been sitting all through the day.

"Are you Mr. Katz's daughter?" she asked.

Karolina didn't care to explain the complicated relationship between them, so she lied. "Yes," she said.

"Well, your dad's okay. We think he had what we call a grandpa stroke. It's better now, we're not finding any trace of it on the imaging. It can cause the elderly to be confused, lose their memory for a little while, but usually it's temporary. He's got high blood pressure—we'll write him a prescription for that. But he needs to rest and take it easy for a while."

When they got home, all Milton said was, "Time to hit the hay."

His walk toward the staircase was so tired, so filled with evident sadness, that Karolina stopped him. She said, "Milton, what food your mother is making when you are little boy?"

The next morning, Karolina prepared a chicken soup for Milton, following a recipe from a YouTube channel featuring an authentic Jewish grandmother. Milton ate Bubbe Naomi's soup with her that evening at the dining room table. He was quieter now than before his stroke, she thought, and more docile. She wasn't sure that she preferred this version.

Milton took his first sip and closed his eyes.

"Believe me, my mother never made anything that tasted half this good," he said. "Most of the time she poured the soup out of a can."

Since then, Karolina said, Milton had been even more reclusive than before. She had called Ginnie in Arizona, who had agreed to rearrange her schedule and fly out to New York: she was coming to visit Milton next week. She had thought the news would cheer him up, but when she told him, he had only nodded grimly.

"The party's over," he said.

Karolina looked at Mona.

She said, "Milton will be very happy you are come."

"THANK YOU FOR TAKING CARE OF HIM," Mona said.

Karolina replied by nodding with sedate dignity.

"Everybody will get old," she said.

"Do you have a bathroom I could use?" Mona asked.

Karolina directed Mona to the guest bathroom in the front hall. Barney, swishing his tail nervously, followed her. She didn't have to pee. She just wanted to wash her face. She wished that she had never come, that she had stayed home yesterday, or that she had come much earlier, when Milton was still Milton, not some diminished version of the man. She thought about Phil, who would have bounded up the steps joyfully at the prospect of seeing a demented Milton. Mona was not a good person, she thought, and this was a moment requiring a good person.

Mona had been in her preparations for Lady M. when her sister was first diagnosed. Zahra had asked her to come to the doctor's appointment and Mona, irritated, had refused: it would have meant missing a half day of tech rehearsals. Moreover, she had been certain that Zahra had been exaggerating her symptoms, wanting attention in her distress over Vadim's latest infidelity. Even Phil thought that Zahra would be fine. You can't reschedule a tech three days before previews on a show like that.

Mona regularly imagined walking with her sister out of that first visit to Mount Sinai, pulling their sunglasses out of their purses to subdue the harsh winter sun, then walking downtown together, Zahra saying that she didn't feel that sick, really. There was a leather store on Madison somewhere in the mid-Seventies where Mona and Zahra had admired the handbags over the years. Mona always told Zahra that if she got some big film contract, that's where they'd head, and Zahra told Mona that if *she* ever sold that property on East 58th Street, she'd take her there. It was on their way downtown from Mount Sinai. They could have spent an hour or two at the store, the hospital forgotten, absorbed in the pleasures of soft leather and craftsmanship, walking out with a pair of costly handbags.

Mona returned over and over again to this false memory, elaborating and embroidering it. Sometimes she didn't take Zahra purse shopping; instead they went to the Frick, where in a little-visited alcove there was a portrait of a seventeenth-century Dutch woman whose face was startlingly like Zahra's. Zahra had once considered getting a master's in art history, forever trying to drag Mona to one museum or gallery after another. Now it was Zahra who didn't want to go: "I don't feel like looking at art at all," she would have said. "Thanks for the idea—" But Mona would have insisted. Later Zahra, seated now on the leather bench examining the portrait more carefully (which Mona had noted years before and had intended to show Zahra since forever), would have fallen into a thoughtful meditative reverie— five, ten, twenty minutes passing in wordless contemplation of her own mortality, and the wonder that she had existed before—here was proof!—and might well exist again. They would have walked home silently, thoughtful, not consoled precisely, still anxious, but together.

And still Mona was haunted by other invented memories: a movie, a walk in the park, a spontaneous meal at Jean-Georges where a table for two had been miraculously left vacant. "Is it a special occasion, ladies?" the waiter might have asked. "We're celebrating life," Mona would have replied, ordering a very good champagne.

It tormented Mona that, in a city so thick with distraction, consolation, entertainment, and solace, Zahra had gone home alone from her oncologist's appointment and waited patiently by the phone for Mona to return her phone call, Mona having forgotten the appointment in the course of her rehearsal, and that when Mona finally did call her sister, six hours after she left the oncologist, Mona's first words were a curt "So what's new?"

Mona dried her face and went up the stairs, Barney two steps ahead of her, past the first-floor landing where a thick cream carpet led to one bedroom which seemed to Mona like some kind of crafting studio, disorderly with boxes, piles of fabrics, and aromatic with the smell of burnt sage; then another bedroom, the door closed. Then she walked up another flight of stairs, darker now and narrower, and reached a small landing, where she found a door, partially ajar. Mona tapped on it once, then twice, and waited. When she got no response, she pushed it slowly open, saying, "Milton, it's—" then checked herself. He was on the couch, his eyes closed, unmoving.

For a moment she wondered if he was even breathing. Then he stirred slightly, and she could see that his breath was regular. It had been almost a year since Mona had last seen him, and she was shocked by the change: his hair, now fully gray, had grown much longer than Mona remembered, and his beard was ragged. His cheeks were pink and flecked with thin red veins, like roads on a map. He was an old man wearing a bathrobe, from which emerged his gaunt, burnt legs.

Mona hesitated to walk into the room, but Barney didn't: before she could stop him, he had made his way to the couch and began to sniff Milton's feet. "Barney!" she whispered. He curled himself into a ball on the floor. He began to groom himself. She stepped into the office too. The room was not neat, but neither was it the mess that Mona's conversation with Karolina had led her to believe. There were piles of papers on the desk, Milton's pants tossed across the back of an armchair.

Mona folded up the pants and put them on the coffee table. Then she put herself in the large leather armchair. All she could hear was Milton's breathing and the gentle swish of Barney's tongue, and from time to time, a car rolling slowly down Joralemon Street. She pulled her legs up underneath her and leaned her head against the wing of the chair. Milton turned over slightly in his sleep. The room was dark and peaceful. Before long, she was asleep too.

Mona was in the living room, home from tour. Phil was there, Aaron also, both of them playing with the baby. That was so sweet to see, Aaron playing with his little brother. Mona happy to have the baby now, after all the talking. Then she was confused. "Was I pregnant?" she said to Phil. "We bought him at IKEA," Phil said. Mona was angry. "Without asking me first?" "He was on sale!" Sheila said. Mona dissolving in love, loving Phil, loving Aaron, loving the baby. Mona drifting to consciousness, the baby disappearing.

"Morning," she said, casually.

Milton was sitting at his desk. He had dressed himself since she'd snuck in the room. His long silver hair was combed back neatly. There was a smell in the room, familiar and pleasing, of Milton, the combination of pomade and lotion that Milton, fastidious about scent, habitually applied. He turned around in his chair. He ran his fingers absentmindedly through his beard, as if concentrating on a scene in Burbage.

"Aren't you the sight for sore eyes!"

"I had that dream again."

"Which one?"

"The one where Phil buys a baby."

Mona referencing previous conversations: Milton and Mona at the Trumilou. Caesar salad, bottle of Sancerre. Phil had wanted the second baby more than Mona, after his breakdown. Mona unsure:

what roles she'd give up, how tired she'd be. Milton listening more than talking. She used to have the dream every night.

"You never went for the second one, did you?"

"We thought about it, but you know . . ."

The dream and its sadness began to dissipate. Mona looked around the little office. She squinted at the bright morning sun, passing through the unwashed windows to form two long beams of dancing dust motes, like spotlights, one focused on Mona's feet, another at a stain on the gray-cream carpet.

"What time is it?" she said.

"'What a devil hast thou to do with the time of day?'" said Milton, luxuriating in the open vowels, filling the "thou" with lovely, knowing intimacy.

"Seriously, I'm a bit confused."

"It must be around eleven," he said.

"I've got to call Phil. He's probably worried sick."

"He doesn't know where you are?"

"Nobody knows where I am. But you."

"Tell me more," Milton said, leaning back into his chair and tilting his head at a curious angle.

"I ran away from home. I ruined everyone's Thanksgiving."

"Oh, so you've been a bad girl."

"I just couldn't take it anymore."

Milton said, "In 1978, my wife at the time, my second wife, invited her entire family to Thanksgiving. We were living in a little apartment on West Eighteenth Street. And my mother-in-law, she had thoughts on how to roast a turkey—and other things also. So I threw the turkey out the window into the street below."

Mona laughed in relief. She was sitting with Milton, he was still Milton. She wondered why she had stayed away so long.

"You threw an entire turkey out the window?"

"Right out the window. It seemed important to me at the time that I make a very firm statement to my wife and in-laws about the nature of my masculinity. Which I believe I did. Would you like coffee?"

"I'd love some."

Milton had a drip coffeemaker on the wooden dresser. Standing up was a complicated process of stretching his legs, pitching himself forward, and then slowly bringing his spine to vertical. Mona could see that he was no longer as agile as he once was. But once erect, he moved without hesitation across the room and set the pot to brewing. Then he went back across the room and sat down again. Mona was surprised how natural it was to sit with Milton in his office.

"So, tell me *everything*," Milton said greedily.

"It's not even interesting. I got your card yesterday, I went for a walk with Barney, it occurred to me that I would go insane if I had to spend one more minute at home, and I spent the night on a girlfriend's couch, in the course of which I drank far too much, and now I'm here."

The coffee was ready. Mona said, "Stay. I'll do it," and poured two cups into the chipped pair of mugs on the dresser. She gave one to Milton, then sat back in her chair with the other.

"And how are things with the doctor?" Milton said.

Again the Trumilou, again the Sancerre, now one of those finicky, complicated fishes that require elaborate dissection on her plate. "You will be bored to death and having an affair within five years," he had said. "That is not the thing to tell a girl whose tall and handsome boyfriend the surgeon has just offered her an engagement ring." "I'm serious. Take your talent seriously. No one else will. Trust me." "How many times have you been married again?"

"So I know whereof I speak." That lunch left Mona so furious that she considered for a spell leaving the company, disturbed by Milton's bizarre presumption that he had a role in Mona's most intimate decision. She remembered Jillian D'Amato all those years ago asking, "So is it as culty as they say down there?"

She said, "Speaking of doctors, Karolina told me you haven't been feeling well lately. I'm *so* sorry."

"It happened to my mother also, at the end. Little strokes. One after the other. Took everything away from her piece by piece."

Mona softened. "How are you feeling now?"

"Never been better. In my prime."

"Seriously."

"Seriously? Well, Ginnie's coming out next week to try and put me in a home. Last week I went out to mail that goddamn postcard, the first time in months I find the courage to leave this room, and I got lost."

Milton seemed almost proud of his misadventure.

"Right on Joralemon Street. Mailed the postcard, went out for a beer at Connolly's—not far from here, not fifteen minutes away—and walked out with a splitting headache. I knew right away something wasn't right. Couldn't figure out where I was. Couldn't figure out *when* it was, whether it was 1973 or 1956 or last week. I kept thinking I was supposed to go down to 107 and rehearse, then I thought I was supposed to go work a shift at my dad's diner."

"That sounds terrifying," Mona said.

"Like the worst acid trip I ever had."

"But you seem fine now."

"That's the way it was with my mom, too. At least for a while."

"You know who I am, don't you?"

"Of course I know who you are, sweetheart. You're Elizabeth fucking Taylor."

A crow landed on the railing outside the window and squawked.

"I see that bird every day," Milton said. "She's in love with me. She brings me all the shiny shit she finds. Puts it right here on the ledge. Walks up and down the ledge, squawking her brains out."

Mona didn't know what to say. She sat quietly for a second. The crow looked at Mona with black, jealous eyes.

"Phil's fine," Mona said. "I guess."

Milton raised an eyebrow.

"I think he might be bored with me."

"Bored with you? Now how could that be?"

Mona wasn't sure if Milton was being sarcastic.

She said, "I sometimes have this fantasy, it doesn't make much sense, but the rebels kidnap him. And I don't want him to suffer, it's more about me, how much I miss him and how worried I get about him. And my whole life is just me organizing the campaign to get him back and talking to politicians but basically just praying for him all the time. And then I start to love him so much and then Phil always ruins it—I mean real Phil, not kidnapped Phil—by doing something stupid, like giving me notes or something."

"You pray for him? Like to God?"

"In the fantasy, yeah. I imagine myself down on my knees and I start bargaining with God, 'I'll do *anything* if you just give me back my husband.'"

"Why don't you pray for him in real life?"

"Because I don't *feel* that way in real life. In the fantasy it just comes so naturally, so easily, all this love."

"Interesting," Milton said, in a way that suggested that quality so rare in others and so ordinary in Milton: sincere interest. He waited for Mona to say something else, and when she didn't, he said, "Did you know Ollie Flanagan? Maybe he was before your time. On the board for years, partner at one of the big law firms. Then, sometime in his forties, he quits the board, quits the law, and becomes a Trappist monk at a monastery upstate. Takes a vow of poverty, gives away everything he owned. Over the years we stayed in touch. When he had to come to the city on monastery business— you'd be amazed how litigious those monks could be—I'd comp him a seat. I always thought he was the happiest man I ever saw."

There was a bottle of antacids on Milton's desk. Milton poured one into his hand and chewed it. "You want one?" he asked Mona. She shook her head.

"So back when I was going through the worst of it with Susan— around that time when she came into Burbage with a fire extin- guisher—I drove up to the monastery and spent a day sitting on a bench, just wishing God would talk to me too and tell me to become a monk. They raised sheep up there, made cheese—you remember that beautiful speech from Henry Six? 'O God! methinks it were a happy life / To be no better than a homely swain'?" In any case, I remember talking to Ollie. He told me I had it backwards. That you *become* a monk in order to get that sign from God, that God is *always* talking, but not everyone is listening. That you must learn to listen."

"I used to do that speech," Mona said, not to change the subject, but to encourage Milton, who had paused, to continue.

"And very well too, as I recall. So about ten years ago, Ollie quit the monastery and went back to practicing law in the city. Got mar- ried a little after that. I gave him a call, we went out to lunch. I asked him why he quit the monastery and he told me that God told him to go home. He was glowing, just glowing. It broke my heart a little to see the man looking so happy, to tell you the truth."

Milton scratched his face thoughtfully.

He said, "I always think about that story whenever anyone starts talking about praying."

Mona was quiet a moment. She wondered briefly if she had ever been the basis for some inconclusive story that Milton had told some other actor: "I had this actress in the company—solid talent. Went off the rails somewhere." She was about to ask Milton about his daughter, whom she had met once or twice over the years and remembered as a severe, somewhat humorless young woman, when he said, "You think I should go back?"

"Where?"

"107."

"Is that an option?" she finally said.

"You remember Gloria McPherson, don't you? We did a fundraiser at her place in Greenwich? She sent me this." Milton swiveled on his chair back to his desk, where he pulled an envelope from a drawer. "Have you seen my glasses? There they are. Yeah, just take a look at this."

He handed Mona the card. It was a Christmas card, from last fall. On the inside, in the kind of careful cursive that only the very elderly still employed, was written: *Dearest, dearest Milton. What an adventure we've had over the years. I was so dismayed to hear of your retirement. I do wonder how the place will survive in your absence. If you ever want to come home again, you need only say the word. This forever fan will welcome you from her usual seat in row four, arms as wide open as ever. Fondly, Gloria.*

"That's lovely," Mona said, who had a distant memory, possibly false, that Gloria McPherson might have died over the summer. She could remember Terrence making some sort of announcement.

"Gloria McPherson tells Vijay Singh that enough is enough, they'd bring me back. And there are others also."

"Like who?"

As soon as she said that, Mona wished that she hadn't. It was not necessary to be cruel. She had her points of weakness also; she was proposing to play Cleopatra, after all. A certain degree of delusion was necessary simply to get through an ordinary human day. Milton was not deterred, however. He waved his hand in a vague circle toward his desk, as if to suggest that enumerating one by one the letters, emails, and calls he had received and kept hidden in its nooks and crannies would be as far from the point as describing a tsunami in terms of its constituent droplets.

"*Would* you go back?" she asked. "If they asked?"

"Out of the question," he said. "That ship has sailed."

There was something fine, she thought, in Milton's gallantry.

"It's not the same without you," she said. "We all miss you."

In the rehearsal room, Milton had a narrow-lipped, humorless smile he employed to indicate a false note—a forced laugh, or a mawkish tear.

He said, "107 Avenue C will continue to do just fine in my absence, I suspect. I have not heard rumors of collective suicide. And I understand that Terrence has launched an appeal for the rehabilitation of the rehearsal rooms. I am on some kind of mailing list. He writes to me on a weekly basis asking me to send him money."

"Well, *I* miss you," Mona said.

Milton continued to smile at her, his eyes somber. Was he bored? The room was quiet for a moment. Mona began to think that she might like to go home. Twenty years of entertaining Milton was enough. It took so much energy to keep him amused. She didn't want to talk about Zahra after all. She didn't know if Milton would remember her, or care. Finally Milton said, "Keep up with any of my old chums?"

Mona was relieved that Milton had found a neutral subject on which to extend the conversation. She mentioned a few old members of the company, present and former: one was doing Broadway, another was on that Hulu show—she mentioned a name and Milton looked at her blankly. In any case, she said, everyone was watching it. Not that she much liked it herself. She mentioned a few other names.

"How was my Henriad?" he interrupted.

Mona told Milton the truth: that the show had been good, very good even. He arched his eyebrows in surprise, perhaps disappointment. Mona wished that she had lied, then was angry at herself for the thought: Why should she lie? She described the modern-dress production, the cuts the director had made, and the new actor brought in to play Milton's Prince Hal. As they spoke Milton's face moved through a series of expressions that to an outsider might have been innocuous but to Mona were thick with meaning. Milton was not a good actor. Mona saw his eyes, staring at Mona over the tops of his tortoise-rimmed reading glasses, hard and accusing, and his lips were pursed. She could see the tension in his shoulders.

"What's the matter?" she finally said.

"That show could have been a gem."

"It wasn't bad."

"If you say so."

He was sulking, Mona thought: She had been disloyal, she had thrown in her lot with his enemies. Now Mona understood what Milton wanted: not pity but an avowal of desire, a confession of her enduring need. He had summoned her here to play a confessional scene, to tell him how lost she was, to beg him to give her tips on Cleopatra, to denounce the new management at 107 as incompetents and fools. When the work was bad, he had been known to walk out of the rehearsal room. That was the look on his face now.

"So what can I do for you, Mona? What brings the two of you here at dawn?"

"I got your card."

"The internet stopped working. Karolina turned it off or something."

"So turn it back on, for Christ's sake."

"I don't know how to do that shit."

"You called me out here for *tech* support?"

"I called you out here because after twenty fucking years not so much as a goddamn phone call."

Mona stood up and slipped on her shoes. Halfway to the door, she said, "Come on, Barney." Barney lifted his head but stayed on the couch. "I said, 'Come on,'" she snapped, sharper with the dog than she expected. Still he stayed on the couch.

Mona turned back to Milton.

"I bet everything on you, Milton. I put all my chips on you. I've been dealing with the accumulated weight of your sins for a solid year while *you* just sat here like patience on a monument, wallowing in self-pity and wondering who loves you best. So don't put all this on *my* shoulders. *I'm* the one who got left behind. Not once until your internet went out did you bother to check on me. And now *I'm* the unfaithful daughter? Me?"

Mona leaned over to attach Barney's leash.

The room was quiet for a moment, then Milton started to clap.

"*Bravissima*," he said.

"Don't even try—"

"It's just a remarkable thing you can do. I've never seen an actor go from flat to angry better than you. Like a rocket. You *fill* the room with energy."

There was a moment—just a moment—when Mona felt that she could still storm out of the office. Then it passed.

Milton said, "I could watch you be angry forever. The first time I saw you in Burbage, all those years ago—you were so green. There really wasn't much there. But something popped to me—that I was looking at a future Cleopatra."

Mona unclipped Barney. Then, still holding his leash, wrapping it around her knuckles, she sat back in her chair.

"About last night," she said. "I spent the night at Vanessa Levin's house."

Mona expected a stronger reaction out of Milton than the one she got. "How is she?"

"She's got a little son, she's got her life. She blames you for everything."

Mona sat down again. Milton ran his fingers through his thin silver hair. He started to say something, reconsidered, then started again. Finally he said, "Cleopatra loves the audience. More than anything else in her life, that's her passion: the audience. Not Antony, not her women, not her son, not even herself. No other character in Shakespeare is quite like that. I've always wondered what kind of remarkable boy came into the company, in his late teens or early twenties at most, who could play that role. What a talent he must have been. Only a few actors can love the audience that way. Vanessa Levin, for example, never loved the audience—she was in fact highly uncomfortable in front of the audience—but at the same time she was intensely aroused by the audience. I don't mean *just* sexually but I *do* mean sexually. Now that's a very unusual combination. I suppose that's what made her Isabella so remarkable."

"You know, Milton, she was—she is—a person, not just a role."

Milton sipped his coffee, now cold.

"Sweetheart, I've lived my life. I've got plenty of things I'd change if I could do it all over again. I wouldn't throw that goddamn turkey out the window, that's for sure. But not a minute, not a second, of the time I spent with Vanessa Levin do I regret. And if the price I had to pay for it was this"—Milton waved his hand in a circle to indicate exile, the attic, disgrace—"so be it. I won't apologize, Mona, if that's what you or any other—"

He didn't finish the sentence.

Mona thought of Vanessa sitting on the floor of her kitchen, her round face in tears.

Milton swiveled in his chair so that he was looking away from Mona, and out through the tall attic windows at the facing houses.

"She called me," he finally said.

"Who?"

"Vanessa."

"When?"

"Before the article came out."

"I didn't know that," Mona said.

"Why would you?"

"She didn't mention it."

"She sat right where you're sitting now."

Mona looked down at her chair, then up again at Milton.

"And what did she say?"

"She was—she was lovely. She told me about her little boy, she even showed me a picture of him. She told me about the reporter from the *Times*. And she wanted to know what to say."

"What did you tell her?"

"Mona, I've never told an actor how to play a role. Just tell the truth, I said. 'Speak of me as I am.'"

"How did she take that?"

"She was furious, of course. She didn't come here looking for permission to talk to the *New York Times* about our love affair all those years ago. She wanted to see me beg and squirm. She wanted me to apologize for corrupting her youth and leaving her unhappy, she wanted me to roll around on the carpet seeking absolution for my sins, then she wanted to announce magnanimously that she forgave me. And I simply wasn't prepared to do that. It would have made everything I ever did in my life a lie, and at my age that was too much to ask."

Mona looked at everything for a moment but Milton: at Milton's bookshelf, which housed his working library of Shakespeare; at his desk and its piles of autobiographical fragments; at Barney, indifferent to the moment, still asleep on the couch, his tail tucked close to his haunches.

He said, "The truth that Vanessa couldn't stand—the truth that destroyed us—was that I loved Vanessa's Isabella more than Vanessa. I was fond of Vanessa—of course I was. Very fond. But I was in love with Isabella. My God, I was in love with her. For Isabella I would have been prepared to leave all of this. But not for Vanessa."

"Most people would say that's kind of lunatic."

"But not you, Mona."

"No, not me," she said quietly.

"Either you believe in what we do when we step into that rehearsal room or you don't. Most people don't."

Mona stood up, her motion so sharp that Milton, startled, looked at her.

"Is that your bathroom?" she said.

"Help yourself."

Mona went into the bathroom and closed the door. She didn't have to pee, but she sat on the toilet anyway, and pulled Vanessa's pills from her pocket. She poured three pills in her hand, thought about it a moment and added a fourth. This would allow her to tolerate Milton for another hour, and tolerate herself also. On the wall of the bathroom were a series of lithographs depicting various moments of the fox hunt. Terrified foxes were sprinting across the downs, more shadow than substance, the hounds a cruel mass of red and black on their heels, and behind them, the riders, baying in glee at the spectacle. She couldn't decide if she had ever admired Milton more, or had a greater contempt. She didn't want to think about the problem either. Mona felt a visceral longing for the hour of suspended judgment in the palm of her hand. On her nearly empty stomach the pills would dissolve in minutes, no more, and Mona would be capable of sitting at his feet for another hour in affectionate, commiserate sympathy. She would not mention her sister. She would play the role of his daughter. This might be the last time, after all, that she ever saw him.

Only the thought that she had a show this evening caused her to hesitate. She could play the part on technique alone—there was a level she would never go below. She knew that. The audience would be fine. But there were heights you could reach also, even as Maria, and she didn't want to foreclose that possibility. She had made a promise to herself.

She put the pills back in the bottle and flushed the toilet. She washed her face at the sink with cold water. She took a little of Milton's toothpaste, put it on her finger, and brushed her teeth as best she could. It was time she headed home.

When Mona walked back into the office, Milton inspected her carefully. He looked at her the way he looked at his actors in Burbage when some detail was amiss, some subtle error of inflection or rhythm, some position of the arms not quite true to life.

Finally he said, "Your nails look awful."

Mona looked down at her hands. She had done the nails earlier in the week, but they were already chipped and dirty. She had chewed on them last night.

"I could do them for you, if you want."

"I don't think so, Milton. I need to go home. It's been—"

"C'mon, lemme do the nails," he said.

"No."

"I used to do them for Susan when she was sick. She couldn't get them done in the salon, she didn't have the strength for that. And then she couldn't do them for herself because her hands were shaking too much, so I would do them for her. I'm good at it."

Mona hesitated.

"I've got a lot of colors here, let me show you," he said.

Milton opened his desk drawer and pulled out a shoe box. There must have been twenty different bottles of nail polish inside. He put on his glasses and squinted at them. He said, "We've got, what's this, Desert Nights, we've got You Do Blue, we've got Cherry Red, Cherry Crush. Metallic Haze, huh. This one's called Moonbeam."

Milton handed the nail polish bottles to Mona, who looked at them.

"They're pretty," she said.

"Yeah, I've got all the colors here."

"I have a show tonight," she said.

"Who're you playing?"

"Maria."

"Oh boy," Milton said sympathetically. "They stuck you with that, huh?"

"Someone's got to do it."

"Yeah, this would be okay for that."

He handed her a bottle of Cherry Red.

"She'd pick You Do Blue," Mona said.

"Your call. Sit down right here, ma'am. I'll take care of those nails for you."

"Thank you," Mona said, sitting down on the couch. Milton took her hands and started massaging them. His hands were strong and soft.

"Have you seen my glasses somewhere?" Milton said.

"There. On your neck."

Milton put the glasses on his nose.

"Let's get this old polish off," he said. "This wasn't right at all, this stuff. What were you thinking?"

"I dunno," Mona confessed.

Milton rummaged in his shoe box and found a bottle of nail polish remover, and some cotton pads. Mona could smell the acetone as he wet down the cotton pad. She had always liked that smell, which reminded her of doing nails with Zahra when she was a girl, but also made her feel momentarily light-headed and clear-thinking. She started to say something about Zahra but stopped. Milton started taking the old, beige polish off her fingers.

After a minute she said, "So how does it work around here. Karolina cooks for you?"

"She puts a tray outside the door. It's okay. Not good, not bad."

"Why don't you go downstairs and eat with her? Have some company?"

"Why don't *you* go downstairs and eat with her?"

Mona laughed.

"You know, when I was lost last week or whatever it was, it occurred to me that I've been pursuing women my whole life. And when I left 107, my first thought wasn't that I was out of a job, it was that no woman was ever going to talk to me again. I had been exiled from the world of women."

Milton took a nail file out of his box and started shaping and buffing her nails, one by one. He started with her thumb. Mona was surprised how dexterous his thick, short fingers were.

"So what do you do all day?" she asked.

"I do some writing in the morning." He gestured at his desk. "I'm writing a memoir."

"And that's going all right for you?"

"First few hours in the morning, I can get some work done. I'm doing fifth grade now, sixth grade. Maybe I'll make it to high school before I'm done. Listen, your nails are in terrible shape."

"I know," she said.

"I'm serious, you've got to take better care of yourself."

"I know."

"Someone needs to tell you these things."

"I know."

Milton painted the clear polish on the fingertips. "This is what makes it solid," he said. "A lot of people skip this, but you'll get chips in a couple of days if you don't do it right."

"Why did Karolina turn off the internet?" she asked.

"She decided I was depressed. She thought I was watching too much porn and eating too much salt. She thought turning off the internet would get me out of this room."

"Why is she here at all?" Mona asked.

"Because I'm scared, Mona. I'm scared that if I'm left alone in this house I'm going to end up like my mother, stroked out in the shower."

It was time to lay down the first coat of You Do Blue. But before he got started, Mona said, "I changed my mind. I want red. I want Cherry Red. I haven't worn red nail polish in I don't know how long."

"That's a good decision. I always liked a woman with red nails and red lipstick."

Milton didn't talk while he painted her nails. He concentrated carefully on staying within the margins of the nail bed, avoiding the cuticles and finger.

"There you go," Milton said. "That'll be forty-nine ninety-five, plus tip."

"Thank you, Milton," she said.

"Altogether my pleasure."

It felt like it was time to leave, but Mona's nails were still wet. She could hear from somewhere in the distance a wind chime ringing like church bells.

Milton said, "Mona, about Cleopatra. Just don't forget that she hasn't read the play. She doesn't know how it's all going to end. Don't let her give up hope. As soon as you lose hope, the play is a fucking bore."

Mona waved her fingers in the air to dry them.

Mona said, "Can I tell you something? I did a bad thing."

"Welcome to the human club," Milton said. "I'm a member."

"Reach in my pocket. My fingers are still wet."

Milton leaned over and pulled the bottle of pills out of Mona's vest.

"I stole these from Vanessa's medicine closet," she said. "And I feel terrible about it."

"Oh, you have been a very naughty girl," he said.

The look of mischief in Milton's eyes told Mona straightaway that she had made a terrible mistake. She felt as if she had entrusted a violin bow, fragile and irreplaceable, to the inspection of a toddler, who was now waving it wildly around the room. She was aware that she was salivating slightly, and she swallowed.

Milton stood up.

"What are you doing?" she said.

"Just a second," Milton said, walking toward the little bathroom.

"Milton, don't you—"

Then she heard the toilet flush. He walked out and handed her the empty bottle.

"No more problem," he said. "Problem solved."

"God damn it, you had no right," she said.

Mona felt a deep and probing sadness. She knew now that she had been correct to take the bottle from Vanessa's medicine cabinet, she understood that it had been an act of foresight and goodness. She could think only of the happiness she had lost, the hours of family joy and tranquility now forsaken, how irresponsible she had been to put it in Milton's hands.

After a minute, Milton's crow, who had been watching the proceedings with fascinated, inhuman calm, began to caw. Then she flew off and Mona stood up and went to the bathroom. She wanted to wash her face. She saw the remnants of unflushed pills floating in the water of the toilet; she thought about sticking her head in the bowl and drinking deeply. But instead she flushed the toilet again, and the decomposing pills spiraled away.

When she came out, Milton said, "How's your sister doing?"

4

Did she die at home or in the hospital? (At home, which she wanted but I don't know if it's better because it's so scary.) Why was it so scary? (You don't want her to be in pain, you don't want her to have seizures, anything could go wrong. I mean, everything's going to go wrong, you know that, but . . . you know.) She was in the bedroom? (We rented one of those hospital beds and put it in the living room. Because it makes it easier. You can raise it when you need to feed her and lower it, it's got guardrails. It made more sense. Also, she liked to look out the window. We could raise her up and she could look at this tiny sliver of the East River you could see from her window. It was like *this* much East River and that's why she bought the apartment.) Who was there with you? (I was there most of the time. Rachel—my niece—she was there too. Vadim was there sometimes. He had his own apartment, but he'd come by every day. Rarely at night. And Mr. Butterfield.) Mister— what was his name? Butternut? (Butterfield. Yeah, that was his real name. He was this Jamaican nurse we hired. He just did . . . *this*, people dying. But he was good at it.) What made him good? (Very calm. He prayed a lot. He didn't make a big show of it. I guess he was just ghoulishly calm. Sitting there all day waiting with his eyes closed and praying.) How old was Mr. Butterfield? (Maybe about sixty? But he was one of those guys you couldn't tell. He could have been younger or older. Old enough that this dying business wasn't a completely abstract subject to him, you know what I mean?) And he was there the whole time? (No. Most of the time. We hired him full-time, but it was a lot of people in the apartment. We thought it wasn't going to last that long, that's what Phil said.) (To tell you the truth, Mr. Butterfield kind of drove us insane. Vadim wanted Mr. Butterfield there and Rachel didn't care and I didn't have an opinion, you know? Because Mr. Butterfield, he was always saying these things, like, "Sister is passing now," or "Sister loves you very much," or "Sister is with God now." He had literature with him, from his church. He'd sit on the couch and read his pamphlets, and he'd just leave them there, like, *Oh my, I forgot my evangelical literature right here, go ahead and read it.* And if Zahra could have heard that shit, she would have gone nuts. And I think she could hear, she just wasn't paying that much attention. But we wanted him there because we were scared if something happened, we wouldn't know what to do, which I guess made sense.) (Also Mr. Butterfield didn't like dogs. I mean, he didn't make a big deal out of it, but if Barney was sleeping on Zahra's bed and she needed to be turned, he'd be like, "Please will you put your dog on the floor." And he'd make this fake little smile, like he thought it was disgusting that Barney was sleeping next to Zahra.) (To tell you the truth, all I can really remember about Zahra's last week was Mr. Butterfield. I was totally obsessed with the man. He was just there, all the time.) Why didn't you just ask him to go? (We were scared. And he wasn't doing anything wrong. I've never seen anyone die before. Were we supposed to give her water? You don't want her to be thirsty but then you think, *Maybe she'll drown.* Were we supposed to give her food? For example, I was supposed to give her liquid morphine and you're supposed to dropper it in the back of her throat. But I couldn't get her to sit upright and she started to moan like I was strangling her. And you kind of need three hands to do it. Then, this was before she couldn't walk at all, she had to go to the bathroom. Rachel was sleeping and Vadim had gone out for a smoke, and I dropped her. She fell right on the floor. So I didn't want to be alone with her.) I'm not quite getting it. Where was everybody? How was it all organized? (Zahra's living room. Zahra in a hospital bed near the window. Two doors, leading into the back bedrooms. Vadim asleep in one, Rachel in the other. There's a couch. I'm asleep on it, or Mr. Butterfield sitting there. The guy never slept. Just sat there praying and muttering. "Sister is going now. Sister will be very happy soon to see mother and father. Sister is going with Jesus now." Barney on the hospital bed or on the floor beside Zahra. Zahra on the bed. Not looking bad. Honestly. I put lipstick on her because she wanted that. Rachel did her hair. Just the noises she was making were kind of terrible.) How long did this last? (She was still up and walking around until a couple of days before she died. She was even able to go outside a little bit, but it left her pretty tired. In my mind this phase was something that could go on for months maybe. But then it got worse very fast. Like today she was outside and tomorrow Mr. Butterfield showed up. And from basically the time he showed up she stopped talking.) She never talked again? (One time. It was strange. She had been gone for a couple of days. Really gone. Just breathing, like a breath . . . another breath . . . another breath. You keep thinking that she won't take the next breath. And then just this one time she came back. Rachel was asleep and Vadim was smoking and I guess Mr. Butterfield was out of the apartment, I don't know where he went, and it was like all the circuits got turned on at once. I was looking out the window and she said, "Will he ever shut up?" and I turned around, I said, "You're here!" and she said, "He's driving me nuts." I said, "You mean Mr. Butterfield?" and she said, "No, the other guy." Then she woke up a little more, like someone coming up from a dream, and I sat on the bed and held her hand. I asked if she wanted to hear some good gossip, because I had this thing I had wanted to tell her and I knew she would love it. It was about an ex of hers, Nicholas Fine, this finance bro who—well, he treated her like shit. In any case he got arrested just the week before for insider trading and I knew that would make her happy. And she loved hearing that story. She asked me all sorts of questions, she was there with me, right there. "Did they perp-walk him? Was his wife crying? How many years is he looking at?" It was so strange. It was weeks and weeks since she had been so there. We were just sitting on the bed and she was laughing, all normal, so happy, and she looked so beautiful. I asked if she was scared. She said, "It'll be fun." And I said, "What will be fun?" And she was just about to tell me when Mr. Butterfield came back into the apartment and he said, "Oh, Sister is talking," and she never said anything again.)

5

Mona, Milton, Karolina, and Barney stood outside the brownstone waiting for Ahmed to arrive. Karolina glanced at her phone and announced that he was seven minutes away, then Milton, who had never taken an Uber, said that he didn't understand—Ahmed was Mona's friend? Mona explained all over again that you just clicked on the phone and a car showed up, and Milton nodded, clearly confused by the concept.

Milton turned toward Karolina. "Do you know the history of this street?" he asked. When Karolina gave no answer, he took her by the arm and said, "All this used to be farm country . . ."

Mona stamped her feet a little to warm up her legs and blew in her hands. She wasn't sure quite how it happened that Milton and Karolina were coming home with her. The threesome had been drinking tea in the kitchen when Mona mentioned Zabar's. Karolina said that she had never been to Zabar's, to which Mona said that this was like living in New York and never seeing Central Park. Milton, who was eager for a change from Karolina's bland, unsalted food, declared that they needed to go. He wanted to stock the house. "What is got into you, Milton?" asked Karolina, pleased to see Milton so full of energy. Mona explained that she often went to Zabar's—it was near her apartment. They could all go over together. In fact, she added, Milton's long-suppressed vim now contagious, they could have lunch at her place, which must be filled with leftovers.

Milton had his hand on Karolina's shoulder as he pointed out the place where Teunis Joralemon kept his famous saddlery. Mona wondered if Milton was courting Karolina. She was listening attentively and smiling.

There had been a little scene just before leaving the house. Karolina had intercepted Milton at the threshold of the house, considered his wardrobe, and said, "Milton, today is now very cold." "I'll be fine," Milton said. Karolina, however, refused to take no for an answer. She pulled out scarves and hats from a hall closet and began fussing over him.

Now Milton stood stiffly in his brown and yellow scarf and cap, his thin legs poking out from under the coat. Karolina listened with due attention to his monologue. Two mothers walked by, pushing strollers, and Mona waved at the little girls sitting in them. They waved back.

"So where's this Ahmed?" Milton said.

"He is coming, Milton," Karolina said. "Four minutes. You see?"

She pointed the phone in Milton's direction. "I can't see that," he said. "I don't have my glasses." Mona wished that she had peed before she left the house. Milton's crow, directly above them, carefully inserted a shred of tinfoil at his window ledge.

The humans, self-absorbed as always, did not notice that Barney had wandered halfway down the block. The smell had found him first: something rich and fat and eggy, with bottom notes of bread and top notes of cheese. Then he could see it. At the end of the block, on the ground beside a garbage can. It sat on a single sheet of butcher paper, unwrapped, an inexplicable apparition: a bagel, with scrambled eggs and cheese, and four slices of fatty bacon. Barney approached the bagel with an increasing sense of unreality. He began to drool. Arriving at the bagel, he paused to smell the thing, then ate it in three sharp bites. Eating that bagel was the closest thing Barney had ever felt to a spiritual experience, although, of course, like all of us, he lacked the words adequately to describe it. The best that can be said is that, as he ate the bagel, he felt that he lived in a world that, despite its sorrow, had been made for a creature such as him. He felt that he was loved. He felt that the universe had meaning and structure and order. He was a changed dog, and he longed to tell others what he knew now. When he was done, he trotted back to the people, wildly wagging his tail. Nobody had noticed his absence.

ACT FIVE

LEONTES

If this be magic, let it be an art
Lawful as eating.

Mona was not particularly nervous as she waited for the Uber, and the chaos in the car kept her from thinking much about her arrival at home. But just as soon as the car turned into the familiar streets of her own neighborhood, Mona's excitement turned to anxiety. She wondered if she would be welcome home at all, or whether she would find her furniture and treasured objects piled up on the sidewalk in front of the doorway, Mona left, once again, to hang, beg, die, or starve in the streets.

When they arrived at Mona's building, there was, inevitably, a confrontation with Ahmed the Uber driver over the damage to the vehicle. Mona listened with only half an ear as Ahmed cursed their little party. Milton defused the conflict with an unexpected suavity, pulling out his wallet and giving Ahmed a large tip. Mona led her entourage into her building. The four of them took the elevator up, the floors ticking by with excruciating slowness. As Mona walked down the long, echoey corridor, past the Finklers, the Greenes, and the apartment that was always on AirBnb, it occurred to her that in addition to everything else she had forgotten her key the day before. Between the sounding of the doorbell and the fumbling at the deadbolt, Mona had time for a brief waking nightmare: the door would open and behind the door only an unfamiliar face. "Is Phil there? Is Aaron? Is Rachel?"

But it was Sheila who answered the doorbell. She had changed her pink sweat suit from the day before to a lime green one; she was still Juicy, though, and her hair was still lacquered with hairspray into a neat, conical dome. "Oh my," she said, surveilling for a moment the invaders arrayed on the doorstep. Sheila saw Milton, whom she had not seen in years, his hair disheveled, diminished in size. "Goodness me, Milton!" she said. Then Sheila saw a large woman in overalls, her silver hair in thick pigtails, glossy-faced, arms gyrating spasmodically, covered in some kind of vomit— Sheila wasn't sure *what* vomit, precisely. Sheila saw Barney, his tail still waving from side to side with missionary zeal. In the middle of all this, eventually she found Mona.

Something about Sheila's shocked, nervous expression melted Mona's heart; the fact that Sheila *was*, and Sheila *persisted*, that she had opened the door, seen Mona, and *smiled*.

Mona launched herself at Sheila and hugged her.

"We were *so* worried," Sheila finally said.

The foyer was soon thereafter in chaos. Bruce had heard the arrivals and crawled off the kitchen stool to greet them. Barney's newfound faith in the goodness of the Bagel had been subdued by his episode of nausea in the Uber. Now, seeing Bruce, his faith was fully restored. He whimpered, moaned, spun swiftly in an energetic circle, then began to jump as high as could, reaching somewhere around Bruce's crotch. Bruce leaned over to pet him, saying, "You *are* a good dog, oh yes you are, you son-of-a-gun." Barney threw himself on his back and slithered from side to side, displaying his taut, rounded belly. His ears flopped to either side of him like wings. Bruce slowly got down on one knee to scratch his tummy.

Soon Bruce looked up from the overwrought dog to see Milton Katz. His reaction to Milton's presence in the apartment was no less joyful than Barney's reaction to him. He stood up, pushed his wife out of the way, and grabbed Milton's hand, which he pumped vigorously. "Good to see you, sir, very good to see you," he said. Shaking Milton's hand didn't seem enough. He wrapped him in his arms, so tightly that Milton began to squirm. Barney continued to launch himself at Bruce's crotch.

In his excitement, Bruce ignored Mona's return entirely, despite the fact that he had barely slept all night, wondering what had happened to her and worrying about her safety.

"Barney barfed on Karolina," Mona said. "In the Uber. I think he ate something."

"Oh no!" Sheila said. "You poor thing."

It was to Sheila's credit that she asked no further questions, that her instinctive reaction when presented with a strange woman covered in dog puke at her door was compassion.

"Let me get you some clean clothes," Sheila said, leading Karolina by the elbow to the back bedroom, where neat stacks of freshly laundered sweat suits were arrayed in colorful stacks on the closet shelves.

Mona walked into the apartment. She felt as if she had been away for a very long time. She looked at the apartment as though it were on StreetEasy or Zillow, staged for sale by an aggressive real estate agent. It had good bones, that much was clear: the living room was flooded with strong, southwest light, and the corner windows ensured that it would stay in sunlight all through the afternoon. She noted the dark parquet floor, gleaming with wax, and the original plaster ornamentation. Nobody ever believed the price that Bruce and Sheila had paid for the apartment when they bought it back in the seventies, but they had bought the apartment not as an investment—no one imagined back then that the neighborhood would turn around—but inspired by a genuine love for the space, its quirky angles and subtle architectural details. It occurred to Mona, looking at it, that they were drawn back to the apartment over and over again because it was the place where they had felt their greatest happiness over the years. It was for this reason that they had sold it to Phil and Mona, and for this reason, despite their avowed intentions to golf the winters of their old age away, that they drifted back to the apartment with unexpected regularity.

Rachel was sitting on the couch. She had started to stand when Mona presented herself at the door, then sat down again when she saw Milton, unsure how to interpret or react to this unexpected development. She picked up her phone and tapped out a quick message to her followers: "She's home." Mona did not know it, but the messages Rachel had been typing through the night to her social media audience had been neither mocking nor ironical but simply sad. She had confessed, in an excess of adolescent self-importance, her innermost conviction that she and she alone had been responsible for driving Mona out of the apartment. Strangers on diverse continents had prayed for Mona all through the night; had tweeted of their own dark nights of the soul; and had condoled, consoled, and comforted Rachel, some of them finding in Rachel's story an unlikely source of succor to their own troubled lives. Now, even as Mona made her way to the couch, Rachel's phone transmitted back to her an instantaneous wave of globe-encircling joy, manifesting itself in the form of happy-face emojis, memes of talk-show hosts bursting into spontaneous dances, and GIFs of pinkish orange sunsets illuminating placid oceans.

Mona sat down beside Rachel on the couch, so close that she could feel the warmth of her skin and could smell the last diminishing traces of rosemary and lime on her skin.

"I'm sorry," both of them said at the same time.

"Why?" Mona asked, genuinely confused.

"You know. Just sorry."

"But I'm the one—"

Mona picked up Rachel's hand and kissed her wrist, and Rachel put her head on Mona's shoulder. Mona felt Rachel's short, soft hair brush against her cheek. Mona did not want to move or even breathe. Mona could see herself but not Rachel in the mirror above the mantelpiece. She wished that she could explain to Rachel in a convincing manner just how great her hair had been. She wondered if in the dozens of photos various guests at Vanessa's party must have taken, one photo of her and her hair had survived. Only Rachel would be excited to see that photo, would understand how meaningful her hair had been. Phil might have been (or might not, she admitted) aroused by her hair, but he would not have understood its *importance*: the hair had been a proof that despite the degradations of time and sorrow, something new could flourish and survive, like a daffodil bursting through the stony soil of the prison yard.

Rachel for her part had revelations of similar intensity that she longed to impart. She had dreamed again of her mother, just before dawn. They had gone on safari together, and Zahra had insisted that the lions were tame, that despite the warnings of the guide, she could approach and pet them. The details of the dream were fast disappearing in the light of day, but she knew that Mona would want to know of the existence of the dream, would be willing to consider the symbolic meaning of the lions.

Mona and Rachel might have sat like that for much longer, but across the room Bruce sneezed. When this proved insufficient to disrupt the general tranquility, he cleared his throat with such vigor and vitality that both Rachel and Mona looked over. Mona forgot about her hair, and Rachel her dream. There Bruce stood, his face flushed with pride and happiness, leaning over Milton in a gesture of pleased possession. Milton for his part stood surveying the room, his features conveying his usual sharp intelligence, his eyes the only place of emergent doubt.

Rachel looked at Mona. "Milton?" she said. "Really?"

"Go and say hello."

"Will he lick me?"

"He might," Mona conceded. "But be nice anyway. He's having some issues. Where's Phil? I forgot my phone—"

"We *know* about the phone," Rachel said, in such a way that Mona understood that her phone had been dialed, redialed, dialed again, texted, messaged, and sought after by every possible electronic modality nearly every minute of her absence. "He had to go out. I'll let him know you're home."

Rachel tapped on her phone a few minutes, passing the message to Phil. Mona felt a mild sense of disappointment in her husband, as if her disappearance should have provoked a total suspension of all ordinary chores. It felt wrong that he had left the house, despite the fact that he was in constant contact with every member of the household, alert instantly to any possible change in Mona's status.

Rachel said, "He'll be back in ten minutes."

Sheila led Karolina back through the living room. They were dressed now like the besties they were fast becoming: two juicy women in their prime in the colors of bright tropical fruit. They settled themselves in a pair of comfortable armchairs—the only furniture that had survived in the apartment from the time Sheila had lived here as its mistress. Sheila was already discussing her book group, and the latest insult from Nora Weiner, who just last night had sent an email to the entire group complaining that Sheila's choice of books, the latest from Jonathan Franzen, was a little slow. Her complaints fell on the most sympathetic pair of ears. Karolina did not know who Jonathan Franzen was, but she understood what it was to be dismissed and insulted. "People are so funny," Sheila said, and Karolina nodded, as if it had never occurred to her that people, who could be so wicked, so mean, so devious, and so unworthy of her trust, could be funny also.

———

MONA KNOCKED ON AARON'S DOOR. "Come in," he said, and when Mona saw him sitting at his desk, staring at his computer, his earphones on, she rushed across the room and hugged him. "I'm so sorry, Aaron," she said. "Were you worried?"

"No," Aaron said, his voice revealing that he had, in fact, not been worried.

"You must have thought something terrible happened to me."

"Not really."

Mona was prepared to throw herself at his feet for forgiveness. "I'm a terrible mother," she said.

"Could we talk about this later?"

Mona wasn't ready to retreat. "Was Ultimate fun?"

"Ultimate?"

"Yesterday? You know, throwing Frisbees?"

"Oh," said Aaron, dredging from the mud of memory the fossilized ruins of an event now long past. "It was okay."

"Did your dad have fun?"

"I guess. I didn't see him much."

"Was his friend there? Melanie? The girl he went to high school with."

"They're all his friends from high school."

"I forget her last name," Mona lied. "Melanie McSomething?"

"I just played Frisbee."

"What does she look like anyway? Is she cute?"

"I don't know, she's a mom, I guess."

"So am I, honey, and men are throwing themselves at my feet day and night," Mona said.

"I don't want to think about that," Aaron said.

Mona stood by Aaron's side, remembering the way, when he was small, he used to chatter at her. It never used to stop: the things he wanted to build (a space train, a submarine), or the Lego set he wanted for his birthday, or, when he was a little older, the precise details of various naval battles he learned about on YouTube. She had just about lost hope that he would say anything when he looked up at her.

"There was a fox," he said.

"A fox?"

"At Ultimate. It ran right through the lawn."

"Wow," she said.

"Do you remember Foxy Fox?"

Foxy had been a stuffed animal that lived no more than a foot from Aaron's hand all through his early childhood, until he got lost on a family vacation in Bermuda. For almost a year after his disappearance, Mona had written letters to Aaron from Foxy—even took them to the post office and sent them—recounting for Aaron Foxy's various adventures as he made his way around the world: Foxy on a container ship to Africa. Foxy rides a camel in the desert. Foxy goes to the moon.

"Of course I remember Foxy," Mona said. "I wonder where he is now."

"I think he lives at Ralph Perrimeno's house in the Hamptons," Aaron said.

"Poor Foxy must be bored shitless," Mona said.

Aaron laughed.

"No kidding," he said. "I am never going to one of Dad's high school Frisbee things again."

———————

BRUCE AND MILTON MOVED SIDE BY SIDE in the direction of the couch. Rachel, seeing them approach, scurried away, like a bather at the beach seeing the first flash of lightning. She went into the kitchen and, not knowing what else to do, decided to make coffee, although she didn't really want any—she'd drunk and peed an entire pot this morning. But she enjoyed the invisibility the activity offered: one was always so much more obvious just sitting still.

Most of the time Rachel wished she could simply disappear. Not into nothingness, mind you: she was quite happy to be alive. She just found that she enjoyed the world much more when she could settle into a corner and observe it. She liked to watch people's faces and hands, their little gestures and involuntary facial expressions—the things people revealed when they thought they were revealing nothing at all. Most of the time, she liked better sitting in a restaurant by herself and listening to other people's conversations, than being forced to converse herself. Rachel didn't understand how anyone could ever be bored on the subway, or in a doctor's office, or at a book group attended by a half dozen squabbling older women. She could amuse herself at any time just by watching people and telling herself little stories about them—what they had for breakfast; whether they got along well with their mothers; what secret passion lurked in the hidden recesses of their souls.

Now she looked at the four old people in the living room. Milton glanced at her from time to time. She had given him a little wave but hadn't dared to talk to him. She still didn't know if she had done the right thing. There was a look on his face now of mild bewilderment, as if he was not quite sure just where he was and whether the faces that surrounded him were friendly.

"Milton, would you like some coffee? Or we have orange juice, water, tea . . ." she asked.

He looked up at her. "Thank you, sweetheart. What I'd love is a beer, if you have one. I can't remember the last time I had a cold beer."

"I'll take one too," Bruce said, as if Milton had given him permission to ask for something forbidden.

Rachel was still puzzling over the strange encounter she'd had with Bruce last night. He had surprised her, just after Mona had swept out of the apartment announcing her intention to buy parsley, by dropping their argument in its entirety, declaring, "Well, I was young once too," then retreating to the back bedroom, where he disappeared for the better part of the afternoon. Later that evening, at the end of that uncomfortable Thanksgiving dinner—which began with Phil's hesitant declaration that they should probably just eat without Mona, he didn't know where the heck she was, and concluded with Mona's telephone call reassuring them that she was in fact alive—Bruce had disappeared into his back bedroom, then come back and handed Rachel a check for five thousand dollars. "A libation to the gods of youth and adventure," he'd said. "Do something fun." Then he made a courtly gesture of picking up her hand

and kissing it. Both the check, which Rachel had not yet decided to cash, and the kiss left her utterly mystified.

"Anyone else like a beer?" Rachel asked, looking over at Sheila and Karolina. She had to ask twice, so immersed were the pair in their conversation. They glanced at one another, like teenage girls. Neither Sheila nor Karolina had drunk a beer at this hour in decades, and had the other not accepted, both would have refused; as it was, first Sheila, then Karolina, said, "Yes, please," and giggled.

Rachel had sat up late last night with Sheila. Neither of them had felt like sleeping: Mona's disappearance had thrown the house into emotional chaos, and while Phil, Aaron, and Bruce had reacted to the uncertainty by retiring at midnight each to their own bedroom, there to do whatever men did in moments of crisis, Sheila and Rachel took comfort from the other, sitting at the kitchen table with a pot of chamomile tea. The subject of conversation chiefly had been Sheila's marriage. She and Bruce had recently celebrated their fifty-seventh wedding anniversary. She told Rachel that Bruce had gone last year to the annual convention of the Edward de Vere Institute in Oxford with a host of like-minded anti-Stratfordians, leaving Sheila at home for a week. Sheila had looked forward to that week with giddy abandon, thinking of the sheer pleasure of a week to herself, the first she could remember since Bruce's retirement. But the intensity with which she missed her husband shocked her, she told Rachel. The house felt painfully lonely, a precursor to the empty house in which she would one day dwell if Bruce died before her. Sheila drifted from room to room, unsure what to do with herself. Soon, she found herself consumed by jealousy— intense, physical, carnal jealousy, which ate at her insides and kept her from sleeping at night. She imagined him laughing with a younger woman, a fellow attendee, who shared his passions and admired his command of the "evidence," and who saw him now as Sheila had seen him once so many years ago. His absence had been a week of perfect torture. "People are just so funny," she said. "An old bird like me, sitting up nights unable to sleep because of a man I've known since I was twenty-two." So intense was her jealousy, she admitted, that one afternoon she did something "crazy": she went online and bought a last-minute ticket that very night to London, intending to surprise her husband. She was packing her little suitcase when he called. He was in the hospital in Oxford: he'd taken a little stumble on the paving stones and hit his head. They were keeping him overnight for observation. "You sound fine to me," she said. "Of course I'm fine!" Bruce boomed. Bruce began a transatlantic lecture on the evils of socialized medicine: he had waited in the emergency room almost four hours, only to be treated by a "lady doctor" who could have been no older than twenty-five. She had insisted on a battery of unnecessary tests. He began to rant about Obamacare. Sheila unpacked her suitcase as he spoke.

Rachel had an urge to tell all her stories. She had started keeping a little notebook in which she wrote things down, and sometimes—rarely—almost never—but *sometimes* the little stories she wrote made her smile. She wondered if she would ever find the courage to show them to anybody else.

Rachel opened the refrigerator and found the beer. It was her Uncle Phil who made sure the house was always stocked with beer made by his personal brewer, who lived in the furthest fringes of Brooklyn and made a limited-edition IPA infused with grapefruit zest and thyme. She remembered that Uncle Phil had danced—literally begun to hop around the kitchen in a clumsy jig—when the email arrived, informing him that his name had come off the waiting list and he now had the right to pre-order up to six cases per season. Rachel pulled out four bottles, thought about it a moment, and added a fifth for herself.

———————

MONA WENT BACK TO HER BEDROOM and closed the door. She could see Phil's big, rumpled outline on the bed, her own side of the bed smooth and neatly made.

The bed had been one of the first splurges of Mona's life together with Phil. She first saw it in the window of a furniture shop in the East Twenties. The salesman had told her the bed's "story." A woodworker who lived upstate had carved it out of Japanese maple, a process that took the guy almost a year, from lumber to completed object. Mona wanted some part of this upstate woodworker's peace and calm and concentration in her bedroom. Mona couldn't stop stroking the wood with her fingertips, it was so smooth and lustrous and shiny.

Mona had liked the bed so much that she took Phil to see it. She had been surprised, however, when Phil insisted they buy it. He saw in it what she had. It was before they were married, when they were still living in Phil's old apartment in Harlem. They could have lived somewhere nicer—Phil earned a doctor's salary—but he had been determined to pay off his student loans as quickly as possible. Neither of them had thought of themselves as particularly well-off. Buying that bed was the first sign he gave her of the extent to which he was willing to go to see that she was happy, how intense a project that would be for him. There were a few scratches on the beautiful headboard from Mona's rings, dragging back and forth.

Mona remembered the early days of their courtship. He had taken her out of this bed a few times back then, when he was on call and needed to go to the hospital. She used to go with him. He invited her to watch him perform various minor procedures. "Am I even allowed to?" Mona said. "Of course," Phil said, in a way that indicated his absolute mastery of the surgical suite. Then to the patients on gurneys, he said, "I'm your doctor and I'll take care of you today." Those words aroused Mona from head to foot. The nurses would scrub her in, gown her up, and she'd sit very quietly on a stool in the corner of the surgical suite. The whole thing fascinated her: the confident manner in which Phil instructed the nurses assisting him, the look of concentration in his eyes as he attended to crucial detail after crucial detail, the high seriousness of the place. A change in hospital policy shortly thereafter ended her visits to the operating room, but Mona still thought from time to time about how she felt watching Phil work, like her whole living body was vibrating under her surgical gown.

Mona began to undress. She needed to take a shower. She took off her yoga pants, her underwear, her brassiere, and tossed them into the hamper, where they lay on top of Phil's underwear and the T-shirt he had worn yesterday to Ralph Perrimeno's house in the Hamptons. She stepped into the bathroom, where she turned on the hot water, letting the shower steam up before she got in.

How much simple pleasure there was in life from one's own soap, shampoo, and conditioner! Aaron had bought her the soap, together with an accompanying body lotion, as a Christmas present the year before: it had sat unused under the bathroom sink until Mona found it the month before. She discovered to her surprise that Aaron had selected *her* smell. She hadn't known it was her smell before she used it—she had thought she was more roses and floral—but she was wrong: this was incense and the Orient, smoky with spice and bergamot, not the least bit cloying, imaginative and rich. She thought about Aaron in the store, preparing to spend more money than he could afford, patiently sniffing bar after bar of soap until he found one that he supposed she would like.

When Mona was done with her shower, she leaned over and shook out her hair, then stepped out onto the yellow bath mat. Phil had insisted on installing in the bathroom an anti-fog mirror so he could shave. Now Mona looked her naked body up and down, considering herself. She winced. None of it was the way she wanted. Mona felt that she was trapped in a stranger's body, some saggy, short-limbed, turkey-necked, mildly repulsive loser. She had felt this way her entire life.

Mona wondered how a woman who looked like her would ever play Cleopatra. But the same thought must have occurred to Cleopatra herself; every morning Cleopatra looked at herself in the mirror and was obliged to convince herself that she was capable of playing the role of Cleopatra just one more day. Cleopatra would teach Mona to play Cleopatra. Mona imagined herself standing before the audience naked, as naked as she was now, to say, in a voice mingling irony, laughter, seduction, and uncertainty, Cleopatra's first line in the play: "If it be love indeed, tell me how much." That was Cleopatra's question not to Antony, but to the audience. You only had to ask that question, not knowing the answer, and everything else would follow.

Mona wanted to spend the rest of her day in bed. But she was aware that the house was filled with people. So she dried her hair, dressed herself in clean underwear, pulled on a different pair of yoga pants and a new T-shirt, and went back out there to see how everyone was doing.

———

"SHAKESPEARE WROTE THE PLAYS," Milton said. "You're an imbecile if you think otherwise."

"I just don't think, good sir, that you are on top of the literature," Bruce said. "You're just not following the work that independent scholars are doing."

"Bruce!" Sheila said, embarrassed by her husband's behavior in front of her new and sensible friend. "Nobody wants to hear about that stuff now."

Mona felt a terrible sadness for Bruce. The look of frustration and betrayal in his eyes was heartrending. A kind of doubt worse than despair entered his soul: either he was wrong on one issue of primal importance—the authorship of the plays of William Shakespeare—or on another—the infallibility of Milton Katz. He was trying to puzzle out some solution to the problem, but none was at hand: he was at the cliff's edge, stampeding herds of bison behind him. He needed to make a choice, to jump or be trampled.

"We'll continue this," he said, with a brave chuckle. "I must ease myself."

He stood up on shaky legs and left the room for the hall bathroom, where, Mona suspected, he would sit on the floor and cry.

Mona was trading amused glances with Rachel when Barney began to whimper at the front door. This was how he inevitably heralded Phil's arrival in the long corridor leading from the elevator to the apartment. He could hear and smell him long before the others.

This was the moment Mona had dreaded. Her heart began to beat swiftly as she heard the key in the lock. But Phil was not alone. Vanessa and Elias were right behind him.

"Come on in," he said. "The bathroom's right over there."

Phil glanced at Mona—Mona could not quite interpret his eyes—but Barney's overflowing joy at seeing him dominated the moment that followed. Barney told Phil about the Bagel by rolling on his back, by insisting on attention, by licking his master's face, by wagging his tail and moaning.

"Just down the hall," Phil said.

Vanessa gave a little gamesome wave at the many occupants of the room. "Be right back," she said, perhaps not noticing Milton on the couch. She waved her fingertips in Mona's direction. "Little emergency here." Then she ushered Elias in the direction of the toilet.

Mona was so surprised by Vanessa's entrance into her apartment that she stopped thinking for a moment about her marriage. She tilted her head at Phil at a quizzical little angle, as if it had been Phil and not Mona who had gone out to buy parsley just ten minutes ago and come back with unexpected guests.

"Hey," he said.

"Hey."

Phil walked across the living room, where he gave Mona a kiss on the cheek. This might once have bothered her—the occasion *clearly* called for a dramatic embrace—but she had long understood that Phil reserved his most passionate moments for private occasions, that he was deeply uncomfortable onstage. Phil only indicated the full flush of his feeling by putting his hand on Mona's shoulder.

"I was worried about you," he said.

Then he explained to Mona that he had called her this morning, very early. It was Vanessa who had answered the ringing phone and explained that Mona had spent the night on her couch and forgotten her phone. They had agreed to meet out front of the Museum of Natural History at noon, where she was taking Elias to see his favorite dinosaur; she would give him the phone there. Once met, they had started walking together, comparing notes on Mona as they walked in the direction of Phil's house. The last few blocks Elias had been hopping in obvious distress from foot to foot, so Phil had invited them up to use the bathroom, on account of Elias's refusal to use the bathroom in the neighborhood Starbucks.

"I like her," Phil said. "Why didn't I ever meet her?"

Phil and Mona stood in the living room, Phil dressed in the pale blue cashmere sweater Mona bought him for his birthday and the handsome slacks they had bought together from J. Crew. He was almost a very good-looking man, with his head of salt-and-pepper hair and lean, chiseled jaw; his head was just a little too narrow for his bony shoulders, and his ears a little too protuberant. Mona had been struck by his appearance on that very first evening all those years ago in this apartment. His hair was already turning gray, even then. Sheila had made a chicken cacciatore and Bruce had opened a bottle of expensive Chianti, insisting on showing Mona pictures of the very vineyard where he and Sheila had purchased a case. Mona had noticed the dignified, kind way Phil had helped his mother, who was having some back issues at the time, into and out of her chair. When she winced, he said, "Show me the spot," and then massaged her lower back with his practiced hands. "You know, my back hurts too," Mona said with a little smile, and Phil said, "Let me see if I can work on it for you too." There had been a few other guests at the meal, to make it less embarrassing for Phil and Mona, but Phil sat himself next to Mona, and was clearly only interested in her. He was a little boring, she thought, and nothing in the next two decades of life together would change that opinion. But she liked how different he was from everyone else she knew. She knew straightaway that she could make an appointment for coffee with Phil six weeks in the future, and that he would be there, absolutely. It was Phil who had asked if she wanted to see his childhood bedroom, but once there, it was Mona who had kissed him, surprising him so much that he stumbled back, his face opening into the widest smile.

Mona stood in the living room now and, for the first time since he walked into the room, looked carefully at him.

There were a pair of lines in the Scottish play. In the first, Duncan says, "There's no art to find the mind's construction in the face." Mona always thought this was a pretty dumb thing to say, and so did Lady M., who, not ten minutes of stage time later, checks out her husband and says, "Your face, my thane, is as a book where men may read strange matters." When they rehearsed the play, Milton had remarked, "And that, my friends, is a dumb king and a good marriage."

Now Mona looked at her thane's face and she knew, no question about it, that Phil had spent the night in torment. She had completely misinterpreted the conversation of the night before: that had been Phil putting on a brave front. Phil's gray-green eyes had not shown such an active, probing interest in her in years. His eyes were asking the same questions, over and over again: *Where were you? Who were you with?* Then Mona knew that he had been awake at three in the morning, imagining Mona with Vikram Gupta in some Midtown hotel, his fantasies hot. She saw Phil pacing in the night from bedroom to living room and back to bedroom; pouring himself a shot of Lagavulin from the bottle he'd bought a few years back and never touched; then abandoning the project of sleep somewhere well before dawn. She could see every variety of betrayal in his eyes. She had not suspected Phil of such lurid imagination or such intensity of emotion. Mona could see that Phil was trying to hide his jealousy, but he was a poor actor. Only now, as first Vanessa and then Milton made clear who her companions of the previous twenty-four hours had been, was the fever of his jealousy diminishing.

Phil looked at Mona and Mona looked at Phil and then Phil realized that his house was full of strange people. Phil believed deeply in the responsibilities of a host, and he was grateful for the distraction. He was all jumpy. He wasn't sure what to say to Mona, what questions to ask, whether she was angry at him or if he should be angry at her. He saw Milton on the couch, holding his now-empty beer. He walked over and said, "Well, if it isn't Milton Katz, right here in my own home." Milton said, "Well, how do you do, Doctor, how do you do," and shook Phil's hand. Phil leaned over the kitchen counter to give his mother a kiss on the cheek and introduced himself to Karolina. "Is that a Polish accent I hear?" he asked. Phil had attended a conference in Warsaw a few years back and learned a few phrases. He asked Karolina in thickly accented Polish if the bus went to the airport. Karolina laughed in delight and said something he didn't understand in reply.

"Has anyone seen Dad?" he asked.

"I think he's in his room," Mona said. "I'll check on him."

The walk to the back bedroom wasn't long but Mona used the time to calm herself. She had a sense of dawning triumph. Poor Phil! He was such a good husband, and so bad at marriage. Thank goodness she hadn't married a man like Vikram, who could match her move-for-move. Vikram would never have thrown away all his advantages like that, walking into the house with a face like that, showing the whole world just who he was. Mona knew that the only place you should be totally honest with the world was onstage.

Mona at that moment loved Phil beyond all measure: his grizzled head; his strange, barking laugh as he watched television, but never at her jokes; his good, earnest soul. Mona of infinite variety surprised herself as she inevitably surprised others. She was happy. How good it was to have the luxury of time. Some other time there would be time, she decided, to wrangle with Phil, to fight, to be jealous, to discuss with Dr. Billy, to fight again, to make peace, to confess, to negotiate, to rehearse, perhaps to succumb to Vikram, to sulk, to compromise, to sleep in separate beds, and then to reunite. All of these were problems for another day.

Thank goodness, she thought, that there was time enough for that. All things considered, time was nothing but a gift.

———————

MONA FOUND BRUCE ON HIS LAPTOP, clicking madly from Reddit page to Reddit page, in a desperate attempt to gather the evidence that would convince Milton.

She rubbed his shoulder and said, "Are you hungry?"

"I could eat," he said. Then he added forlornly, "The evidence is so thick now. I don't see how anyone could doubt it."

"I wanted to talk to you about that," she said. Not even the most sensitive observer would have suspected that she was anything but another lunatic. "I read some of those articles you sent me—and you may have a point."

"Of course I have a point!" Bruce boomed. "That goddamn William Shakespeare!"

"Milton's not going to change his mind," Mona said. "Milton's old and stuck in his ways. But we know the whole story. Isn't that enough?"

Mona could see that he was not entirely convinced—gaining

Mona was meager compensation for losing Milton in the battle against deception and untruth—but he was willing to be consoled.

"I suppose," he said, and followed her back down the hallway.

———

BACK IN THE LIVING ROOM, Mona asked if anyone was hungry. Vanessa was talking to Rachel—she had yet to salute Milton—and Elias was on the floor, rubbing Barney's tummy.

"Can we stay?" Elias asked his mother. "Please?"

He had seen the dinosaurs many times, an experience made no more interesting by repetition. But he liked dogs, and this warm, sweet-smelling apartment, and he liked Mona too, who knew how to play.

Vanessa looked at Mona, who said, "Oh please, stay! It's the *least* I can do."

Mona didn't know if Vanessa knew yet that she had stolen her painkillers. She didn't think she would tell her if Vanessa did not figure it out for herself. If the subject came up, she intended to blame the woman in red leggings.

"Do we have leftovers in the fridge?" Mona asked.

Sheila looked at Phil, who looked at Bruce, who looked at Rachel, who explained that the leftovers had been sent home yesterday with Harry and Susanna. "We were all so worried about you," Sheila said. "We just couldn't think about that."

"And Susanna could?"

"She even brought her own Tupperware. It was just so easy to let her pack everything up."

A gloom fell over the crowd at the prospect of organizing a spontaneous lunch for all these hungry people.

"Don't worry," Mona said. "I've got leftovers in the freezer."

Mona had an entire Thanksgiving meal shoved in the compartments and alleys of her freezer, odds and ends not just from last year's Thanksgiving, but from diverse years before that as well. It was all in neat, labeled pouches. She began to pull them out of the freezer, each one hard and gray, like things aliens on a planet of ice and snow would eat. Soon the microwave was spinning dizzily. To accelerate the meal, she put pans on the stove and threw stuffing in one, dropped a brick of gravy in another, a square of green beans in a third. She turned on the oven and threw into it a dozen rock-like dinner rolls. It would all taste terrible when it was ready—but wasn't that the spirit of Thanksgiving? In the meanwhile, she thought, it was a wonder, watching the food bubble and thaw in the pans.

Mona stirred what she thought might have once been mashed sweet potatoes and thought about Paulina. At the end of *The Winter's Tale*, when Leontes, aged and despairing, thinks that he has destroyed everything, it is Paulina who enacts the mysterious rites by which his dead queen returns to life. There were few characters in Shakespeare more beautiful than Paulina, who stood for truth, and justice, and spoke honestly with passion.

"Is that stuff even edible?" Rachel asked.

"It is required you do awake your faith," Mona said.

Mona stirred the various pots and pans, dashed to the microwave to tap buttons, made sure nothing burned. "'Tis time; descend; be stone no more," she whispered to the food. The food began to melt and acquire color.

Milton alone in the room had understood Mona's allusion. Nothing in Shakespeare moved him more than the late romances, which seemed to him always magically to float on a countercurrent to despair. It was wonderful to be in the rehearsal room again. He sniffed the air curiously. "If this be magic, let it be an art lawful as eating," he said.

A potholder in one hand, a wooden spoon in the other, Mona looked at Phil and said, "You come here."

He trotted over, with the air of an animal expecting a blow. Barney followed at his heels.

"I missed you," Mona said.

The look of relief, intermingled with desire, on Phil's face was overwhelming. He leaned over and gave her a gentle kiss, then, sensing that his emotions were reciprocated, a more forceful one.

"I thought I lost you," he said.

Soon the house was filled with the smell of defrosting turkey, congealed and lumpy mashed potatoes, the strange Lebanese stuffing, spiced with cumin, that side by side with Zahra she had prepared years before. Mona remembered Zahra in all her glory, waving her knife in dangerous little circles and complaining about Vadim. They had prepared this entire meal, she now remembered, in this very kitchen, burning and overboiling and underspicing in what even the most generous critic would admit was a failed attempt to reproduce their father's Thanksgiving meal, in the process drinking several bottles of wine by themselves. Now that food was coming back to life.

"Go together, you precious winners all; your exultation partake to everyone," Mona said.

She dipped a finger in one sauce and then another. She could not explain it, but the meal's long hibernation had transformed it. Everyone in the apartment was aware of the wonderful smells coming from the kitchen. They turned and looked at one another in amazement.

Mona handed out plates from the cupboard to Vanessa, Rachel,

Karolina, and Bruce and told them to set the table. Milton stood up from the couch, and Milton—even Milton!—asked if he could help. "You can open a bottle of wine," she said, handing him the bottle of Barolo that Ralph Perrimeno had sent them last year for Christmas. She told Elias, who had been staring at her, to help her in the kitchen. Soon she had him on a stepstool and told him carefully to stir the cranberry sauce. It was turning from gray to red in front of her eyes, bubbling. All of the guests obeyed Mona's orders, pulling open the eaves of the big dining room table, arranging plates, opening the folding chairs, transferring the food, now hot, to serving dishes and putting it on the table. She found a job for Rachel. "You could put on some music," she said, and Rachel played with her phone until an acoustic guitar, lovely and calm, came piping through the speaker. Bruce handed plates to Karolina, who said, "Thank you," and Milton gave plates to Vanessa. Neither of them had spoken to one another yet—maybe they never would. But Vanessa took the plates from his hand and arranged them neatly on the table. Soon the smells coaxed even Aaron out of his room, and he too was assigned his task, lighting the candles, which he completed like the rest with cheerful acquiescence. Barney stood guard for the scraps which he knew would inevitably fall. The only one who didn't work was Phil, who stood on the fringes of the open-plan kitchen, a look of patient, hopeful wonder in his eyes, as he watched his wife work miracles.

Acknowledgments

I owe a significant debt to Jessica Bennett's article "Nine Women Accuse Israel Horovitz, Playwright and Mentor, of Sexual Misconduct" (*New York Times*, November 30, 2017), from which I drew inspiration for Angie Steinmetz's article. From Ms. Bennett's article, I borrowed the factual events described in the lede, and the adjective "forcefully," used in both articles to describe a catastrophic kiss.

My character Milton Katz is not based otherwise on Israel Horovitz but shades of a number of departed great directors who may be discernible in the character of Milton.

When Milton describes the act of playing Shakespeare ("We catch these people at a time in their life . . ."), I have put into his mouth almost verbatim the wonderful words of Glen Byam Shaw, quoted by Barbara Jefford in Oliver Ford Davies' *Performing Shakespeare: Preparation, Rehearsal, Performance.* The description of performing for Milton ("a whole theater laughed and cried") was in fact Christopher Plummer's description of rehearsing for Tyrone Guthrie. Milton's observation that it is easier to insert a knife than to withdraw it is from an interview with Ron Cook, cited in Ron Destro's *The Shakespeare Masterclasses*. Milton's preference for "cool" Shakespeare comes from John Barton's preference for cool Shakespeare; anyone interested in seeing remarkable demonstrations of the difference between "cool" and "hot" Shakespeare should watch Barton's series *Playing Shakespeare*, available on YouTube. This might be my favorite nine hours in all of YouTube's many millions, and was the place where this novel began.

Hafez's account of Maria Callas playing Medea at La Scala draws on Arianna Huffington's biography *Maria Callas: The Woman behind the Legend*. Huffington's account is based on an interview with the conductor Thomas Schippers, who imagined Callas's thoughts as she stared down that hostile audience.

———————

JAMES SHAPIRO, LISA HARROW, Jeffrey Horowitz, Torrey Townsend, Keith Chappelle, and the numerous performers, participants, and organizers at the Shakespeare Forum were all immensely generous with their time. I am grateful to them all.

If you are reading this novel now, it is because my agent Susan Ginsburg did not give up on it—or on me. This novel found difficulties in its course to publication of which it is useless now to complain; only Susan Ginsburg could have surmounted them. She did so with unfailing patience, steady wise counsel in moments of despair, and a degree of personal kindness that is, I suspect, unique in the world of publishing. "I can no other answer make but thanks, / And thanks, and ever thanks."

It was to my editor Pete Simon and the team at Liveright that Susan eventually navigated this novel. Mona, Milton, Vanessa, Barney, et al.—*my* disorder'd rabble—could have hoped for no more congenial stage on which to perform. Pete's editorial interventions (with important prompts from Kim Bowers and Kadiatou Keita) improved the novel at every turn. His confidence in the novel sustained me. His courage, and the courage of his house, should be a model for publishers everywhere.